More delicious praise for [barcode: D0393199]

"The divinely demented Adam Rex strikes again! *Cold Cereal* is exciting, strange, and deliciously different. His deft mixing of myth with modernity is flat-out fabulous."
—Bruce Coville, award-winning children's author

"Warning—this book contains the following ingredients in dangerously high quantities: wild fantasy, dynamic action, great satire, and silly jokes. I loved it. Second helpings, please!"
—Jonathan Stroud, bestselling author of The Bartimaeus Trilogy

". . . . Rex takes his magically delicious premise seriously, finding the thin line between absurdity and comedy, while giving this story more gravitas and depth than might be expected."
—*Publishers Weekly*

"An expansive cast of colorful characters (including Merle Lynn, an accountant) keep the surprises coming. . . . Reader interest and suspension of disbelief never flag in this humorous, consistently entertaining, well-spun yarn."
—*The Horn Book*

"Rex supports his centrifugal imagination with tight storytelling, effervescent characterization, and strong imagery and metaphor. Will leave eager readers anxious for the sequel."
—ALA *Booklist*

AND NOW A WORD
FROM OUR SPONSOR

CLOVER
Is this any way to start y'r day?

GIRL
It's Clover!

CLOVER
Top o' the mornin' to ye! Time to
put some burlap in yer lap!

Part of this nutritious breakfast!

CLOVER
Burlap Crisp—another good cereal
from the good folks at Goodco.
There's a Little Bit of Magic
in Every Box!

CO

CER

ADAM

OLD
DEAL

REX

BALZER + BRAY
An Imprint of HarperCollinsPublishers

Balzer + Bray is an imprint of HarperCollins Publishers.

Cold Cereal
Copyright © 2012 by Adam Rex
All rights reserved. Printed in the United States of America.
No part of this book may be used or reproduced in any manner whatsoever without
written permission except in the case of brief quotations embodied in critical articles
and reviews. For information address HarperCollins Children's Books, a division of
HarperCollins Publishers, 195 Broadway, New York, NY 10007.
www.harpercollinschildrens.com

Library of Congress Cataloging-in-Publication Data
Rex, Adam.
Cold cereal / Adam Rex. — 1st ed.
    p. cm.
Summary: A boy who may be part changeling, twins involved in a bizarre secret
experiment, and a clurichaun in a red tracksuit try to save the world from an evil cereal
company whose ultimate goal is world domination.
ISBN 978-0-06-206003-7
[1. Cereals, Prepared—Fiction. 2. Magic—Fiction. 3. Adventure and adventurers—
Fiction. 4. Twins—Fiction. 5. Brothers and sisters—Fiction.] I. Title.
PZ7.B26615Co 2012   2011019538
[Fic]—dc23   CIP
                                                                    AC

Typography by Joel Tippie
14 15 16 17   OPM   10 9 8 7 6 5 4 3 2
❖

First paperback edition, 2013

More than ever, for Marie

PROLOGUE

In the busy airport, baggage turned slowly on a carousel. A crowd of people stood around it, arms crossed and waiting, some of them staring at a silent television bolted to the ceiling. The closed captioning at the bottom of the screen was seven seconds late and often misspelled, so though the newscasters were back and reporting on the death of billionaire Sir Peter Humphreys, the words still read:

BURLAP CRISP—ANOTHR GOOD CEREAL FROM
THE GOOD FILKS AT GOODCO//
THERES A LITTLE BIT OF MAGIC IN EVRY BOX.

The people were passed by an airport employee in a stiff airport shirt carrying a cage that couldn't ride on the baggage carousel because there was something living inside.

People stole glances at the pet carrier in his hand and said "Cute, a little dog" and "Look, somebody's dog was on the plane." Then he set the cage down by a cluster of unclaimed bags and went into an office for some paperwork.

A woman with a tight ponytail that hoisted her face into a permanent, painted grin bent in front of the cage.

"Aw, hewwo, widdle Chihuahua," she said. "Hewwo." Then she rose to go wherever it is people like that come from.

Next at the cage door was another woman, wearing a sweatshirt decorated with an appliqué hot dog.

"Oh, Martin!" she called over her shoulder. "It's a dachshund! Just like the one I wanted at that pet store! Come see! Martin!"

When it became clear that Martin was not going to come see, she left, and immediately another face appeared. A man's. He peered into the pet carrier, looked over his shoulder in disbelief at the hot dog woman, then back in the carrier again.

"You ain't a dog," he told the thing in the cage. "You a tiny little man."

The tiny little man in the cage, the tiny old man in a red tracksuit with a face like a rotten apple, brightened and turned to the door.

"You see me, lad!" he said. "Don't you? Lord, it's been a while. Quick, now, an' open the door."

"Not a dog," the man muttered. "A little man in a box."

"Quickly, lad! Let me out! She'll come for me soon!"

The wide face only stared back.

"Thing is, see, you somebody else's little man. You ain't my little man. Maybe you supposed to be in that box."

"*Please*, lad," the little old man pleaded. "I've been kidnapped. I've been in this chicken coop for *three days*. I'll ... I'll make it worth your while. Riches. Gold! Anything that's in my power t' give—"

But the man outside the cage was already getting up. As he stood he said, "None of *my* business," and walked away.

The caged man pressed his face against the cold door and watched him go. Then a little fist clutching a Barbie doll struck him in the nose, and he withdrew to the back of the carrier.

"Puppy!" screeched the girl with the Barbie as her face filled the door. "PUPPY!"

"I must be in New York," the little man said. "I always hated New York."

CHAPTER 1

"Lucky," said Polly at breakfast. Scott looked up from his cereal and frowned. It was just the two of them in the kitchen, but "lucky" seemed like such an unsuitable word that he was tempted to see if someone was standing behind him.

"Me? Lucky how?"

"You're going on a field trip," Polly reminded him. "On your first day of school. The girl down the street with the cool bike told me that *my* class is doing the president's Physical Fitness Test."

Scott understood. Privately he thought the president should mind his own business about how many chin-ups everyone could do, but his mom was always getting after him to set a better example for his sister.

"It'll help you make a good first impression," he told her, borrowing a phrase they'd been hearing from Mom a lot this past week. "Because you're so good at sports."

"Well . . . ," said Polly. "Well, you'll probably impress everybody in dork class with your dorkness."

"Shut up."

"Hey," said their mother as she entered the kitchen. "Don't tell your sister to shut up."

"But she called me a dork—"

"Maybe if you listened to her more she wouldn't have to get your attention that way. And don't call your brother a dork."

Polly said, "*Sorry* are you going out with Daniel tonight? Are we having videos and scrambled eggs and—"

"I don't need a sitter," said Scott.

The look on Mom's face brought them both up short. "I . . . won't be seeing Mr. Trumbull anymore," she said. "But we can still have video night. Yeah?"

So he was Mr. Trumbull again, thought Scott, and he knew his sister thought it too. He wasn't to be called Daniel now. Soon Scott would forget the man's name, just like what's-his-face. A pall fell over the kitchen, an unscheduled Moment of Silence.

Polly broke the silence, but then she usually did. "Is it because we moved? It's only ten miles."

"No, no. Things had been building toward this for a while. Leaving Philadelphia was just the . . . last straw, you know?"

6

For a while it seemed impossible to say anything but the wrong thing. Leaving Philadelphia and their old school behind had been sort of a last straw for Scott, too. But it was a curious requirement of Mom's new job at Goodco that she live in the company's town of Goodborough, New Jersey, alongside all its other employees.

He raced his last few cereal puffs around in the milk with his spoon. "It's not 'dork class,'" he said finally. "It's called Project: Potential."

"Yeah. That's much better."

Scott glanced at the clock. "I have to go," he said, rising from the dinette.

"It's kind of early still," said Mom. "This school starts later than your last one."

"I know. But I wanted to get there before the other kids to . . . meet my teacher and stuff."

Polly dork-coughed into her hand.

"That's a good idea," Mom said, smiling. "See you tonight."

Three schools in three years, thought Scott as he pedaled through the crisp November air. *They should give me a punch card. Five schools and I get a free soda.*

He steered toward the local park, down the storm drain shortcut he'd discovered yesterday, dodging broken glass and a man with a rabbit head, up the embankment toward the gap in the fence and was that a man with a rabbit head? Scott braked hard, grinding a black snaking skid behind him. The rabbit-man stopped, too, and looked back. His tweed pants and white dress shirt were creased and dirty. His necktie was askew. His rabbit head was a rabbit head.

Around the rabbit-man the air looked vivid and alive.

"Hey! Kid! Thtop! Thtay there!" He picked his way back through the garbage and glass on big rabbit feet and rushed toward Scott, who tensed and tried to stand up on his pedals to get away; but there was no time. In an instant he had a five-foot-tall rabbit-man all up in his face.

"You've got to *help me!*" said the rabbit-man in a throaty warble. "Hide me!"

"Um—"

"They're coming! I don't want to go back! I don't *want* to go back!"

Scott dismounted and let his bike clatter to the ground. He stepped backward, stumbled, and fell against the grassy hillock behind him, and the rabbit-man pressed close.

"Okay, calm down," he said. "Everybody calm down. Nothing to be afraid of. What I need . . ."

"Y-yes?"

". . . ith for you to take me to your houth . . ."

"What?"

8

". . . and *hide* me . . . in your *bayth*ment."

Scott was leaning back as far as he could without falling over, his chin against his chest, breathless. When he finally inhaled, he smelled sweater and cookies.

"You're not real," he said softly, closing his eyes. "You're imaginary. You are a . . . neurological event." And sure enough, when Scott opened his eyes, the rabbit-man was gone.

No, there he was. A little ways off now, running toward the drainpipe again on his swift, imaginary legs.

"THTUPID KID!" shouted the rabbit-man, and he disappeared into the pipe.

The things he passed shimmered and changed. The air itself seemed to flinch and shiver at his touch. Dead leaves uncurled and flushed with new life; broken glass appeared, for a moment, to be bright jewels; a stray cat was a unicat.

Scott blinked and looked again, but it was only a cat, of course. What had appeared fleetingly to be an animal with a single spiraling horn in the center of its forehead was merely a smoky gray housecat, thin and twitchy and watching Scott with blue-green eyes. Then it suddenly and theatrically began to clean itself in that way cats do when they want you to know what a big deal you aren't. Scott whistled to get its attention, but the cat turned its back to him and licked its paw with such ferocious indifference that he soon gave up and pushed his bike into the park.

"Not today," he whispered as he walked. "Come on. Please."

A large white van was creeping through the soccer field, right over the grass, and the man in the passenger seat studied Scott through tinted goggles. Rose-colored glasses, actually. Scott kept his eyes on the horizon and breathed great mouthfuls of calm air.

Thirty minutes wasted, and now he fidgeted in his orange plastic chair. He hated the first day at a new school. Around him other kids were chattering, excited about the field trip maybe, staring at Scott like he was a brightly colored fish, describing their weekends. But Scott only watched the empty chair at the front of the room and nervously traced his fingertip through the grooves of a swear word carved into his desktop. Some former student had left it there, maybe years before, but it pretty well summed up his feelings. The word could have been a jittery neon sign buzzing inside his chest as he waited for the new teacher to arrive.

And now he was getting a headache, of course. Of *course*. Perfect.

Specifically, he got migraine headaches, which was a useful thing to know—the word didn't mean much to most of the other kids, but from their parents it drew gasps and unexpected charity. Once at parent-teacher night the mother of a fifth grader had become so flustered by the word that she'd given Scott five dollars.

He'd get a pain behind his eye, another at the base of his skull and down his neck. And then there were the hallucinations, the seeing-things-that-weren't-there.

"We call them auras," a doctor had told him and Mom. "A lot of people get them before getting a migraine. Not all, but a lot. I understand they can be scary, but they'll be a signal that it's time to take one of these pills I'm going to prescribe for you."

In the present, in class, Scott fished a small pill case out of his pocket and removed a white triangular pill. He took it without water and felt it draw a bitter chalk line down his throat.

"What happens to other people when they get these auras?" Mom had asked. Scott understood that what she'd really wanted to know was if anyone else claimed to see a mermaid in the community pool, like Scott had the week before.

Some people saw strange lights, the doctor had told them, or distorted shapes. Zigzagging lines. Some even smelled odd smells or heard things. It was different for everyone.

In the end Mom had left it alone.

The pills usually worked. Scott prayed they would work against the nauseating tendrils that were just now beginning to twist themselves through the back of his neck.

And now the door opened and there she was, a petite woman with a mess of papers in her hands and a pencil sticking out of the bun in her black hair. By the end of the day there would be three pencils in that bun and Scott would think she was pretty, but for now he only frowned and thought, *Where were you? I got here a half hour ago to tell you about my name, so where were you?*

"Sorry I'm late," Ms. Egami said to the class. She dropped her papers, which scattered in that special way papers do when one is running late. She gathered them as the briefly quiet students began to stir as if someone were gradually raising the temperatures of their desk chairs. "Quiet down," she said, and produced the class list to call roll.

This is it, thought Scott.

"Brett Adamson?" said Ms. Egami.

"Here."

It's not as if I'm at the end of the alphabet, Scott thought, chewing his lip. *I get called almost right away, when everyone's still paying attention.*

"Jamie Cassanova?"

"Here."

Probably next.

"David Christiana?"

Okay, next then.

"Here."

"Sco—Scottish Doe?"

Kids all around him were snickering, looking his way, whispering comments to each other behind their hands.

"Here," said Scott.

"Is that right?" asked Ms. Egami. "'Scottish'?"

More snickering. Giggling, even.

"I prefer Scott," he said. Not that it mattered. They'd been told that his real name was Scottish, and it would take them the whole rest of the year to forget it.

"Wow," said Ms. Egami. "Scottish Doe. Scottish P. Doe."

Scott flinched. There were middle initials on the roll? *Now she's going to ask—*

"What does the *P* stand for?"

Laughter was batted back and forth like a squeaky balloon as the kids shared their private thoughts about what the *P* did or should stand for.

"That's enough," Ms. Egami said to the class, but she was obviously new to teaching and hadn't yet learned how to scold and make it stick. It was only a second before the balloon was in play again. This had to end.

"PAUL," Scott said, a little too loud. "The *P* stands for Paul."

The *P* might as well have stood for "pin" or "porcupine" the way it took the air right out of the balloon. The class was silent. There was nothing funny about the name Paul and never would be.

"Oh," said Ms. Egami, and she sounded almost disappointed. "Paul. For a second I thought it might be . . . something else."

"No."

"Oh, well. Right. Allie Fabares?"

"Here."

The roll call went on, and Scottish Doe, whose middle name was not Paul, exhaled slowly and sat back in his seat.

Three sixth-grade classes crammed into one big yellow bus for the field trip to the Goodco Cereal Factory, so when Scott stepped up and through the doorway, he found that most of the seats were occupied by kids who already had all the friends they needed or would ever need. Except for a seat right up front, on which sat one very small and delicately pale eggshell of a girl. And exactly no one else.

Scott glanced around the rest of the bus. He caught a few students looking his way and mouthing "Scottish" to their neighbors, as well as some shorter, sharper words that seemed just now like the clacks of locks or the clicks of closing doors. He could walk down the aisle of this bus like the stranger-come-to-town in a cowboy movie and watch all the locals hide behind shutters and rain barrels. Or he could just sit down next to the girl nobody liked and take his cooties like a man. He sat down next to the girl.

She flinched. Quickly made and then broke eye contact. In that moment Scott could see that her eyes (which, years later, her driver's license would claim were brown) were really very nearly pink. Her hair was as thin and blond as corn silk. She was not short or skinny so much as small, tiny boned. Her head was wired with orthodontic headgear, such that she looked to Scott a little like a lab mouse caught in a trap. Which she was, in a way, but we'll get to that.

"You *must* be new," she whispered.

"Yeah. I'm Scott. Scott Doe."

"Emily Utz."

The bus cleared its throat and rumbled forward. Scott risked a look around the bus and found that everyone appeared to have forgotten him. He had a talent for being forgettable.

"You look familiar," Scott told Emily. After he'd registered at Goode Junior High, the school administrators had sent a welcome packet that included the last issue of the school paper. He recalled a photograph of kids with eggs—eggs in old footballs, eggs with parachutes and little plastic hang gliders—and among these a pallid little girl holding a geodesic globe of balsa sticks like it was a live pigeon. It was topped with a blur of whizzing propellers, and if you looked closely you could see the white egg at its center. "You were in the newspaper," he added, "holding this thing."

"I called it the Ovothopter," she told him. "It was for Egg Drop Day." And when Scott stared back blankly, she explained that the eggs were all dropped from a local news helicopter over the baseball field. If your egg didn't break, you won a prize. Emily's didn't.

Scott smiled. "What was your prize?"

"They didn't give me one."

"That's not fair."

Emily shrugged. "Technically my egg didn't drop, so I was disqualified."

CHAPTER 2

Scott's first day of school happened to coincide with the arrival of a yellow scroll tied up with pink ribbon earlier that morning. It was just sitting there on the dining room table at Erno and Emily's house, the first thing they saw when they came downstairs.

Erno was a lean and rumpled kid—his clothes, which looked fine on their hangers, always looked on Erno as if he'd found them in the road on the way to school. He had bronze skin and chocolate-brown curls. Emily had milky-white skin and pinkish eyes. Standing side by side, they looked like a box of Neapolitan ice cream.

Erno and Emily were twins, somehow.

Erno frowned at the pink ribbon. "Maybe it's just a birthday present," he said. Emily lifted the yellow roll from the table and tugged at its bow.

"Our birthday isn't until the end of the month," she

said as the ribbon fell away and the pages unfurled in her hands.

Two flimsy, canary-yellow papers—one for each of them, probably. Both had the same verse printed in dull black:

WHERE DOTH THE CLAW OF ARCHIMEDES REST?
IN YELLOW PAGES START THY QUEST.
BY VETERANS DAY YOU SHOULD HAVE GUESSED
THE KEY TO THIS, THY CURRENT TEST.

"Oh boy," said Erno.

Emily looked up from her page, tilted her head. It was like you could see her thinking. In point of fact, the light-bulb in the wall sconce above her actually flickered on just then. Bad wiring.

"That's clever," Emily whispered, smiling. Like she already knew the answer.

"Like you already know the answer," Erno scoffed. He told himself she must be bluffing, despite all historical evidence to the contrary. She looked over at him with an apologetic half smile.

"I don't know the answer. Not . . . not really."

There was an awkward silence, and Emily plucked absentmindedly at a wire of her facebow. Hers was mag-nificent headgear, if you were into that sort of thing.

Orthodontia had sort of been invented in Goodborough, and the intricate curves and veiny filigree of Emily's hardware suggested that the practice had flowered here into a kind of art form. Dentists routinely stopped her in the street, often in tears, and demanded to know who had done such beautiful work. Some doctor at Goodco, she'd tell them. She didn't know the woman's name.

Erno watched Emily shrug and slip out of the room with her yellow page. He could hear her trying to sneak up the creaky stairs with it before Mr. Wilson came down for breakfast.

They didn't used to be so secretive about the tests. Or games—Mr. Wilson usually called them games, when he called them anything at all. They used to talk about them a lot. They used to loudly announce that they had to go potty, too, but you get older and some things become more private. The games were one of those things—you worked on them in private; you solved them in private; if you had the right answer, you expected some acknowledgment from Mr. Wilson to come privately, possibly when he wasn't even around.

Erno couldn't remember the last time they'd played one of the games out in the open. Not during the Great Vocabulary Mix-up, and that had been five years ago. Not during the Prime Number Treasure Hunt. Nor the Geography Costume Contest. Nor Anagrammania.

It felt a little like shame. But why? *Why did people feel shame over things that everyone did?* thought Erno, and he counted the games among these things because he assumed other families played them too. He had no idea how alone he and Emily were.

Erno poured himself a bowl of Puftees and sat down with the curled yellow paper, the floor groaning under the weight of his chair. He wondered if he should Google the whole verse—their foster father didn't usually write in old-timey language like this. Then the man himself walked through the dining room and into the kitchen, and Erno stuffed the poem into his lap.

"Puftees," Mr. Wilson acknowledged in passing. "How are they?"

"Fine," said Erno. "The same. Why, did you change them?"

Mr. Wilson called from the kitchen. "There's slightly more xanthan gum in the puff meal this quarter. Only in northeastern markets. You can't tell?"

"No. Should I . . . should I be able to tell?"

"Not consciously, no."

Emily came back downstairs, poured herself a bowl of Puftees, and joined Erno at the table. "I'll be a little late coming home from school, Dad," she told Mr. Wilson. "I have an errand to run."

Mr. Wilson grunted.

"Field trip today," Erno reminded her. That morning the sixth-grade classes were visiting the Goodco factory—just as they had in the fifth grade, just as they had in the fourth and third.

"I remember," said Emily. "I'm containing my excitement now so I can really go crazy when we get there."

"Heh. Well, I just noticed you forgot to wear your Goodco Team sweatshirt."

Emily smiled. "And my big foam finger."

"I told Denton and Louis that I'd sit with them on the bus."

Emily's smile faded.

"They asked," added Erno, "so . . ."

Disappointing Emily was another thing that everyone did. They sat in silence for a moment as Mr. Wilson clattered about the kitchen. Then Emily pushed back her chair.

"I just have to brush my teeth and take my eardrops," she said, "and then I'm ready to go." She was leaving without clearing her bowl. Erno supposed the least he could do was clear it for her.

"You didn't finish your cereal," he called.

"I don't think I like Puftees anymore," she answered. "Who can stand all that xanthan gum?"

● ○ ★

The Goodco Cereal Factory was housed in a humorless brick of a building attached to three generations of grain elevators. You could tell they'd tried to jazz up the main entrance in the 1980s with mascots and marshmallow shapes and a pink dragon, but now that every surface of these was bristling with metal spikes to discourage pigeons, the whole thing came off as kind of unfriendly. The children filed inside under the flaking arched neck of the Goodco dragon. And it was here that Erno noticed that his class was joined by a boy he'd never seen before. A new boy. He supposed the kid must have been around all morning.

A field trip on his first day, thought Erno. *That must be kind of confusing.*

The kids and their teachers crowded into a tiled lobby and were met by a young blond woman with preternaturally white teeth. She beckoned them to come stand before a large television screen that was cycling through a slide show of breakfast tables and cartoon mascots.

"Hi, sixth graders! I'm Stephanie, and I get to be your tour guide today! Are you kids ready for a little bit of magic?"

Erno and Emily shared a wry smile. They already knew that the "magic" included a lot of not talking and keeping your hands to yourself and watching men in

shower caps attend to slow, slow conveyor belts. Breakfast Technicians droning on about cocoa stock and ricemeal density. Listening to people tell you for two days afterward that your hair smells like corn. But it was worth it just to get the free admission coupon to Cereal Town that they handed you on the way out. Cereal Town was in Lancaster County, Pennsylvania, and was staffed almost entirely by polite, sixteen-year-old Amish kids. It was like living inside a commercial—floating down a river of milk on an oat bran inner tube or screaming through the loops of the Cereal Killer Koaster—and it was also just about the only fun outing Mr. Wilson ever took them on.

The slide show faded, and a photo of the factory filled the screen. "The Goode and Harmliss Toasted Cereal Company," said Stephanie, "was founded in 1858 by Nathan Goode and Jack Harmliss in their hometown of Goodborough, New Jersey." Sepia-toned pictures of Goode and Harmliss drifted across the television. One was round faced and mustachioed and had hair that looked wet. The other was lean with bushy sideburns and hair that looked wet. Erno could never remember who was who. "Once just a small factory nestled between the Delaware River and Camden Tributary, today Goodco cereals are manufactured in fifteen countries and sold worldwide. But it's still headquartered here in Goodborough, in the Centennial Building atop a man-made island in the center of Lake Meer."

Clover the Leprechaun appeared on the screen behind Stephanie, and she said, "Now, who recognizes this little scamp?"

Sixty-five dutiful hands went up, though the question was at best a formality: Goodco had reams of market research to tell them that Clover was more recognizable to the average American than Gandhi, Elvis, and all the current Supreme Court justices put together. Stephanie told them this, in fact, and Erno imagined all the Supreme Court justices put together into some kind of giant super-justice. His attention was wandering.

"But do you know that in the early days of television, Clover wasn't a cartoon at all? He was played by a real little man on live TV!"

The screen changed to a black-and-white clip from *The Spencer Tracy Comedy Hour*. The show didn't break for a commercial; the camera just panned to another part of the stage where a group of pretty white children sat in a horseshoe around a tiny old man on a big plaster clover. He was dressed in a jacket and waistcoat with comically large buttons, a tricorn hat, short pants, and big-buckled black shoes. He looked as miserable as a dog in a Halloween costume.

Each child had a spoon and a white cereal bowl with the label BRAND X written on its side.

BLOND BOY
Breakfast! The worst meal of the day!

BLOND GIRL
Why can't we have a cereal that's *fun* to eat?

SECOND BLOND BOY
And will help me to grow up big and strong like President Eisenhower?

BRUNETTE GIRL
<gasp> A leprechaun!

BLOND BOY
Let's steal his gold!

LEPRECHAUN
. . . Why ask for gold.
How about a golden
sweet cereal.

BLOND GIRL
Breakfast magic!

BLOND BOY
Burlap Crisp makes morning
fun! Let's eat!

LEPRECHAUN
I don't care what you do.

ANNOUNCER
Burlap Crisp! A
good cereal from the good
folks at Goodco! There's
a Little Bit of Magic
in Every Box!

The screen resumed its slide show.

"Clover didn't seem like he wanted to be there," muttered Allie.

"That was his character," said Stephanie. "Back then he was called Clover the Angry Leprechaun."

"How did they make the bowls change?" asked Dubois.

"Camera tricks!"

"But you said it was live."

"Oh my goodness!" said Stephanie. "What a treat—children, look behind you!"

Erno didn't have a good gauge of Stephanie's enthusiasm yet, so when he turned, he half expected to see the Snox Rabbit or an actual coconut vampire and not a pair of middle-aged men in short sleeves and ties holding briefcases.

"Wow," Denton muttered. "That *is* something."

It sort of *was* something, though—one of these men was Mr. Wilson. Erno didn't know the other one.

Emily virtually sparkled beside him. "Dad!" she said. She waved her hand, then put it away again when the other sixth graders began to snicker.

Mr. Wilson had the uncomfortable half smile of someone who was being forced to sit quietly while people sang "Happy Birthday" at him. He nodded and grunted some acknowledgment.

"Children," said Stephanie, "about twice a day two

representatives come to take samples from each of the product lines so they can compare them to small batches of 'perfect cereal' back at headquarters! We never know quite when they're going to show up. Gentlemen, don't let us keep you from your very important duty!"

Mr. Wilson and the other man proceeded through the lobby and through a door marked AUTHORIZED PERSONNEL ONLY. Stephanie ushered the sixth grade into a public hall and gestured to a long window that ran the length of the left wall. "Let's just watch these men do what they do."

Mr. Wilson and the other man stood in a white room atop a grating while a Hydra of nozzles blasted them from every direction with compressed air. Mr. Wilson's combover flapped festively and settled over the wrong ear. Kids snickered again and stole glances at the twins. After their decontamination the men stepped forward to select pink matte rubber suits off the wall. They pulled these on, complete with gloves and a hood with something like a diver's mask in front. They still had their briefcases. They looked like marshmallow men going to work.

Stephanie and the kids watched from behind a barricade as the marshmallow men stepped out onto the production floor and collected cereal samples in their briefcases. The conveyor belt operators in their shower caps and white smocks stood at crisp attention as the marshmallow men moved about. Erno could no longer

tell which figure was Mr. Wilson until they both reen-
tered the white room, removed their suits, handcuffed the
briefcases to each other's wrists, and left.

Erno heard the new boy whisper "That was your dad?"
to Emily.

"Yes. Erno's too."

Erno looked at the new boy, and the new boy smiled
back. Then he lost him as the tour began moving again.

They were back at school in time for lunch. Some days Mr.
Wilson gave them money to buy their lunch, and other
days, like today, he made them lunches himself. Erno had
some money he'd earned by house-sitting for neighbors,
and he hoped the school cafeteria was serving something
he liked. Mr. Wilson made really terrible lunches.

It so happened that they were serving pizza, or more
accurately a kind of impersonation of it, as though the
whole concept of pizza had been rather poorly explained
to the cafeteria workers by people who'd only read about
it in books and didn't really like children much. Erno's
brown bag, on the other hand, contained a baloney salad
sandwich, thick with mayonnaise and pickle. Bad pizza
beats good baloney salad, he decided. After buying lunch
he tossed his bag in a waste bin.

It wasn't easy to decide where to sit. Erno had joined
Emily for lunch the day before, but he'd disappointed her

on the field trip bus. And now he could see her there, at the big table in the corner, all alone with her baloney salad and orthodontic headgear. For years she'd had a friend named Jill, and things had been simpler: he would sit with Emily when Jill was absent, and occasionally when Jill wasn't absent, so it wouldn't be so obvious. But Jill's family had moved to Michigan.

"You sitting with Frankensister today?" Denton called loudly to Erno, so Erno sat down next to him if only so the boy would have no further reason to shout.

"Frankensister *love* Erno," moaned Louis. He did it at least once a day.

Because one day Roger had remarked that Emily was pale like a vampire, and Louis had pointed out that her metal headgear made her more like a robot, and then it was generally agreed without any help from Erno that the halfway point between a vampire and a robot was a Frankenstein. Which was why today and every other day Erno had to listen to the three boys make Frankenstein noises and wave their arms around.

"Doesn't even sound like her," Erno muttered.

"Lighten up," said Denton. "Hey, did you guys see the new episode of *Agent SuperCar* last night? With all the explosions?"

Roger and Louis had, and they immediately started talking loudly about it, quoting their favorite parts. Erno stayed quiet, thinking it best not to remind them once again that the Utz kids did not own a television.

"And remember when Agent SuperCar said 'Regular or unleaded?'" Denton shouted. "And then he sprayed the polar bears with gasoline and they all exploded?"

"That was so great."

"Explosions are the *best*."

Erno ate his pizza and watched Emily across the cafeteria. Back when Jill had been around, Erno and his friends had had an unspoken arrangement: he let them make fun of Jill, and in return they didn't make fun of Emily—not to her face, at any rate, nor his. But now these so-called friends had begun to circle Emily like hyenas. Erno realized with a start that he didn't know what the deal was anymore.

And as he watched Emily she turned—very suddenly, in fact, considering she didn't have full use of her neck—and looked directly at Erno. She looked at him looking at her. After a moment her attention returned to a small slip of pink paper in her small, pink hands. She studied it as though it was a diabolical puzzle, which it probably was.

"Oh," Erno said softly. "Oh no."

Denton stopped speaking midsentence and faced him. "What did you say?"

"Nothing. I'll . . . be right back."

"Whatever. Free country."

Erno stood miserably and shuffled back to the garbage can in which he'd tossed his lunch bag and sighed. The can squatted there in the corner, short and fat and topped with a quivering mound of trash and half-eaten food. Breathing deeply (through his mouth), he rolled up his sleeve and plunged his arm into the mess, pushing wrappers and pizza crusts aside. He dug, ignoring banana peels and peanut butter and the insults his behavior was beginning to draw from the rest of the cafeteria crowd.

"What's the matter, Utz? Aren't they feeding you enough at home?"

"Erno! Over here! You can have this pudding I dropped."

"What are you doing?"

Erno looked up at this last remark. He hadn't noticed the new boy standing just across the can from him. It was a fair question.

"Um, I lost my lunch bag in here."

"You're not still gonna *eat* it, are you?"

"No! No, it just has this piece of paper inside it I need. With . . . a phone number written on it."

"Oh," said the boy. "Well, here." He used his binder to shovel some of the garbage aside, and with this help Erno quickly found the bag.

Inside, beneath the carrot sticks and sandwich, was a tight roll of pink paper secured with tape. He pried free the tape, and the paper uncoiled like a party favor, and the secret message, which was most plainly not a phone number, divulged its hidden mysteries:

THIS IS NOT A CLUE.

"Son of a—" said Erno, and he threw the paper back in the trash.

The other boy was eyeing him strangely. Well, maybe not so strangely, considering.

"Um, thanks," Erno said. "I think I'm gonna go wash my hands."

"I'll come with you. I want to wipe off my binder."

They walked out of the cafeteria and through the wide halls. Erno couldn't help liking this new kid: he had a kind face that was unassumingly handsome, if that was possible.

"Thanks again," Erno said. "You didn't have to help."

"My name's Scott," the boy answered. "I just started here this morning. I'm in Ms. Egami's class."

"I'm Erno. I'm in Mr. Klum's class, right next door to you."

"Erno? Erno Utz?"

"Yeah," Erno said, surprised.

"We're in Project: Potential together," Scott said.

Project: Potential was a separate class that the gifted

students went to for an hour each day. The name was supposed to make it sound exciting, like Code Name: Cursive or Mission: State Capitals. While the regular kids took spelling tests, the P: P students learned things like architecture or mythology or Latin. All the things a smart kid was supposed to want to learn and none of the things he really needed to know, like how to shrug off the embarrassment of attending a class called Project: Potential.

"How did you know my name?" asked Erno.

Scott smirked. "You're supposed to be the smartest kid in the sixth grade."

Erno looked at the jelly sliding down his wrist. "That's not true. I'm not the smartest."

"But everyone says—"

"Yeah. They just say that because they hate my sister."

CHAPTER 3

Project: Potential was in the afternoon, in a mint-green room that smelled like mentholyptus. It was taught by Ms. Wyvern, a musty, clown-faced woman who spoke with an unplaceable accent that was thick with gurgling r's and sneezy vowels. Her black bowl-cut hair was interrupted in front by a white skunk stripe, which she claimed appeared right after the Soviets launched Sputnik in 1957. And she seemed to have no idea how much she spat.

Erno sat staring at the yellow paper from that morning and was not listening to Ms. Wyvern read them a story from a fat book titled *Legends and Lore*. "'King Vortigern's mens rrrebuilt the tower, but aaagain the tower fell down. Sssso he called to him his wise men.' Julie, would you continue the readink?"

Julie read, "'The wise men advised King Vortigern to find a boy with no earthly father and kill him, and mix

37

his blood with the mortar of the tower.' Gross. 'Only then would it stand strong. So the king made to search the countryside, and soon they found a group of boys in the midst of a quarrel.'"

Veterans Day is the eleventh, thought Erno. He copied every eleventh letter from the verse and then every eleventh word, but each yielded only gibberish.

Julie passed *Legends and Lore* to Gerald, behind her.

"'Two boys taunted a third,'" read Gerald, "'saying, "Boy with no father, no good will come of you." So Vortigern's men seized that boy and brought him to the ruined tower. And when he learned he was to be killed, he was exceedingly wroth.' Wroth? Um, 'He asked King Vortigern, "Who has set you upon this course? Bring them here so I may question them sith they would have my blood." And when the wise men came forth, he asked them to explain why the tower always fell. But the wise men did not know the answer.'"

Erno scanned the last line of the poem: *"The key to this."* Maybe *this* was the most important word in the whole clue, and he had to find the key to it? He was grasping at straws.

"'"If you wist not why the tower falls,"'" read Brandon, "'"how can you claim to know the solution?" he asked them, and the wise men were dolorously beshamed. Then King Vortigern asked the boy his name, and the boy answered,

"I am Merlin, and I know why your tower falls.""

Brandon tried to pass the book to Erno, but Erno didn't notice, so engrossed was he in the little poem. He also didn't hear Ms. Wyvern ask him if he'd like to share his note with the rest of the class, so she had to ask him twice.

"*MESTER UTZ*. Woult you like do shaaare thad note with the rrrest of the class?"

The other students giggled. Erno blinked and looked up at Ms. Wyvern.

Nobody, of course, ever wanted to share their note with the rest of the class. Erno didn't understand why they always asked. It had given Erno the idea a while back to make up a dummy note he could keep ready to exchange, with a little sleight of hand, for any real note that got discovered. The dummy note read:

TEACHER'S DOING A GREAT JOB TODAY, ISN'T SHE? CHECK YES IF YOU AGREE.

But he'd never gotten to use it, and he couldn't use it now—it wasn't on yellow paper.

"Um, sorry," said Erno. "It's not a note."

"Et looogs like a note."

"It's . . . it's not. It's a puzzle."

Ms. Wyvern brightened. She suddenly appeared quite pleased, which was not a good look for her.

"Vaaabulous! Perhabs the whole class can heelp you wid thes puzzle."

Out of the corner of his eye Erno saw Emily tense up in her seat and frown.

"I'm supposed to do it myself," said Erno.

Ms. Wyvern's smile fell, and she made a faint hissing noise, as though the air had been let out of her cheeks. She was uncomfortably close now, her breath medicinal. Emily and Erno had argued once over whether Ms. Wyvern wore actual makeup or instead allowed herself to be bitten repeatedly on the face by mildly poisonous spiders; but now, at close range, Erno was prepared to admit he'd been wrong about the spiders.

"Es thes puzzle a . . . schoooool assignment?"

". . . No."

Her arm lashed out with reptile speed, and before Erno could think, the paper had left his hand. He blinked, and there it was: long and curled between the pursed tips of Ms. Wyvern's scaly fingers.

"Don be greeedy, Mester Utz." She pulled the paper taut, then read:

> "Whaare doth the claw uf Archimedes rrrest?
> In yeddow pages staaart thy quest.
> By Veterans Day you should haf guessed
> the key tooo this, thy gurrent test."

"Fmpf," she added. "Not ferry good poetry."

"Archimedes was a mathematician," blurted Ethan from the back of the room. "And he was Greek. And he invented things." Ethan was the sort of student who was always keeping score—if he couldn't be the first to declare his knowledge of something, he would make certain you understood that he'd known it already. One day he would be declared the winner, and there would be a Smartest Boy trophy and a parade.

"Yess, yess, Archimedes," Ms. Wyvern agreed. "Great man. But whoo knows uf the claw uf Archimedes?"

Erno had looked that up, and he was pretty sure Emily knew about it as well. But neither sibling raised their hand.

Ms. Wyvern revived her laptop, which was projecting on the whiteboard behind her. "Hode on, I'll focus. Lights, pleeease."

The room went dark, and an encyclopedia entry emerged from the digital fog. It featured a detailed etching of something like a huge crane with a claw at the end of its tether. The crane strained over a seaward stone wall to pluck a warship right out of the ocean.

"The claw uf Archimedes, allegedly uuused to defend his Sicilian home frrrom the Romans."

"I knew that already."

"Well done, Ethan," said Ms. Wyvern. "Sssooo . . . whaare doth the claw uf Archimedes rest?"

"In Sicilia?" said Carla.

"Sicily."

"That's what I meant."

Erno knew this wouldn't be the solution. It was too easy.

"Maaaybe. Maaybe. Veterans Day is on the eleventh—you haave nine days, Mester Utz."

Erno looked over at Emily, but she just shook her head sadly and put her face in her hands.

"Messes Utz, do you thenk you can do better?"

Emily flinched. Ms. Wyvern and the whole class were staring at her.

"Maaaybe you thenk you can solve thes theng, hahn?"

Emily looked down. "We're supposed to do it ourselves," she said softly. "We're not supposed to *have* help."

The other kids laughed. They laughed whenever Emily said *anything*, like it was unnatural, like she was putting on a show.

Ms. Wyvern harrumphed like a backed-up toilet and returned to the screen.

"Soooo, whazzizzit? What haf you figured out, Mester Utz?"

Erno sighed and said, "Well, the answer probably isn't something you can just find on the internet. That's not how they usually . . . it's probably something you can find here in Goodborough."

"A-hahn."

"So," Erno continued, "the claw of Archimedes rests on a ship, right? Maybe the answer is on one of the boats in the harbor. Or maybe the science museum has a model of the claw, or . . ."

"A-hahn. Eenyone else?"

The boy who had helped Erno at lunch had been sort of half raising his hand for three minutes, but the way Ms. Wyvern suddenly flinched and noticed him you'd have thought he'd popped out of a box.

"You—new boy. What do yoou thenk?"

"Scott. My name's Scott."

"Yes, yes, new boy Scott. What you thenk?"

"It's like one of those claw machines. Where you try to grab prizes." The class laughed at this, and Scott flushed.

"Was your prize that you got to keep the ship?"

"I think your prize was not getting killed by Romans."

Project: Potential ended for the day as a freshly photocopied stack of poems was passed from hand to hand. Each student was instructed to work on the puzzle at home. They filed out of the room in twos and threes, except for Emily. Erno sidled up to Scott.

Then Carla Owens turned to face Emily and everyone else. Carla was a big girl who wore purple, and she had long, bright purple fingernails, which she used to scratch

43

and pinch out small punishments to people she didn't like. She didn't like Emily.

"*We're supposed to do it ourselves,*" Carla said in a nasally whine that was meant to sound like Emily, but didn't. "*Don't help Erno!* Oh, *don't help him. He's not supposed to* HAVE *help.*"

Many of the other kids laughed. Project: Potential kids could be a little bloodthirsty: some of them loved to see others abused. They loved it because it wasn't them, the way people used to love watching gladiators get eaten by tigers.

Emily ignored the taunt and tried to walk briskly by, but Carla blocked her way.

"Leave me alone," Emily said quietly.

"What? What did you say? You're so scrawny I couldn't hear you, Pinkeye."

Erno stepped forward. "Just leave her alone, Carla."

Carla's eyes blazed. Her mouth quivered. "Shut up, Erno! I was taking *your* side! She—if she wasn't your sister, you'd hate her too!"

"No, I wouldn't," Erno said, and he was pleased to realize that he meant it. "And you weren't taking my side. If I needed a cheerleader I could do a lot better than Carla Owens."

"You're just like your sister!"

"If only."

Carla's face looked pink and sweaty, like a hot dog. She said, "No wonder your mother's dead," and suddenly nobody was laughing anymore. "When she saw Emily's ugly little rat face, she decided she'd rather *die* than be your mother!"

There was a seasick silence. Emily was swaying a little and breathing fast, the way she always did when she got one of her spells.

It seemed from her expression that even Carla Owens knew she had gone too far. Everyone stared at her, and at Emily, mouths slack, and for a quiet, poisonous moment, nothing happened. Nothing except for the sudden appearance of a thin line of blood between Carla's nose and lip, like a red mark on her great mistake of a face.

"Your nose is bleeding, Carla," said someone.

Carla looked cross-eyed at her own nose and tried to dam up the flow with a slip of tongue. "How did . . . ," she muttered, then looked fearfully at Emily. And Emily attacked.

For an instant it was like watching a nature film of a tiny white mouse pouncing on some garish South American toad. The mouse scrabbled and bit, and the toad's eyes popped at this unexpected turn. But nature soon corrected itself, and the giant toad knocked the mouse aside with the long, purple fingers of her long, purple arm.

Emily got to her feet with a cut on her cheek. She

seemed ready to leap again, but this time Erno stopped her and held her fast as she flailed at Carla.

"You don't know anything about my mother!" Emily's tiny voice screamed. "You don't know anything about anything! You're only in Project: Potential because your dad's the vice principal! YOU READ AT A THIRD-GRADE LEVEL!"

Erno pulled Emily back, and Carla quickly walked away. The other students scattered, and Emily began to cry, and the twins stood together in the school quad, alone and late for class.

CHAPTER 4

After school Scott found Erno outside the bike racks, so the two of them walked home together. He supposed Emily was home already—Carla Owens had concocted some story about the day's events that made herself look blameless and Emily look like a rabid animal, so she'd been suspended for fighting.

"Has she ever done that before?" Scott asked.

"What, attack someone?" said Erno. "No. She usually just says nothing and walks away when people tease her. Or else she falls over."

"Falls over?"

"Yeah, she gets these dizzy spells when she's stressed out. Ear infection. She falls right over unless I'm there to catch her."

"She's lucky to have a brother in the same grade."

Erno shrugged. "She'd be lucky if Carla Owens got

swallowed by a volcano, but until that happens . . ."

Scott huffed. "Some things . . . some things you probably can't even get a volcano to swallow, you know?"

Erno smiled a little. "Yeah. She probably tastes like a prune."

They fell into an uneasy silence, discomfited by the mystery of what, if anything, Carla Owens tasted like.

"I've been thinking about what you said in class," Erno finally spoke. "It would be just like Mr. Wilson to hide the answer to one of his games in a claw machine."

"Mr. Wilson?"

"Our foster dad."

"He thinks up these puzzles for you?"

"Yeah, and Emily was right: we're supposed to do them ourselves. They're our tests, you know? So it sort of ruins the test if we get help."

Scott's eyes narrowed. "So . . . your dad pits you and Emily against each other, to see who's *smarter?*"

Erno frowned as if he'd never really considered the implications before. Scott was sorry he'd asked.

"Well," he added, "it's funny you mentioned the science museum, because that's why I thought of claw machines. We just moved here, you know, and the move was kind of . . . hard, and my mom wanted to do something nice for my sister and me. She's a scientist—my mom, I mean—so she took us to the science museum last weekend. And they have a claw machine in the lobby."

Erno raised his eyebrows. "A claw machine in the science museum . . . man, that's *gotta* be it. Hey, are you . . . are you expected at home right away?"

"Not really. My mom's at work, and Polly's staying after school." Scott frowned and scanned the horizon. "To be honest, I'm not sure I remember where my house is."

The boys hustled to the science museum, a squat little building by the high school with an entrance that was roped by a thick double helix of plaster DNA. SCIENCE IS FUN! read a banner of Albert Einstein on a bike. Because nothing says fun like a picture of an old person riding a bicycle.

They burst through the doors, and there it was: a claw machine behind the admissions kiosk. And inside the Plexiglas case, perched atop a pile of plush owls and dolphins and dolls of Einstein riding a bicycle, was *another yellow scroll*.

Erno turned to the woman inside the kiosk. "Do we have to pay admission to play the claw machine?"

"Well," she said, "no. But we have a wonderful exhibit on the life cycle of rain clouds! Or, ooh! A photosynthesis workshop at four o'clock! Yeah?"

"Um," said Erno, and he looked at Scott.

"Just the claw machine today, I think," said Scott. "Can you make change?"

The woman sighed and reached for their five.

"Jeez. Fifty cents a game," said Erno as they pressed close to the machine to examine the scroll—another yellow page tied in pink ribbon, just like the first one.

"It'll be easy," said Scott. "It's right on top."

Erno slid a dollar into the slot, watched it get spit back out again, tried once more, smoothed the bill against the corner of the machine, tried a third time. The game's little claw of Archimedes shuddered to life. Erno jerked it in place over the scroll and pressed a button labeled DROP. The talons closed, and traced the edge of the paper tube as if testing its quality, and then rose and retreated to the chute in the corner, empty-handed. This claw was not so certain it *wanted* a yellow scroll. This claw was merely browsing.

"You try," said Erno.

Scott tried. The claw pinched the scroll, raised it up by its end, and dropped it again—too early. It rolled off an owl's mortarboard and came to a stop against the glass.

"We still have four dollars," he said.

Four dollars later they had accidentally won two owls

and a dolphin, but the scroll remained in the case, lodged between Einsteins.

"I don't have any more money."

"Neither do I."

"Are you guys done finally?" asked someone behind them. It was a younger boy with a juice-stained face and two shiny quarters in his chubby little claw.

"Um. Okay," said Scott, backing off. "But . . . can you do us a favor?"

The boy frowned. "A *favor?*" he asked, over-enunciating the word like he'd never used it in a sentence before.

"Yeah. Could you not try to get that yellow scroll? We're trying to get that."

"Yellow . . . you mean that roll of paper? I don't want paper. I want an old man riding a bicycle."

"Of course," Erno muttered. "The one thing we can't trade him for his quarters."

"That's great," Scott told the boy. "Never mind, forget I said anything."

The boy squinted at the scroll. "You guys want *that?*"

"Yeah, but you don't, so—"

"Why? Is it good?"

"No," said Erno. "It's totally boring. You don't want it, seriously."

The boy looked at the scroll, then back at Scott and

Erno, and then he stepped up to the controls. A second later it was clear to everyone present that the boy only had eyes for the scroll, and when the claw dropped, it hooked through a loop of pink ribbon.

"Oh man," said Scott. "Are you kidding me?"

"Little jerk," Erno muttered under his breath.

The scroll dropped down the chute, and they could hear it thap lightly against the door of the slot below.

"We'll give you two owls and a dolphin for it," said Scott.

The boy had the scroll in his hands. "Stuffed animals are for girls. You two are girls," he said with a sticky pink grin. Then he pulled at the ribbon and unrolled the page and stared at its inky center.

"What does it say?" asked Erno. He sounded desperate.

"Why should I tell you? It's mine. It's really awesome, though."

"We'll give you two owls and a dolphin and . . ."—Scott searched his backpack—"an eraser shaped like Agent SuperCar and most of a pack of gum."

"Strawbubble?" the boy asked, looking at the pack.

"Very Cherry."

"Okay," he said after a moment. "Deal."

"Thanks," Erno said to Scott as they exchanged their gum and toy eraser and stuffed animals for the secret message as if they were the sissiest spies alive. The boy ran off with his haul.

"Suckers!"

Erno unrolled the page, and together he and Scott read the single, typewritten line:

THIS ISN'T A CLUE, EITHER.

Erno sighed. "This is child abuse, right?"

"I wasn't going to say anything."

CHAPTER 5

Erno was beginning to consider inviting Scott to the house some afternoon, so now he couldn't help seeing it as if for the first time, the way Scott would. It was old and cramped—full of hiding places but so creaky as to make for really noisy hiding. Deep down Erno knew they were all a little old for hide-and-seek anyway, but he'd have to have *something* to suggest after breaking the news that the Utz kids had no video games or television.

The only board games they owned were Monopoly and Risk. Either one on its own might be considered by most sixth graders to be boring and overlong, so most sixth graders would not be able to appreciate what Erno and Emily had made when they combined the two into a bewildering supergame called Ronopolisk that was now in its fourth year and didn't really encourage a third player. And wouldn't it be a shame to stop now? Just when the Scottie Dog was poised to invade Poland.

So no TV and no games. No games but *the* games, and Erno wasn't supposed to share those, either.

The discarded pink bow still lay like a scribble on the dining-room table. Was that significant? Was it a clue? Erno tried to tease some meaning out of its shape. It sort of looked like an ampersand.

There were sounds coming from the library, the dry swish of a broom against the floor. It was Wednesday, and on Wednesdays their housekeeper, Biggs, came to clean and cook, and mend anything that needed mending.

"Biggs!" Erno called into the next room. "Did Mr. Wilson say anything to you about this ribbon?" He looked down at the table, then back at the doorway, and was startled to find Biggs standing next to him.

"You all right?" Biggs asked in his dull way.

"Yeah. You sneaked up on me." Even as Erno said this he could scarcely believe it, looking up at the man. What would Scott think of Biggs? He was, as always, *enormous*. More than eight feet tall, he stooped to get through every doorway. Even when he sat down, as he did now on a dining-room chair, he seemed too tall, and his knees pointed up at the ceiling like churches.

"Good day at school?" asked Biggs, scratching a huge hand over his cheek. As impressive as Biggs was, his hands still seemed two sizes too large, and were as thick

and pink as hams. They were outmatched only by his feet. Which admittedly Erno had never seen, sure, but they had to be gigantic because why else would he wear such shoes? So long and tapered and to all appearances seaworthy. Like kayaks.

"School was fine," Erno answered. "Did Mr. Wilson mention anything to you about this ribbon? Like, did he tell you not to touch it?"

"No," said Biggs, scratching the back of his neck. "Just never disturb stuff like that."

Erno nodded. Of course Biggs knew all about the games. As housekeeper he would sometimes uncover hidden clues meant for Erno and Emily, and he'd been asked in these cases to leave them as he'd found them.

"I think Emily's figured it out already." Erno sighed. "The new game, I mean. Or she's figured out how to figure it out, which might as well be the same thing."

Look at me, thought Erno. *Talking about it.* It felt *good* to talk about it. You could tell Biggs anything.

The only answer that came from Biggs was a sort of whuffling sound. He was sniffing the air, the great nostrils of his broad pug nose yawning wide. Erno had to stifle a yawn just looking at them.

"What is it?"

"Washing machine's done," said Biggs.

Erno smelled nothing but didn't argue as Biggs rose and

walked soundlessly away. He'd never noticed it before—
everyone else in the Utz house made the old wood creak
and whine when they moved. Everyone but Biggs.

Nothing was said about the scroll at dinner that night. Of
course. They mostly sat in silence.

Mr. Wilson said, "Erno, could you pass me the square
root of one hundred and forty-four peas?" So Erno began
to portion them out onto his foster father's plate using
chopsticks that had been laid out for just that purpose.

"Emily," he continued, "would you please spear your
father another piece of moribund domestic avian mus-
cle?" And so Emily served him some chicken. This was
ordinary dining-room conversation in the Utz house, but
Erno still strained to catch every word, worried that it
might contain some clue. It made dinner exhausting.

It was days later when it hit him, and he called Scott right
away.

"Archimedes is an *owl*," he told him.

"He is?" said Scott. "I thought he was a Greek guy."

"He's that too. But . . . have you ever read *The Sword in
the Stone*?"

"No. I've seen the movie."

"There was a movie?"

"Sure. They show it sometimes on the Disney Channel."

"Oh. Well, we don't have a TV."

"You don't . . . what?"

"Have a TV. We've never had one."

There was a longish pause, during which Erno occupied himself by imagining Scott's horrified face. He was used to this kind of reaction. He may as well tell people that they didn't have a toilet.

"Well, I haven't seen the movie in a while," said Scott. "I don't remember the owl."

"He can talk, and his name is Archimedes. He belongs to Merlin. That story we read the other day made me think of it."

"Sooo . . . the claw of Archimedes rests . . ."

"On Merlin? On Merlin's shoulder? I'm sure I'm onto something here. I . . . there was a new scroll sitting on my nightstand today when I got home."

"What did it say?"

"In yellow pages find the name
and pay a call to end the game."

"It was a hint." Erno sighed. "I bet you a hundred dollars Emily didn't need a hint."

"'In yellow pages find the name,'" said Scott. "You think

59

you're supposed to find the name Merlin in the original poem? Hold on." Erno could hear Scott muttering to himself before his voice came back clear, and clearly excited. "In the first poem there are two *M*s, eighteen *E*s, seven *R*s, four *L*s, and three each of *I*s and *N*s. Two-one-eight, seven-four-three-three."

"That's just enough digits to be a local phone number."

"It said to . . . what, make a call?"

"Pay a call," said Erno. "Doesn't that mean to visit someone?"

"The phone number's worth trying anyway, isn't it?"

"Yeah. I'll call you back."

Erno hung up, tried the number, then dialed Scott's again. "Didn't work," he told him. "I got one of those 'The number you've dialed is no longer in service' messages."

"Well, but listen to this: in the original poem, the first *M* is the twenty-fourth letter. The first *E* is the third. If you check them all like that you get two-four-three, four-one-four, two-three-three-four."

"That's long distance," said Erno. "What area code is that?"

"It's the Congo. In Africa. I just looked it up."

Erno bit at a hangnail. "If this isn't the answer, Mr. Wilson is gonna kill me for calling the Congo."

"Can you do it as a three-way call?"

Erno could, and soon both boys listened as the number rang for the second, third, fourth time. Then voice mail:

"You have reached the voice-mail box for THIS ISN'T A CLUE, EITHER. If you'd like to leave a message—"

Erno opted not to leave a message.

CHAPTER 6

At lunch the following day, Erno sat at the end of the table and glared at the yellow pages, too antsy to care much what Denton or Roger or Louis thought anymore. Veterans Day was in two days.

"What is that thing again?" asked Denton.

Erno mumbled, "It's a class assignment," which was now technically true.

Suddenly a big book fumped down on the bench beside him: a fat brick of flimsy yellow paper. The Yellow Pages. Scott stood over him.

"Not *those* yellow pages," he said, pointing to the poems in Erno's hands. "*These* Yellow Pages."

"Have you been carrying that around all day?"

"No, I just borrowed it from the school office."

"Um, guys," said Erno to the guys. "You remember

Scott, right?" They each nodded or grunted or didn't do anything at all.

Scott sat down. "'*In yellow pages start your quest. Find the name.*' Well, look at this." He thumbed through the book to a page he'd marked, then traced his finger down to a small box in the corner:

MERLE LYNN
C.P.A.
Tax and Financial Planning

211 E. Ambrose 215-5937

"Start your quest?" Denton scoffed.

"*Nerd* quest," said Louis.

"The quest for the . . . the quest for the . . . magical . . . ." said Roger, struggling to finish, ". . . calculator. Am I right?" He grinned, palm in the air, and awaited his high fives.

"If this doesn't work I can just run away from home," said Erno later after school. "There are probably all kinds of other families that would be happy to have me. I'm not *completely* stupid, right? I could play their games and take their tests and beat the pants off their biological kids."

"I don't think other families have tests," Scott answered. "Sorry my little sister is tagging along."

"It's fine. Long as she doesn't mind visiting Merle Lynn,

C.P.A., on her way home."

"Stop talking about me like I'm not here," said Polly. "Ooh! Yard sale! Kid's yard sale!"

A girl of seven or eight stood in her front yard behind a TV tray and a bright orange poster that read FOR SALE.

"We don't have time," said Scott. But Polly was already bounding up the yard, singing, "Yooou only say that 'cause YOU'RE mean, an' you have abandonment tissues."

Erno looked at Scott. "'Tissues'?"

"She means *issues*."

"So your mom's a scientist?"

"A physicist, yeah."

"Factory or headquarters?" asked Erno. There was no question that she worked for Goodco in some capacity. Why else would a family move here? Scott said his mom worked at headquarters, and Erno was relieved to hear it. HQ kids and factory kids didn't mix much.

The yard girl was selling those kinds of toys that were popular in drugstores and dollar shops. Action figures with SOLDIER HERO printed on their uniforms. Fashion dolls with names like Marbie and Babbie. Polly examined a stiff little figurine of a prince nobody had ever heard of with a lean sword and a shield shaped like tree bark.

"Where'd you get him?" she asked the girl.

"Cereal box."

Polly paid fifty cents for the prince, and she marched

him up and down Scott's backpack all the way to Ambrose Street.

"Stop that," said Scott.

Erno nudged him. "This is it."

They were standing in front of a high-peaked row house: all eaves and gables and a tall turret topped with a conical cap. A plaque on the porch read CERTIFIED PUBLIC ACCOUNTANT. Two filing cabinets sat like young lovers on the porch swing.

Scott and Erno approached the front door while Polly hung back a few steps, suddenly shy. Erno rang the bell, and a man answered.

He was an ample, bowling pin–shaped man with a gray beard trimmed close. He wore a threadbare blue bathrobe over his boxers and wifebeater. The robe was pilly in places and no more than a meager crosshatch of thin gauze in others. It appeared to be worn not so much out of modesty as out of a sense of loyalty to the garment itself.

"Hey," said the man. And when none of the kids immediately answered, he added, "Selling candy?"

"Um, no," said Erno.

"Too bad."

"Are you . . . Mr. Lynn?"

"Call me Merle."

The hall behind Merle was cluttered with plastic

binders and cardboard boxes. And dust. Erno didn't know what he was supposed to do. If this Merle was in on the game, he wasn't being very forthcoming about it.

"You have an owl," said Polly behind them. The boys followed her gaze past Merle into the house—and then they too could just see a live barn owl watching them from a fireplace mantel in the next room.

"That's true," said Merle. "Do you like him? Is that cool?"

"It's . . . a little weird," said Scott.

"Yeah. You don't know the half of it, kid."

Polly abruptly raised her new figurine and told him, "I've got a little prince."

"Sweet. Well, if that's everything—"

"Wait," said Erno. "Did my . . . dad give you anything to give me, or . . . anything?"

"Who's your dad?"

"Augustus Wilson."

"Oh!" Merle blinked. "Yeah, well, I'm finished with his taxes, but your sister came and got 'em a week ago."

Their mother had died in childbirth. That's what they'd been told. Their real father had possibly never been in the picture.

Though they'd always lived in the same house, they'd had a revolving team of foster parents, photos of whom still climbed the wall above the stairs: a mother with a

face like a fist, posing stiffly with the infant Utz twins as if caught between two car alarms. A picture of Brad, a very nice man who got a very nice job offer in Maryland and left after only ten months. A candid shot of Erno and Emily with their second foster mother, taken by her husband in Cereal Town at Christmas. The old woman was yanking Emily's arm over some misdemeanor in front of Marshmallow Manor while Erno scanned the park for a place to hide. It was remarkable both for its Hansel- and Gretelishness and for the fact that it was the nicest picture anyone had of this woman. And there were more recent photos with Mr. Wilson, who had thus far outlasted each of the others by four years.

The one and only constant in their lives had been Biggs, the housekeeper. He'd helped care for Erno and Emily when they were small. Biggs seemed to be good at everything he did, be it knitting them sweaters or fixing a carburetor, and he was a competent nanny, though he approached every task with the same dull demeanor and apparent lack of interest. Now Biggs only came on Wednesdays, and Erno wished it were more often. Dull as he was, Biggs was always helpful, and tireless, and hugely loyal. It was like having a horse that could cook. Erno thought about visiting him from time to time, but neither of the twins knew where he lived. Erno would have been astonished if you told him that Biggs lived at the top of a tall oak tree in Avalon Park, though Emily probably would have just nodded thoughtfully.

Erno hurried home. He unlocked his front door, and there was Emily, sitting in the stairwell with a bag of candy in her lap.

"Merle Lynn, C.P.A.," he told her.

"Here," she said, and offered the bag.

He sat down beside her. "Where did you get all this?"

"It was my prize for winning the game. I saved some for you. There's a lot of chocolate, and those peanut butter things you like. And a lot of gummi. You know how much I hate gummi."

Erno sat down beside her and reached into the bag. He took a peanut butter roll, and Emily ate a toffee.

"Don't people do their taxes in the spring?" he asked.

"Dad was having the last seven years refiled. To see if he could get more money back. He cashed in a bunch of investments, too."

Erno nodded politely. Money stuff was beyond him. "How long ago did you solve it?"

"The day I got suspended."

"Well. On Monday your suspension will be over, but Carla will still be ugly."

"You shouldn't say things like that," said Emily, and she looked him in the eyes. "I'm ugly too."

Erno started to say "No you aren't," but Emily cut him short.

"I've just been thinking about it, is all. Carla hurts people, but I think that's all she has. That's her *thing*. Making fun of her just makes her worse."

Erno's face was hot. "Well, *you* made fun of her. You called her stupid."

"I know. I shouldn't have."

Erno knew she was right, but he was a little sore from being lectured to by his sister. "For someone who understands people so well, you sure don't know how to deal with them."

"I know," said Emily. "I think that's *my* thing."

She released a long sigh.

"I'm so SICK OF SCHOOL!" she added, loud enough to send a flock of sparrows in the front yard out of their tree. "I wish we could just QUIT!" In that same moment, a lightbulb in the front room burned out, almost as if Emily had startled it.

"You know," she said quieter, a guilty look in her eyes, "sometimes I think we could. Quit. We already know more than the teachers do, anyway."

"Maybe *you* do. I don't." But Erno agreed that theirs was

maybe not the most rigorous school. So much busywork, so many movies and field trips. "Do you remember that February when we celebrated Slacks History Month?" he asked. "I think that just started as a typo."

Emily looked at him imploringly. He could tell she wanted permission to say something. He could even roughly guess what it was.

"I . . . I'm not trying to brag, or anything," she said.

"It's okay," said Erno halfheartedly.

"It's just . . . well, you know how much I read at home."

"Sure."

Emily glanced around, making sure the school's spies weren't listening in.

"Well, I haven't actually learned anything at school since the second grade. Not one thing."

Erno assumed she was exaggerating. But then he recalled Egg Drop Day, and Emily's Ovothopter rising pluckily into the western sky as two hundred other eggs rained down like a biblical plague. Emily didn't exaggerate; Emily was an exaggeration.

"Everything they teach us is already in my brain," she said, a look of haunted wonder on her face. Then she ate another candy. Erno stared at the candy.

"That new boy, Scott—I think he thinks the games are kinda . . . weird. Kinda mean."

Emily swallowed hard so she could speak. "Mean?"

"Yeah. The idea of Mr. Wilson making us compete against each other."

"What did *you* say?"

Erno opened a little bag of gummi shapes. "I didn't say anything really."

They were quiet for a while, eating candy. Erno broke the silence.

"Where on Earth do you think Mr. Wilson found gummis shaped like the Greek alphabet?"

"I think he made them himself," Emily answered. "He does things like that, because he loves us so much."

They were quiet again. Then Emily rose, leaving Erno with the bag.

"I think a lot of kids aren't fortunate enough to have a dad who invents games for them," she said as she marched up the stairs.

By Veterans Day the Ovothopter was videoed as far west as Denver. Both Emily and the National Weather Service agreed that the egg would probably come down somewhere in the Rockies, and that it wasn't worth the effort to go see if it had broken or not.

CHILD ONE
G-g-gosh, what a spooky
old forest.

CHILD TWO
Look, a castle! Maybe we can
stay the night.

CHILD THREE
And tomorrow morning
we'll enjoy the delicious
taste of KoKoLumps!
Part of this nutritious
breakfast!

{The castle portcullis rises}

ALL THREE CHILDREN
It's Kookie! The coconut
vampire!

KOOKIE
I'm loco for coco!

CHILD ONE
Don't let him get our
KoKoLumps!

CHILD TWO
Look! The sun's coming up!

ROOSTER
Coco-doodle-doo!

KOOKIE
Ai ai ai! Curse you kids!

CHILD THREE
Crazy Kookie—vampires don't
eat breakfast!

{Kookie crumbles to ash.}

CHILD THREE
KoKoLumps—another good
cereal from the good folks at
Goodco! There's a Little Bit
of Magic in Every Box!

CHAPTER 7

"Lucky," said Polly at breakfast. It was a Tuesday, the last school day before Thanksgiving break. And for Scott it was barely a school day at all.

"Maybe in a few years you'll have Ms. Egami for homeroom," he answered. "Maybe she'll take *your* class to New York."

"Ms. Egami," Polly sang. "Oh *Ms. Egami*, I *love* you. If only I were older, and not such a dork."

"Shut up."

"Hey," said their mother as she entered the kitchen. "Don't tell your sister to shut up."

"But she called me a dork—"

"Maybe if you listened to her more she wouldn't have to get your attention that way. And don't call your brother a dork."

Polly said, "*Sorry* are you going to go out with Coach Steve again? He asked me to ask you after soccer practice, but he told me not to tell you he asked."

Mom gave a wincey little head bob. "I don't know. He's a very nice man."

"And good at soccer."

"That's not as important to me as it is to you, honey. Honestly, there's no point thinking about it now—we'll see when I'm back from Antarctica."

Goodco was sending Mom on a scientific expedition. To Antarctica. Something to do with optical anomalies and strange waveforms—Scott didn't really catch most of it, nor understand what, if anything, it had to do with breakfast cereal.

"They should make a kids' book about us," said Polly. "They should call it *Too Many Daddies*."

Scott smiled weakly and stared into his oatmeal. Why did everybody always want to talk about everything?

"Coach Steve isn't your daddy," said Mom.

"It could be a lift-the-flap book. Daddy number one is on the television. Daddy number two is in the station wagon, driving away. Daddy number three is honking from the curb so he doesn't have to ring the doorbell and talk to us."

"Oh, come on—do you mean Tim? I only went out with him twice."

"I'm going to go," said Scott, rising so quickly that the table shook. "Sorry," he added, and patted his napkin against a trickle of milk that had hiccupped over the side of his bowl.

"It's earlier than usual," said Mom.

"Yeah, but the field trip, remember? It's today. We're supposed to be on the bus and ready to go by—"

"Right, right."

"And I'll need a ride because we won't be back until four thirty—"

"I know," said Mom. "I'm on it. See you then."

There had been a lot of daddies. There was Daddy number one, Scott and Polly's real father, but he'd left when Scott was five. They hadn't seen him in years—not in person, at any rate. Afterward Mom remarried, divorced, and dated other men, some seriously, some not. Scott knew that other members of the family talked about her. There'd been talk as far back as her first wedding.

A lot was made of the fact that she'd caught her own bridal bouquet. Picture her with her back to the bridesmaids and other single women, covering her eyes anyway, throwing the bouquet high—maybe too high—over her shoulder. Then the half-funny, half-serious shuffling of ladies' feet, the just-kidding-but-not-really contact of elbows against ribs as each woman vied to catch the bundle and therefore maybe—who knows?—be the next to marry. But as Mom turned to watch the flowers fall, a gust of wind howled through the courtyard like the ghost of weddings future and buffeted the bouquet back into her open hands.

Mom had laughed then; everyone laughed. Mom waved the roses for the crowd and laughed, but she didn't throw them again. She kept the bouquet.

Had she known? Had she known in her gut that she was marrying a man who would get famous and leave them? It made for a better story if she had, and Scott believed—without knowing he believed it—that a good story was truer than truth. And so he'd never asked.

His father, John, hadn't always been so famous. He was something called a triple threat—that meant he could sing and dance and act—and before Scott was born he had been trying to get someone in New York to pay him to do any combination of the three. Scott's mom, Samantha, was working to support them both while John pursued his dream. They'd agreed he had five years with his dream before he had to get a real job and give her a chance to go back to grad school. He could feel the five years coming down on him like a slow curtain.

Then Samantha got pregnant and started hinting that the plan needed a good looking at. If she finished her degree in physics, she could make real money. Not big money, maybe, but steady money. And so far John had only won a few small parts in commercials.

It had been after one of these arguments that John retreated to the fire escape of their Brooklyn apartment.

"That you, John?" came a voice from the landing above. John tilted back to look.

"Hey, Diego."

"Another fight with your lady, eh?"

"The same fight, actually. She's given me a new deadline. Lord, I need a good part! A great character." John exhaled, leaning back against the railing. "If I could play just one great character, I swear I'd name my firstborn after him. I'd tattoo his name on my chest."

"What roles are you up for?"

"A kind of small but really juicy part in an off-Broadway play about the war; the lead in an all-singing, all-dancing version of the Scottish Play; and a meerkat."

"Scottish play?" Diego had said as John's cell phone rang.

What John had actually auditioned for was the leading role in the Shakespearean tragedy *Macbeth*. It's the story of a Scottish general, and of his power-hungry wife, Lady Macbeth, and of their murderous plot to seize the throne. But actors are superstitious people. They'll tell you it's bad luck, for example, to rehearse on a Sunday. It's bad luck to have real flowers onstage, or a mirror. It's bad luck to say good luck. And they never say "Macbeth." In conversation they usually refer to it as the "Scottish Play."

John was especially superstitious.

"You're kidding . . . ," he said into his cell phone. "If this is a joke, I swear I'll . . . no, of course . . . so when do . . . okay, thank you, Steven! Thank you!" John finished, and closed his phone.

"What was that all about?"

"I should . . . I should tell Sam first," John said with his eyes on the bedroom window. "Oh, well, she's still mad at me—that was my agent! I got a leading role!"

"*Qué bueno!*" said Diego, grinning down the stairwell. "Which one?"

Scottish Play Doe was born at 4:13 a.m. on September 6. The ink was barely dry on his father's new tattoo.

Their whole lives, Polly and Scott had been under a general gag order not to tell anyone that their father was an actor and recording star. Polly was always a little itchy with this secret, and she'd been known to slip up on occasion—as she had at their previous school when she'd promised the other girls that her famous dad would get them all their own Nickelodeon series if they'd only make Polly captain of the soccer team. But a lot of the other players hadn't believed her, and the captainship had gone to a girl whose mom brought cupcakes. It had been a rough campaign.

Scott, for his part, had never had any trouble keeping his promise. He *could* tell; but then there'd be a lot of fake friends, birthday parties every weekend, people calling him on the phone ... who wanted all that attention?

Speaking of attention, Scott almost collided just now with a strip of police tape. Until today he'd been avoiding the shortcut through the park where he'd seen the imaginary rabbit-man, so now he was surprised to find the end of the storm drain surrounded by yellow bands and marked with orange cones. He had to dismount his bike to duck under the tape, and that was when he saw the unicat again.

He glared at it. It glared at him. He glanced away and looked back, blinked a few times, gave the animal every opportunity to resume being an ordinary housecat; but it remained stubbornly fanciful. Scott sighed and walked his bike out of the pipe while the cat circled around, keeping its distance.

"Give me a break," he called back to it. "A *unicat*? That's not even a thing." Scott read a lot of fantasy books, and if his brain was going to hallucinate mythical creatures, he felt strongly that they should at least be something he'd heard of.

And now he was going to get a migraine, of course. He fished out his pill case and found it empty. The pills were expensive, so he never carried more than one or two in there. He hadn't refilled it after the last time.

A headache and a two-hour bus ride. Outstanding.

Scott was the first to arrive. The migraine was coming on slowly, but it was coming. He hung around the bus until the driver noticed him and called down through the doors.

"You one of the New York kids?"

Scott said yes.

"This is your bus, then."

Scott sat down near the back and checked his permission slip for the third time that morning.

"What you going to New York for?" the driver shouted back.

"What?" said Scott. He'd heard the man fine but often said "What" reflexively when people asked unexpected questions. It gave him a moment to think.

"I said, Why New York?"

"We're going to see a play. On Broadway."

"Is it *Makin' It?* I saw that once."

"No. It's called *Oh Huck!* It's a musical *Huckleberry Finn.* We just finished reading the book, so . . ."

"Uh-huh. I saw the original cast of *Makin' It*, with Reggie Dwight and Ashlee Starr. My sister knows someone, got us tickets."

"That's great."

Kids began filling out the bus. Erno and Emily squeezed into the seat next to him.

"Hey."

"Hey."

"Hey."

"This is gonna be so cool," said Erno. "Going to New York, I mean. Not the musical."

Emily gazed at Scott with a knowing look. Emily was all about knowing looks. "You're getting a migraine," she said.

Scott nodded, very faintly.

"You are?" said Erno. "Now? That sucks."

"A bus ride isn't going to help you any," said Emily.

Ms. Egami charged up the steps.

"Who's ready to go to New York?!"

Emily was right, as always. The bus ride made it so much worse. The drunken lurch of it sent the nausea slithering round and round his head and all through his insides. Under another set of circumstances he might have actually *wanted* to throw up—vomiting sometimes made the pain and the sick feeling go away—but to throw up on the school bus? In front of his whole class? He'd have to change his name and move to another city. *Again.*

Erno distracted him with talk of fantasy baseball and pretended not to see the way Emily stroked Scott's hand so gently, so sweetly, it made Scott want to cry. He could almost have kissed her, if not for the very real danger that his vomit and her orthodontic headgear posed for them both.

"Tell me," said Scott, "how the new game is going." Emily dropped his hand.

A few days ago Erno had realized Mr. Wilson wasn't using the letter *E*.

It was the word *flapjack* that had tipped him off. You couldn't help noticing a word like that, jostling past like a clown car. When Mr. Wilson had said,

> *"Do you want an additional flapjack? Or bacon?*
> *If not, I'm going to want to wash your dish. Okay? Okay.*
> *Hurry up, now, you don't want a tardy at school."*

he'd realized something was going on. Mr. Wilson always said *pancake*.

"I don't understand what he's doing now," Erno told Scott. "You know he started by not using *E*'s for a while. Then it was *R*'s. Then he was using every letter again, but he wouldn't say the word *no*. Turns out a person can only say *nope* or *negatory* so many times before it gets obvious."

"Right." Scott sighed.

"Then it was the word *and*, and then the letter *M*, then *L*, and *E* again. But now I have no idea. He's definitely using every letter."

Emily sulked. Scott rubbed his neck.

"Maybe he's not using a number," he suggested.

"I thought about that, but how would you know? How would you know if someone was avoiding a number?"

"You could just ask Mr. Wilson to count to ten or something," said Scott. He was already sorry he'd brought it up.

"Yeah," admitted Erno, "except that we're supposed to be more sneaky than that, when we're working on the puzzles. We're not supposed to be so blunt."

"We're not supposed to *talk* about them, either," Emily growled.

A wad of paper sailed backward over rows of heads and seats to hit Emily in the shoulder. The three kids did their best to ignore it.

"I mean," Erno continued, "what if Mr. Wilson stopped saying *robot*, or . . . *esophagus*? It could be years before we—"

"Stop TALKING about it!" Emily shouted, spitting just a little involuntarily.

She'd been too loud. Even *her* tiny voice had carried, and kids in the bus turned to look. A single incident of fighting had given Emily a reputation, and now everyone waited for her to lunge across the seat and start chewing on someone.

"What's going on, Erno?" she continued, quieter. "The

games have been working just fine for ten years, and now you're breaking rules just because Scott thinks they're weird?"

"It's not that big a deal, Emily—"

"Oh no? No? Do you think Dad will agree? What do you think will happen when he finds out you've been getting help?"

"What difference does it make, anyway?" Erno steamed. "You always solve every puzzle first. No wonder you like them so much."

Emily's frown dissolved, and now she just looked hurt. Scott resisted the urge to tell them both to shut up and let him die in peace.

Finally they reached Manhattan, and then the Port Authority Bus Terminal, and then a spot outside some Port Authority restrooms where Ms. Egami asked if anyone had to go and Scott raised his hand so energetically he heard his back crack.

He rushed into a narrow stall and was punched in the nose by the smell. The toilet showed signs of having been visited by either a very large man or a very small horse, but Scott didn't feel he had the time to be picky. He spun out enough toilet paper to vandalize a house and carefully cleaned the seat.

Dizzy, he nearly dropped his backpack to the floor,

then got a closer look at the floor. Instead he looped it over a hook on the stall door and then a great vinegar wave crashed over him and his knees gave and he gripped the seat and sputtered his breakfast into the bowl.

A minute later he flushed and turned.

Afterward, he'd realize he didn't think about it at all—when he saw the hand appear over the top of the door and reach for his bag, Scott lunged forward and seized it at the wrist. The tiny wrist, attached to the tiny hand on an arm like a doll's. A real ugly doll made from dried fruit and old footballs.

The hand squirmed. Scott looked down beneath the stall door for the thief's feet. There were no feet. Scott considered his options, and so did the thief.

"Well now, son," said the thief in a voice that was both high and coarse, like a kazoo. There was something a little foreign about it too. *Australian, maybe, or Irish?* "It seems you've got me. So wha' d'yeh suppose you'll do with me?"

Still holding the tiny wrist, Scott unlatched the door and opened it just enough to poke his head around. It was a tiny man, this man who was trying to take Scott's bag. He couldn't have been more than two feet tall, with a miniature red tracksuit and his arm hooked over the top of the stall door. His tiny old-man face was pug nosed and underbitten like some overbred kind of dog, and it seemed puckered with sadness. Not to mention oddly

familiar. If it wasn't for this familiarity, and for the feel of the man's arm in his hand, Scott would have mistaken him for another aura.

"Yeh don' happen to have somethin' to eat, do yeh, lad?" the little man asked. "I'd be in your debt. 'Tis always a blessing to have one o' the Good Folk in your debt."

Scott glanced around the restroom. Men and boys were coming and going, but none were paying any attention to what he considered to be a fairly unusual tiny-man-hang-ing-on-a-toilet-door situation. *That's New Yorkers for you,* he supposed.

"Except when it's not a blessing, yeh know," the thief continued. "Speakin' fair, the blessings o' the Good Folk can be worse than the curses."

"You could have just asked in the first place," Scott muttered. "You didn't have to try and steal my bag."

"Asking is begging. Pitiful. Want to punch myself in the eye for even tryin' it. Stealin' is good, honest work," said the thief, puffing out his chest.

"Well, not honest, strictly speaking," he admitted, after a moment. "Or actually good."

They were interrupted by Denton Peters, who barged through the men's room door, shouting Scott's name like it was a swear word.

"I'm right here," said Scott.

"Ms. Egami wants to know what's taking so long," said

Denton. "You got the squirts? Should I tell her you have a bad case of the squirts?"

"No! I'm just . . . this guy was trying to steal my backpack."

"Yeah? And you're scared he's gonna come back?"

Scott gaped at Denton.

"Need yeh to let me go now, son," the thief said to Scott.

"Are you telling me you can't see the . . . little . . . guy hanging here?" Scott asked Denton.

Denton frowned in the little man's general direction, and then Scott thought he saw a flash of recognition on the boy's face. He'd seen *something*. Denton Peters squinted, titled his head, crossed his eyes like he was trying to cope with an optical illusion.

"I can . . . sorta see," he whispered.

"Just sorta?"

"He's like a mirage."

What Denton Peters saw next was a sort of prismatic blur, and then Scott jerked back his arm, yelping with pain. Scott pushed past him and scowled into the distance.

Denton followed his gaze to the men's room door.

"Uh . . . what just happened?"

Scott unhooked his backpack. "Your mirage bit my hand."

● ○ ★

90

Oh Huck! seemed like kind of a lousy musical, but Scott supposed he might have been in the wrong mood.

His migraine vanished shortly after leaving the bus terminal, but on the way to the theater Denton staunchly denied having seen *anything* unusual in the men's room apart from the new kid hiding from imaginary elves. Denton had by this time already forgotten Scott's name, however, and most of the other kids didn't know who he was talking about, and Scott had hidden behind Carla Owens until it all blew over.

Scott was quiet as they returned to the bus terminal through the toy store dazzle of Times Square.

"I just don't think they should have made the raft a separate character," said Emily.

"Riff-Raft?" said Erno. "But she's the narrator. She told you what was going on."

"Mark Twain didn't need a talking raft in the book. *Or* a rapping scarecrow."

"Scott, tell my sister that everything doesn't have to be exactly like the precious book."

Scott started. "What?"

"You're still upset," Emily told him. "About Denton teasing you."

"No. No, I'm fine."

"Forget about it," said Erno. "Everyone else has."

The thing is, they probably had. Scott was nothing if not forgettable.

Back at the Port Authority there was some sort of situation. Two flashing police cruisers were up on the sidewalk in front of the entrance, grille to grille. A crowd had formed, and three uniformed officers attempted to push back these people with outstretched arms and patently false claims that there was nothing to see. Another officer, on horseback, paced the street. And in the center of it all, two more policemen squared off against each other like big dogs.

"Let's not do this here, man," one of these officers was saying in soothing tones. "We can talk about it at the station."

The other man took a step back, took a step forward, his boyish face tangled with fear and anger. "We'll go back to the station when you admit I've *apprehended a suspect!*" he said, pointing to the backseat of one of the cop cars. "This is not cool, guys! I know I'm the rookie and all, but—"

"Not in front of the juveniles," said the first officer, glancing at Scott's class.

"We're not juveniles," Erno muttered.

"It just means *kids*," said Emily. "Nothing bad."

An electronic red news crawl on an adjoining building declared the DOW DOWN and REGGIE DWIGHT PUNCHES

QUEEN and then POLICE DISRUPTION AT PORT AUTHOR-ITY BUS TERMINAL. It flashed like a marquee for the weird bit of drama playing out in front of them.

Scott craned his neck to look at the rookie's car. There *was* someone in the backseat, but the suspect was very small. Smaller than a toddler. He wondered. . . .

If Scott Doe had a talent, it was his ability to walk about unnoticed. When not actually calling attention to himself in bus station bathrooms or by defending his indefensible given name, he was one of those kids who could practically disappear in a crowded room. Inconspicuous. Unremarkable. It had always been that way.

So now when Scott shuffled away from his class and approached the police car, Ms. Egami did not notice. Even Erno and Emily didn't notice, transfixed as they were by the police and the strobing lights. Scott stepped up to the cruiser on the street side, away from the cops, and looked in the rear window.

It was the little man again. He was slumped in the backseat, his round fists ringed by silver handcuffs like tiny planets. He could have just slipped them free if he wanted to. Apparently he didn't want to.

"Look, Pete . . . ," the cop was telling the rookie. "We need to get you some help. There is *no one* in back of your squad car. There is nothing but a pair of empty cuffs."

"Fight!" Denton Peters suggested from the sideline,

and Ms. Egami tried to shush him. "Shoot something!"

The window was open a crack. The little man sniffed and looked up at Scott.

"Oh. 'S you. Come to gloat?"

"I can see you," Scott said quietly into the gap, "and that policeman can see you, but nobody else can."

"You're a regular Sherlock Holmes, yeh are. Quick now an' offer your services to those coppers! They could use a brilliant mind like yours."

"Why can I see you? Am I crazy?" Scott asked, worried suddenly that his headaches were the sign of something else, something festering in his brain.

The little man studied him for a second. "Set me free, and I'll explain everythin'."

Scott looked again at the handcuffs, so large against the man's wrists that they looked like a practical joke. "Why can't you—"

"It's complicated."

"Were you stealing again? Is that what happened?"

"What else am I to do? Work for a livin'? Make shoes?"

Scott breathed, and tested the door. He expected a police car to be locked, but it wasn't.

"Hey," one of the police officers said just then. "Hey, your door is open."

Scott ducked down, and the little man scootched to the edge of the car seat, rattling his handcuffs.

"Quickly!"

Scott pulled them off, easy as anything. And that's when the little man leaped up onto his shoulder, ran down the length of his back, and was away.

"Hey!" said Scott. "Come back!"

The small red tracksuit slipped into the street, dodging traffic. Then the clop of hooves, and the mounted police-woman was towering over Scott, her horse snorting thick, furious clouds.

The officer was shouting. Scott cowered. It might have gone badly for him had the horse not chosen just then to turn into a unicorn, and throw its rider, and turn back into a horse again.

The policewoman landed on the pavement, hard. Scott ducked and dashed back to meet his class as the other officers rushed to her aid.

"There you are," said Erno when Scott turned up beside him, panting. "Did you see that horse rear back like that?"

Scott goggled—at the flashing squad cars, the Keystone cops, the plain brown horse mincing about. Just a horse.

"I'm having kind of a weird day," said Scott.

CHAPTER 8

Scott's headache came back on the way home—not as bad as before, nothing he couldn't handle. He cooled his temple against a rattling windowpane as the bus reeled up the curb and into the school parking lot, where Mom and Polly were waiting in the Hyundai and fogging up the windows with their talk.

"You okay?" Erno asked Scott as they disembarked.

"Getting better."

"I have a theory about your headaches, Scott," said Emily, who was shivering under her puffy blue coat. "I think I can cure them, but you have to not mind being electrocuted a little bit. Do you mind being electrocuted a little bit?"

"Um. Can I think about it?"

"Take your time. I have some soldering to finish first, anyway."

Erno rolled his eyes. "My sister thinks she's in one of those movies where the smart kid invents things and all her friends call her Gadget."

"Yeah. *All* my friends," Emily said, and waved her arm only at Scott. "Good night." She stepped off toward a windowless white van, and Erno followed. Scott heard him protest furtively: "*I'm* your friend. You know, sort of."

Scott got into the backseat of his family's Hyundai, and Polly immediately turned and hooked her fingers over the headrest.

"Because your bus was late we get pizza!" she announced.

"Get in the back and buckle up," said Mom.

"Finally I understand why I have a brother," Polly said solemnly.

There's a story behind Polly's name, too.

Scott's naming had turned out to be so significant that John warned against taking his next child's naming too lightly.

"I *like* Sarah," Mom had said, and often.

"I like Sarah, too," said John. "That's not the point. The . . . universe . . . or the gods or someone will tell us what our daughter should be called. We just have to be patient. It could be really important for us, like with Scottish."

Scott, almost four, lay on the sunny bed with his cheek against his mother's belly, hoping to feel the baby kick. Instead he heard a sound like a wet burp. He flinched and looked up at his mother.

"What *was* that?"

"That," Mom sighed, "was a contraction."

John knew that the modern husband was supposed to be in the delivery room with his wife, not pacing the waiting room like a dad in a cartoon. But he'd been by Sam's side for Scott's birth, and the whole operation hadn't agreed with him. Now he noticed a nurse eyeing him, and he forced himself into a chair.

He cast about for something—*anything*—that could conceivably be a sign, a divine message within the confines of the St. Mary's Hospital waiting room. The time was nigh, the child must be named; but there were no suggestions here for John apart from a magazine about cats and a poster outlining how to give himself a breast exam.

Whiskers Doe? he wondered as he glanced at the open magazine. *Leukemia?* Then a tangle of green just beyond the magazine caught his eye.

"I'm sorry . . . Miss? Nurse? Miss?"

The woman turned.

"What sort of plant is that, Miss? Do you know?"

The nurse glared at him. "Are you being funny?"

99

John straightened in his chair.

"Miss, I have played Puck in the Park. I assure you, if I were 'being funny,' you would be the first—"

"That plant's fake. It's made of polyester."

Polly Esther Doe had been born at 8:03 a.m. on August 14.

John would leave them six weeks later.

"How was the play?" asked Mom. "Did you love it?"

"It was okay," Scott answered. "But I had a headache today." *And I saw a unicorn. And a unicat. And a leprechaun tried to steal my backpack.*

"Oh *no*."

They ordered a take-out pizza and rented a video—an old movie their mother had loved as a girl. It was, coincidentally, one of those movies wherein the smart kid invents things and all his friends call him Data. Scott could sense that his mom wanted it to be a real event—a fun family night. She would be leaving after Thanksgiving (a day care worker from Goodco would be staying with them) and wouldn't be back for a month, maybe two. But Scott's headaches tended to wear him out, and he fell asleep during the big finale with the pirate ship, pretended not to wake when his mother covered him with an afghan, and trudged up the stairs to his bedroom when his official bedtime compelled him to his official bed.

He didn't notice anything unusual in his room that night. He didn't notice anything at all until morning, when he woke up next to a leprechaun.

CHAPTER 9

"GWAH!" Scott shouted, and rolled out of bed in a tangle of sheets. The tiny old man in the red tracksuit was there on his mattress, had been sleeping next to him, sharing the twin bed—maybe all night? From the cold floor Scott couldn't see him anymore, and he held out hope that it had all been some sort of waking dream until the little pug face appeared at the edge of the bedding.

"AHH!"

"Ah, put a cork in it," said the little pug face.

Scott rose unsteadily. "Why . . . why are you here?"

The man dangled his legs over the side of the mattress. He smelled like potatoes. "Didn't thank yeh properly before. In the city. Come to make . . . amends." His tone suggested that "amends" was a dish he could be persuaded to serve but didn't care much for himself.

An early-morning memory came back to Scott, of

cuddling up to his stuffed bear Bongo—a memory complicated by the fact that he'd given Bongo to the Salvation Army three years ago. He cringed at the old man and shuddered.

Mom's voice was at the door. "Scott, are you all right? I heard you call out."

Scott glanced at the little man, who shrugged.

"I'm okay," he said. "I had a weird dream."

Mom poked her head in the doorway. "I'm making waffles. Ten minutes?" She paid no attention at all to her tiny houseguest. Scott nodded at her.

"*I* like waffles," said the man after she left. He was drumming his fingertips together and musing at the ceiling. "If there are waffles to be had. Best thing to come out o' the Middle Ages, waffles. The rest o' that millennium was a bit of a wash. . . ."

"Who are you?" Scott asked. It was the least of the questions on his mind. Though he thought he might have to take the long way to get to the others, which included *WHAT are you* and *Why are you two feet tall* and *Don't you think it's maybe time you were going?*

"Call me Mick." Mick slid down from the bed and circled Scott's small room, casting his eyes toward this and that. He had the impatient look of someone pretending to shop when all he really wanted to do was use your bathroom. Then he paused at the window. It didn't face much of anything apart from the alley, but if you stood at the edge and looked through it obliquely, as Mick was doing now, you could see just a sliver of the town at large: its crosshatched trees and factory on the hill. He took a drink of something from a little metal container in his pocket and grimaced as he swallowed. "Can't believe yeh live *here*. Of all places, this."

Scott frowned. "What's wrong with Goodborough?" It wasn't New York, to be sure—it was small and quiet, and nearly everyone who lived there worked for the cereal company in one way or another. But it was nicer than their last home, and it even got tourists: visitors who loved Goodco cereals so much they left bigger cities to come here, to buy souvenirs, to take the tour.

"Yeh don't even know. Course yeh don't. No one digs in the dirt anymore."

"Uh-huh. In New York you said you'd explain what's going on," Scott said. "If I freed you."

"Aye, I did." Mick turned from the window. "So I am honor bound to tell yeh that I am one o' the Fair Folk, the Good Folk of the daoine sídhe, and I am a very long way from home."

Scott inhaled. "You *are* a leprechaun."

Mick scowled. "I am a *clu*richaun. A clurichaun. I amn't no bleedin' leprechaun. Does my suit look green to you?"

"No."

104

"So I amn't a leprechaun. But I am one o' the Fay, one o' Queen Titania's court, an' probably so are you."

"I'm . . . what?"

"Scott!" called his mother. "Breakfast!"

So quite possibly the most important conversation of Scott's life was just then interrupted by waffles, and there are worse things.

CHAPTER 10

"*You look at that,*" said Reggie Dwight to his publicist, but *en español*. He'd landed in Madrid twelve hours ago and kept insisting everyone listen to his second-semester Spanish. "*You look at that, below to the window, in the street.*" He paced across his suite to another window in the bedroom, then back to the first.

"I saw them," said his publicist, Angela, in English. Below Reggie's hotel window, on the sidewalk of Madrid's Calle Gran Vía, were a camera crew and three lonely Spaniards with picket signs. Two of these signs were in Spanish, the third read GOD SAVE THE QUEEN (FROM REGGIE DWIGHT). He actually found it kind of clever.

"*I have . . . ,*" Reggie began, but faltered. He wanted to say he had protesters, but settled for "revolutionaries."

"It's nothing. Someone on the hotel staff must have blabbed."

"*Is exciting. My heart is fat.*"

"Can you please stop speaking Spanish?" Angela chirped. "I wouldn't ask except it's making me want to stab pens in my ears."

"I'm just saying it's kind of exhilarating. All the sudden attention." Both Reggie's last movie and album had failed to meet sales expectations, and he'd been feeling a little neglected. "There's no such thing as bad publicity, right?"

"Sure," said Angela. "Publicists love that expression."

Three days ago Reggie had punched the Queen of England in the face. He had done it for some very good reasons that he was nonetheless now at a loss to explain to anyone else.

"Okay," he said, still watching the street. "What are we doing?"

"We're still waiting to hear back from the *Late Show* people, but there is no way they're not having you on. And this week everyone you talk to is going to call you Sir Reggie Dwight or Sir Reginald if we have to pin a note to your shirt."

"I don't know," said Reggie, rubbing his neck. "I don't really go in for titles and all that—"

"Please. The only thing you love more than your title is pretending you don't love your title. Everyone will be reminded that you're still a Knight of the Realm and the queen hasn't disqualified or excommunicated you or whatever despite you punching her in the face, so if you're good enough for Her Majesty, you should be good enough for them. I mean, do you realize that even a couple of your stalkers have gone quiet lately?"

"Only a couple?" Reggie joked, but he recognized that the really obsessive fans didn't tend to just fade away. They either loved you or they were suddenly sending you portraits of yourself made with dead insects.

"Well, that one accountant still sends you daily email," said Angela.

"What about?"

"The usual. Bogeymen, secret societies. Rubbish. But here's something nice: Goodco still wants you for that commercial."

"I thought Steven already said no to them. I don't do American commercials."

"I want you to reconsider. It's a huge vote of confidence that they're still offering, and this could be a very good move. That talking police dog comedy you just wrapped is a family film, and you want to seem family friendly. And it doesn't get more wholesome than children's breakfast cereal. You'll look like a nice guy . . . you know, less of a queen-puncher."

Reggie had met the queen once before of course—five years ago, when he'd been knighted. When he'd been made a Knight Bachelor "for achievement in theatre and music and for service to children through his charity Kids First." He'd knelt before the small old woman and rested his knee on an odd stool that had no other earthly purpose but to receive the knees of the knighted. The queen wore a pale yellow suit with squared shoulders like a stick of butter, and she'd smiled kindly at him through her big spectacles. He remembered wishing he could touch her hair, which was gathered about her head like candy floss. He wanted to know if it was as sticky as it looked, but of course he didn't dare—he would never have dared to touch the queen. Except, just recently, to punch her. That apparently he would do. He still marveled at this.

"And of course I'm still trying to put this press release together," said Angela. "So once again, any help you could give me—"

"I told you already. I can't explain it in any way that doesn't just make me sound more crazy."

"Are you taking any prescription medications? Something that could have gone bad on you?"

"Just stuff for hay fever . . . sumatriptan for migraines. You know, I *was* getting a migraine that day."

"Hmm," said Angela as she jotted this down. "It's *something.*"

The second time Reggie met the queen was last week, at the racecourse in Berkshire. He had always enjoyed the races. He had always liked horses, but he'd determined as a boy that while a love of horses might be considered faintly girlish, a love of horse racing made him one of the lads. He was enjoying box seats with two London cousins when a prim man appeared at his elbow. Her Majesty was here, dining with the jockey Sir Gordon Maris. Would Reggie please come pay his respects?

Reggie was led to an elegant dining room that overlooked the track. He'd bowed at the neck to his queen, who was dressed in pearls and another of her squarish overcoats, this one as green as a Williams pear. He wondered if anyone had ever told her that she always looked like something good to eat. Maybe Prince Philip. He decided to keep it to himself regardless.

He was feeling the first twists of a headache as he was invited to sit between Her Majesty and Gordon Maris. The little jockey was no longer a young man, but he still looked like a schoolboy in his blazer. The pink and blue diamonds on his tie reminded you of the garish silks he once wore on the racetrack. *He must have these ties specially made*, thought Reggie, and that's when he saw the fly.

A great fat horsefly, plump as a raisin, helicoptering around the jockey's head. Neither Maris nor the queen gave it any notice as they discussed the National Hunt race taking place that afternoon. Then the bug quit its wheeling and buzzed right for Her Majesty, attaching itself like a fresh wart to her nose.

The queen did not so much as flinch, so Reggie flinched for her.

"The young filly Baker's Dozen is a bit of a wild card," Maris droned, "if you'll permit me to say so. Quite good on the hurdles but rather untested on the steeplechase."

Reggie couldn't believe they were still talking about horse racing. Of course, Maris was old and (Reggie remembered reading somewhere) half blind. But the queen! She'd scarcely moved, and now the fly was plumbing the soft flesh of her nostril with its tiny teeth. Reggie glanced for help at the queen's assistant, who was maintaining a respectful distance and a complete lack of eye contact.

Her Majesty smiled at something Maris said, and the fly crossed the bridge of her nose, leaving behind a watery bead of thin red blood that slipped off its tip and dripped onto the china. The fly continued past her eye, humped over her brow, and parked again on the empty lot of her forehead. And just as Reggie began to think it might be his knightly duty to slay this beast, the queen plucked the horsefly off her face and popped it wriggling into her mouth. Then she cast a sideways glance at Reggie and winked.

Maris said, "You know who has a really good horse-breeding program now is the Danes."

"Er," said Reggie, fully intending to excuse himself and

return to his cousins. But then the woman turned, and he saw the darkly glinting ancient eldritch maleficence in her eyes and did what any loyal knight would when faced with the sudden certainty that his queen had been replaced by an impostor.

A few seconds later the old woman was still wailing and squirming facedown on the floor, and Reggie began to wonder if he'd made a mistake.

In his hotel room now, he realized that this had not been the first time he'd seen something that wasn't there. Granted, it had been a while. How old had he been? Six? Seven? Young.

"Goodco is in Goodborough, right? In New Jersey?"

" . . . Yes," said Angela. "But they don't want you in New Jersey. They want you on a soundstage in Burbank."

Maybe we could change their minds about that, Reggie thought. He was fogging up the windowpane. He wiped it clear with his sleeve and discovered that the protesters and press were already gone.

"I need to see my kids," he said.

CHAPTER 11

It turns out that it's impossible to concentrate on breakfast when there's a two-foot-tall Irishman standing under the table. Scott buttered his fruit and poured orange juice on his waffle, and Mom had to make him another.

"What's with you this morning?" she asked as she poured the batter.

"Sorry," said Scott. "Still sleepy." He passed a piece of buttered pear under the table to Mick, who made a disgusted sort of noise in his throat.

"What was that?" asked Polly, so that Scott was forced to clear his own throat several times as cover. He sounded like he was trying to start a lawn mower.

He wolfed down his new waffle, and when the time came for Scott and Polly to clean up, Scott offered to do it by himself. Polly squinted at him as if he was up to something, which of course he was.

"Why? Why do you want to do it by yourself?"

"Can't I just do something nice for you for no reason?" Scott asked, feeling Mick's presence like a pebble in his shoe.

"I guess I always figured you *could*; you just never wanted to."

"Let me do it. You won't owe me anything."

"I won't owe you anything?"

"No."

After a moment Polly shrugged and went off to do whatever seven-year-old girls do. Scott filled the sink with dishes.

"Want help?" asked the two-foot-tall Irishman under the table.

"No."

"This is undignified," said Mick from inside Scott's backpack. After the dishwasher was filled and he could sneak the little man outside, Scott headed vaguely toward the park with a squirmy yellow schoolbag over his shoulders.

"What did you say before?" Scott asked. "I'm one of the Good Folk? One of Queen Titanium's court?"

"Titania. And I'm sayin' *maybe*. Maybe it's why yeh can see me. Yeh ever see anythin' else yeh can't explain?"

Every week, practically, thought Scott. "Yesterday I saw two different kinds of animals with a horn on their heads."

"Sure," Mick said. "What sort? Unirat? Uniraccoon?"

"What? No—"

"Unipossum? Uniturtle?"

"Are those really . . . no, one of them was just a regular unicorn," said Scott, and he marveled that such a phrase had stormed its way into his vocabulary. "The other was a unicat. And before that I saw a rabbit-headed man."

The squirming stopped. "A rabbit-headed man?" said Mick. "Wha' did he look like?"

He looked like a rabbit-headed man thought Scott. *Is that seriously not a good enough description?* "He was wearing a blue tie and a shirt and pants. No shoes."

"Like the rabbit on Honey Frosted Snox?"

Scott frowned. The Snox Rabbit was just a simple cartoon drawing, and when you meet an actual clothes-wearing rabbit-man, it turns out you don't really make the connection; but yes, Scott said, he did sort of look like the rabbit on Honey Frosted Snox.

"Poor Harvey." Mick sighed. "Where did yeh see him?"

"Right about here, actually," said Scott. They were near the storm drain.

"Let me out."

"Are you . . . are you sure? Someone might see—"

"I'll risk it—mostly folks see wha' they expect to see: a dog in a pet carrier, a chicken in a chicken coop. Mostly they expect to see nothin' at all, an' they'd never look for me here."

Scott grunted and eased his bag down to the ground. "*Who'd* never look for you here?" he said. "Are you in trouble?"

Mick pushed the zippers apart with his fingers and stepped free, and ignored the question.

"Now, where did yeh see Harvey?"

"The rabbit-guy? Back there, by that pipe. It didn't have all that police caution tape before."

Mick perked up at this and began scanning the horizon. "Goodco might've marked it off like that. When a spot has seen a lot of the Good Folk, it becomes special, an' more Fay are likely to turn up there. Glamour attracts glamour."

"Goodco . . ." Scott looked into Mick's dried-apple face and something clicked. "I just remembered where I've seen you before."

"Is it New York? 'Cause I remember that too."

"It was in a commercial. At the Goodco factory a few weeks ago."

"Ugh," said Mick. "My distinguished actin' days. Back when I still had enough glamour to appear on camera. Which one was it?"

"I don't know—I wasn't paying much attention. It was

my first day at school, so I was mostly checking out the other kids and feeling weird."

"Did I seem just annoyed or was I actually abusive?"

"More annoyed, I think."

"'Twas one o' the early ones then. They quit usin' me when I ran low on magic an' kept makin' the kids cry."

"Uh-huh. So what is it," said Scott, "to be one of the Good Folk? What does that even mean?"

"Aw, nothin'," said Mick. "It probably just means you're part fairy is all."

Scott gave Mick a sour look, but the elf wasn't paying attention. "That's hate speech. You're ignorant, and I feel sorry for you," he finished, reciting something his mom had always told him to say in these situations.

Mick was distracted, still looking for some sign of his friend. "What? Who's ignorant?"

"Just because he . . . dresses in weird costumes during his concerts and he's an actor and all doesn't mean you should call him a fairy," Scott finished, his face a little hot.

Mick squinted up at him. "What are yeh talking about, son?"

"My dad. Sir Reggie Dwight. He's a movie star, and a recording artist and stuff."

"*I'm* talking about the Fair Folk, the daoine sídhe. The Seelie Court. Brownies an' elves an' those goblins that can keep from stabbing everything an' sit still a minute. Fairies."

Scott's stomach settled. "Oh. Like you, 'cause you're a leprechaun."

"Clurichaun. *Clurichaun.* But yes. Sure an' your great-great-granddaddy was a changeling or your grandmom a banshee or something similar. It happens."

Scott thought. Maybe it was his paternal grandmother. That woman was nuts.

"Your da's a knight?" asked Mick.

"Yeah. His real name's John. Reggie Dwight is his stage name."

"I knew some good knights back in the day," Mick mused as he returned to his inspection of the crime scene. "Course, nowadays knights are all lawyers an' actors an' writers and such. Useless people."

"So what happens now?"

"Happens?" said Mick. His mind was clearly still on his rabbit friend, though he'd narrowed his search to looking for clues in and around the drainpipe. He picked up a stone and sniffed it.

Scott would not be discouraged—he read a lot, and he knew how these things worked. "Yeah, like, do I have magic powers? Do you teach me how to use them or do I go to a special school?"

Mick put the stone down where he'd found it, then very slowly and deliberately turned to stare at Scott in wonder. It made Scott feel suddenly fidgety and donkey headed.

"No . . . no magic powers?" he stammered.

Mick shrugged graciously. "Yeh may have a tarnished glamour about yeh, sure. Like a celebrity's daughter," he said, and Scott bristled. "Maybe folks don't pay much attention to yeh unless yeh want to be noticed? Maybe when yeh do, you're all they can look at? You're the golden boy."

Scott couldn't remember ever being the golden boy, but he'd never actually made much of an effort there. "Is that it?"

Mick mused. "'S hard to keep one of the Good Neighbors out when they want in. Maybe you're good with locks. Or, if yeh prefer, maybe when yeh decide to get around a lock, yeh find the locker forgot to lock it in the first place. Though that's gettin' into quantum physics and isn't really my area."

"Are *you* good with locks? You couldn't even get out of those handcuffs, which still doesn't make any sense to me."

Mick chewed on his lip. "There was magic in play there. That young constable put on the cuffs an' read me my rights, an' they were like a spell coming out of his mouth. I doubt he knew he was doing anythin' unusual. But we know he was a changeling's boy too or he wouldna seen me in the first place."

Scott sat heavily on the grass and immediately regretted it, as the damp seeped through the seat of his pants. Perfect. "So that's it. I find out I'm magic, but all I can do is sneak around good and unlock things. Gosh, I wonder what I'm going to be when *I* grow up?"

"Don't be shirty; it don't suit you. So—to answer your question from before: what happens now. Now I stay with yeh until I can repay your kindness in New York, with interest."

"Oh, you don't have to do that—"

"I do if ever I want to get my glamour back. Gotta play by the rules."

"Your . . . glamour?" asked Scott. "You keep saying that—do you mean your magic? It's gone?"

"I'm dry as turnips."

Scott didn't think that was an actual expression, but he let it go.

"An' maybe . . . ," Mick continued, wincing. "Maybe in the meantime yeh can help me find Harvey. That pooka never could take care o' himself."

Scott thought. Helping a little elf-man find a big rabbit-man sounded better than whatever he would have done today otherwise. "Okay. Won't that be another favor you owe me?"

"Sure an' it would." Mick sighed.

They started back the way they'd come. Scott considered how someone like Mick might end up repaying him.

"Sooo . . . clurichauns aren't like leprechauns in a pots-o'-gold kind of way, are they?"

"Yeh kidding me? I don't even have a change o' clothes."

CHAPTER 12

They had to take a city bus and transfer twice. Scott pulled his scarf tighter and squinted at the expanse of empty grass. This was Avalon Park: four thousand acres of lawn and old-growth trees that the Goodborough town council had created when they were competing to host the World's Fair of 1893. The town lost to Chicago, but it was still a nice park. Scott didn't really understand what he and Mick were doing in it.

"If I was a rabbit-man and *I* had escaped from Goodco, I wouldn't stay in Goodborough," he told the elf. "I'd get out of town."

"You an' me both," said Mick. "I usually head straight for Ireland. Had two good years in the north o' Dublin before they caught me this last time. Shipped me back to the States in a pet carrier."

"How'd you end up in the Port Authority?"

"'Twas the airline, bless 'em. They mixed me up wi' a Pekingese, sent me to New York instead o' Philadelphia. A lady came an' picked up my carrier, certain I was her little Sweetums or whoever. Let me out to stretch my legs in the bus station, an' you know the rest."

"I guess."

"But Harvey's a bit of a coward, an' he knows they'll be watching the borders. *All* the borders," Mick added with mysterious emphasis.

Scott stifled a yawn and thought, *How about the border of Dullsville? Because we crossed that back by the Porta-Potties.*

They had been walking for three hours, crisscrossing the park through its trails and abandoned pavilions. They'd passed the same statue of Zachariah T. Goode twice. It was the day before Thanksgiving, and everybody was probably warm at home with their families. Nobody came here when the weather got cold.

Actually, there *were* two people, far across the field by a ring of thick trees. They looked like men from where Scott stood, but it was impossible to tell much else.

"Harvey's a weird name for him, isn't it?"

"It's not his True Name. Yeh think Mick is *my* True Name?"

On the bus ride over they'd talked about Goodco, and what the last hundred years of Mick's life had been like. Which meant, of course, that to the few other passengers on the bus Scott had appeared to be whispering to his backpack, but he'd ridden enough public transportation to know that a person talking to a backpack wasn't terribly out of the ordinary.

"My mom didn't know anything about it," Scott said now. "About you and your friend being held prisoner and . . . tested on or whatever. A lot of good people work at Goodco." He realized he was sounding defensive. He'd felt defensive all morning, ever since Mick explained how he and Harvey had been treated.

"We weren't bein' tested on. I told yeh. They were stealing our magic. Bleedin' us dry. That an' using us as bait."

"Bait?"

"Bait for other Fay, an' for magical creatures. Glamour attracts glamour, like I said. They used us to pull others across the border."

There was that word again. "What border?" asked Scott. "You mean like from Mexico?"

"The border 'tween your world and mine. A magical border."

The last time Scott had heard the word *magical* this often he'd changed the channel to a better cartoon. But now he had to admit that even a lousy TV show was better than watching a tiny old man sniff toadstools.

"This isn't what I thought we'd be doing today," Scott said.

Mick eased backward onto the seat of his red track pants and once more pulled a little metal flask from the hip pocket. He unscrewed the cap, and the meadow filled with a thick, eye-watering smell of lilies. He took a pull.

"Helping the clurichaun's no fun anymore,'s that it?"

Technically, it never was fun, thought Scott. "I just don't know what I'm supposed to be doing. Besides carrying the backpack."

"Keepin' your eyes peeled mostly."

"For a rabbit-man."

"For a pooka."

"A . . . what?"

"Harvey is a pooka. Did I tell yeh that? He's one o' the old Irish Fay: a shapeshiftin' fairy-man. He can turn into a rabbit. A full-on, normal-size rabbit. Other pooka can turn into goats or horses or dogs or things. Okay?"

"Okay." Scott sort of resented Mick's tone: lecturing him as if about the four food groups.

"Harvey may not be able to turn into a full-on coney right now. Might not have the magic left for it. But he's still a rabbit-man, and his instinct is going to be to get underground, maybe wait out the winter. Now you an' I both can see Harvey fine, but he's tryin' not to be seen right now, an' with good reason, so I'm sniffin' for some hint o' his old glamour."

Scott remembered that day by the drainpipe. "When

he left me he changed things around him. Made them more . . . magical."

"So yeh said. He was under stress, innit? Fifty years of Goodco's sticky fingers have robbed him o' his control. They had machines. Magical machines," Mick said uncertainly, as though the phrase confused him. "They made the glamour flare up in us, an' then they sucked it out. Don't know wha' they did with it. Put it in cereal boxes, I guess."

"Why?"

The question got Mick peevish. "You tell *me* why. Eh? Why d'yeh got all them Goodco cereals in your cupboard back home?"

Scott shrugged. "My mom gets them free at work. I don't eat them—they have a weird taste."

"Oh," said Mick. He scratched his neck. "Beg your pardon. Anyway, when yeh saw Harvey he was newly escaped from Goodco headquarters—the one on the island in Lake Meer. Those machines wore him out, made it hard to control his own glamour, an' it was just pouring out of him. It's probably trickling out now."

A flash of something across the field caught Scott's attention. The two men were still there. The slighter of the two was closer, in fact. He had his hands up by his head, and then there it was again: two sharp points of light as if the sun were glinting off a pair of huge, glassy eyes.

"I think someone over there has binoculars," whispered Scott. "I think he's looking at us."

Mick tensed. He rose and walked slowly but deliberately behind Scott's legs. "Probably can't see me," he said. "S'probably just noticing you."

Scott wasn't accustomed to being noticed. "Don't you think you should . . ."

"Aye."

Scott kneeled and let Mick into the backpack between the city map and the Tupperware of trail mix. The lean man was crossing the field.

Scott could think of nothing to do but watch him approach. How was he going to explain what he was doing here? He wasn't, Scott decided with an inward nod. He was just a kid in a park. Kids go to parks.

The man had binoculars in one hand, a cigarette in the other. He was as lean and tan as a belt, in skinny jeans and one of those sorts of T-shirts that appear all old and faded but actually cost forty dollars. His hair was bleach-blond and looked like a cake decoration.

"Hey, you," said the man when he was close enough to speak conversationally. "Where are your parents? Your mom here? You shouldn't be wandering off by yourself."

"I'm allowed," Scott answered. He had, in fact, asked for permission to go to the park alone. Mom likely assumed he'd meant River Park, closer to home, but legal loopholes have always been the playgrounds of rich men and children. Besides, he wasn't really alone, a fact that suddenly weighed on his shoulders a little more heavily than before.

"Whatcha doing out here, big guy?"

Scott shrugged. "School project. What . . . what are *you* doing here?"

From across the yellow field came the thin reed of the other man's voice. "Haskoll! Get back here!"

The man called Haskoll gave Scott a prim smile, as though privately savoring whatever it was he was about to tell him. He let the silence tick for three seconds, four, before finally punctuating it with a wink.

"It's wabbit season," he said. "We're hunting wabbits."

Haskoll and Scott approached the other man, whom Scott had already been coached should be referred to as Papa. Scott didn't care to meet Papa at all, but Haskoll had roped his arm around Scott's shoulders, just over the backpack, and steered him across the meadow with a kind of grabby friendliness.

"Now be vewy, vewy quiet," said Haskoll. "Elmer Fudd. Just kidding, though—Papa is a very important man. A great hunter. I think you're really going to like him. Papa!"

The other man was older, square jawed and white haired, with a khaki vest and his pants tucked into boots and a long rifle in his faintly shaking hand.

"I've been calling you," he told Haskoll. "I've found more fewmets. Who is this?"

"This is my new friend, Scotty. Why don't you tell him a little about what we're doing here?"

Papa frowned at Scott. "I don't think that would be wise."

Haskoll spoke to Scott directly. "Goodco has asked us to look for a rabbit they lost, Scotty. It's sort of their . . . company mascot, you know? And Papa here is hot on its trail."

"Hm. Yes. Well, I've found some of the creature's . . . scat." The old man must have recognized the blank look on Scott's face, because he added, "Its . . . *leavings*, you know. I need you to check them, Haskoll. My back, and all that."

"Ah . . . you know what?" said Haskoll. "I forgot the rock at home."

Papa scowled. "Well, collect them for later then."

Haskoll took a plastic bag and tweezers from one of Papa's pockets and kneeled by the man's foot, where there were three droppings the size of M&M'S. Once they were inside the bag he tucked it back in a vest pocket while Papa gazed with quiet dignity at the horizon.

"The spyglass, please."

Haskoll produced a small retractable spyglass from another vest pocket and handed it to Papa. This spyglass had a pink lens.

"I see nothing. What do you see, Haskoll?"

Haskoll used his own binoculars. "Nada," he said, and turned to Scott. "How about you, buddy?"

Scott didn't see anything, either.

"You know what, Papa?" said Haskoll. "I wanna get that poop back to the Batcave, check it against the rock. I'll take the van and be back in thirty minutes, tops."

"Don't be ridiculous. And what should I do without you here?"

"Hunt the beast. Track it. Footprints and, I don't know, tree rubbings and whatever."

" . . . Yes, but—"

"I don't think the world's greatest hunter needs *my* help, right, Scotty?"

This seemed to clinch it. Scott had never seen this kind of manipulation work on an adult before. He felt embarrassed for both of them, most of all Papa.

"Do you see that strip of turf?" Papa announced, pointing at the grass. "Shinier than the rest. Means the blades have been disturbed by some animal's passing, you know."

"There you go. C'mon, Scotty."

Haskoll and Scott walked some distance off before Scott spoke. "Well, I should get going. My mom's expecting me."

Haskoll responded by clapping Scott on the back. Or rather clapping Scott on the backpack and in all likelihood striking Mick in the head. "Oh, don't rush off now. I thought you might like to see our little hunting lodge."

"Ah . . . no thanks."

Just then Scott felt a kick from inside the backpack. He winced.

"Well, on second thought . . . ," he said. "Maybe."

Mick kicked him again.

Had they thought of it ahead of time they might have worked out a "one kick means yes, two kicks mean no" sort of system, but they hadn't; and now Scott had no idea what Mick was trying to tell him.

"You all right, big guy?"

Scott nodded. "Sure. Let's . . . go to your hunting place. Thanks."

And now the backpack was still.

CHAPTER 13

Scott watched helplessly through the van's windshield as the last gas station and bus stop of Goodborough passed behind him and Walnut Crescent lay beyond like the curled body of some huge, regal animal. This was the rich suburb of Goodborough. Scott had never been here before.

"Nice, huh?" said Haskoll from the driver's seat.

"Very pretty."

Each estate sat past a vast lawn of deep pile and tasteful flower beds. Some were behind high walls and massive yet girlishly patterned gates. Even the zoo didn't go to this much trouble.

The van turned in toward one of these gates, which parted and swung open at the touch of a keypad outside Haskoll's window. They pulled up to a house made of great dark beams and old stone.

"I have to go to the bathroom," said Scott as soon as the vehicle came to a stop.

Haskoll let them in the tall front doors and disabled an alarm system that had just begun to beep for his attention. "It's the first door down that hall," he said. "Meet me back here when you're done, and I'll show you the trophy room."

The hall smelled like tobacco and vanilla. Scott closed and locked the bathroom door behind him, and unzipped his backpack. Up gasped Mick like a trout.

"I know you're a super-old magical leprechaun and all—" Scott hissed.

"*Clurichaun*," said Mick.

"—but nowadays, getting into a van with a weird adult is considered a *very bad idea*."

"I only want to find out wha' these two know. I'll have a wander and come back to this bathroom. Please, lad. If yeh get into a pickle, just call an' I'll come runnin'."

Scott privately wondered what the elf could do to help, what with his short stature and complete lack of cool magic powers. "This Haskoll guy might see you."

"Aw, chicken teeth. If Haskoll could see me, he'd have already asked yeh about me."

"I guess so."

"I overheard somethin' about a spyglass. Did it have a pink lens?"

"Yeah," said Scott, remembering. "I saw some other guys with pink goggles the day I met Harvey, too."

"Ultraviolet-vision glasses," said Mick. "Helps regular people see the Fay. They don't work so well in the daytime, though. But, lad—if these two are hunting Harvey, then they'd be really interested in someone like you. Someone who can see the Fay without a pair o' goggles. Watch what you say."

Scott nodded and left Mick alone in the darkened bathroom. It wasn't until he'd returned to the front door that Scott pictured Haskoll's binoculars clearly—heavy and black and with perfectly ordinary lenses.

"There you are. Fall in? Just kidding. Wanna see the trophy room?"

Scott let Haskoll lead him through the marble entry hall to a wood-paneled wall flanked with facing staircases. Between these was a narrow door.

Scott took a breath and forced a question to his lips. They were here to learn, after all. "What was that rock you and Papa were talking about? The one you were going to use to check the . . . droppings?"

Haskoll opened the narrow door and ushered Scott inside with a theatrical bow. "Cold iron," he answered. The hall beyond was dark, with the faintest outline of another door at its end. "Iron from a meteor, 'never heated by any human agency.' We have a few hunks of meteor rock, and we always take the smallest one on a hunt. Go ahead and push through that door—it's unlocked."

Scott did as he was told and entered a high, octagonal room that was indistinctly lit by thin ribbons of blue window glass near the ceiling. But some overhead lamps flickered on, and in the yellow, flickering lights ... heads.

Heads.

From eye line to ceiling, the paneled rear wall was lined with severed heads. Having never hunted himself, Scott had imagined a trophy room filled with silver cups and little marble pillars topped with gold figures frozen in the act of shooting or bowling or whatever; but these were *heads*: heads of the most extraordinary shapes. The head of a dark-haired woman with feline features. An eagle's head that was as big as a lion's. A row of toadish boys with bloodred skin. A giant—an honest-to-god storybook giant, his round pink face as big as a beach ball. A unicorn. It couldn't be anything else, though this was no horse head. It was more like some cross between a horse and a fawn: white as cream, with a long, plaited horn of pearl. It was beautiful. Even disembodied and mounted on a rosewood plaque it was so beautiful it made Scott's stomach turn.

There was a cabinet of skulls. Some were grotesque, with fierce curves of tooth and bone, but many, too many, were to all appearances human. Scott wondered what

pointed ears or elegant, almond eyes might once have adorned these. One set of skulls, seven in all, were as small as dice.

Scott crossed the room like a sleepwalker, toward the skulls and heads, to stand under the unicorn. He looked up at the unicorn's head and neck jutting out from that rosewood plaque. There was a brass plate set into the plaque, just beneath the soft fur of the throat, and an inscription. The inscription read MIDWEST REGIONAL SALESPERSON OF THE YEAR.

Scott blinked and read the plate again. Then he stepped over to the massive head of the giant, who had been the Roosevelt High School District Swim Champ of 1963, apparently. The eagle was either World's Greatest Dad or else his head had been a Father's Day gift—it wasn't clear to Scott. Even less clear was why a row of beheaded toad-boys might be considered appropriate awards for perfect attendance, or even what sort of place you'd have to attend to be given something like that.

Haskoll sniffed behind him.

Suddenly it all came clear to Scott as he felt a headache coming on. He forced a smile and turned.

"Nice plaques. Papa sure has won a lot of awards. I really should be getting home."

"They *are* nice, aren't they," said Haskoll, stepping

forward. "I think that one's my favorite," he added, indicating the unicorn. "Of course, not everyone can see what's so great about them. But you and I can."

So Haskoll was special. Special in the way Scott was special, and Haskoll knew it. He'd probably seen Mick in the park. . . .

"Sure. Yeah, I have a soccer trophy at home myself. Well, not really a trophy, more like a ribbon for participation."

. . . and Haskoll did not strike him as being one of the good guys. Scott would deny everything and get out of there as quickly as possible. It was a classic kid strategy, and he couldn't think of a better one offhand.

"You asked about cold iron," Haskoll intoned. "Look over here."

"That's okay, I really need to—"

"I insist." Haskoll took Scott by the arm to a glass cabinet against the sidewall. Inside were three pockmarked lumps of dark metal on wooden stands. Haskoll opened the cabinet and removed the smallest piece. "A real meteor. Nickel-iron. You can hold it."

Scott held it. A faint trill traveled through his hand and up his arm. He didn't like it.

"Feels weird, right?" asked Haskoll, his face close, his breath hot.

Scott shrugged. "Feels like a rock. Heavy."

"We call them coldstones. Papa and me. Watch this."

He produced the bag of animal droppings and held them near the metal. Scott watched, but not much seemed to be happening.

"These droppings are nothing," said Haskoll. "They're rabbit turds. Now watch this." He reeled Scott back to the cabinet of skulls and tapped the coldstone against the glass. At this it sparked with purple light and gave off angry flashes.

"Weird, huh?"

"I don't see anything," Scott lied.

Haskoll turned to face Scott fully. He stared (with the joyless smile of a boy who likes pulling the wings off things) and said nothing. Then a phone rang. Haskoll stared, and it rang again.

"Is that . . . is that your phone? Are you going to—"

"It's just Papa, calling to tell me that our smallest coldstone has been in his left waist pocket all along."

"Um . . . well, shouldn't you—"

"He's an idiot, Papa. A complete tool. I do all the hunting. All of it. Papa just shoots where I point, because he likes to shoot things."

The phone rang a seventh time, and an eighth, and stopped.

"That backpack of yours looks about ten pounds

lighter. Why don't you call for your little friend, and we'll all talk about this rabbit-man that Goodco misplaced."

Scott breathed. "Okay. Can I see that coldstone again?"

"Sure."

Scott took it and threw it as hard as he could through the cabinet glass. Then he ran back for the front door, screaming.

"MIIIIIIIIIIICK!"

He tore through the narrow hall, slamming doors behind him, and slid to a stop on the marble floor of the foyer just as Mick emerged from the bathroom.

"Trouble, lad?" the elf asked before Scott scooped him up.

"Shh!"

Scott didn't suppose he could outrun Haskoll to the main gate, so he pulled the front door open wide and hid the two of them behind it. He pressed his back against the inside wall and counted to give his mind some focus. He'd only counted to two before hearing the sound of a door, and the patter of feet running past, and then silence. At fifteen, Scott and Mick came around the side for a peek.

"Wore out your welcome fast, did yeh?" whispered the elf.

"Not even. I think we were about to get invited to stay permanently."

They squinted out into the sunshine. There was no sign of Haskoll.

"I woulda gotten us free," said Mick. "I always escape, eventually."

"Remind me to tell you about the trophy room."

Outside, birds were singing. Wind ruffled the tops of trees.

"We're going to have to run for it, aren't we?"

"On three?"

On three they ran. Scott, for his part, thought he'd never run like this before. He was a pinwheel of limbs. He remembered the president's Physical Fitness Test at school and how he'd only earned a lousy Participant ribbon for that, too. If only the president could see him now—he just needed to be chased is all.

Mick was faster than you'd expect for someone with no real legs to speak of. He skidded right between the bars of the gate and stopped to look back.

"Mind your house, lad! He's behind you!"

Scott made for the center of the gate where the double doors met—it was especially thick with curlicued iron that would be good for climbing—but found that it had not quite latched. Luck o' the Irish, or whatever it was he had for being part changeling. He slipped through the gate and shut it firmly behind him, and then Haskoll was there. The gate shuddered as the man slapped against it and glared, grinning, his fists clutching the ironwork, his face straining against the bars. Scott and Mick ran off down the hill before he had a chance to recover, or work the keypad.

"It's been really fantastic spending time with you, Scotty!" he called after them. "I hope you'll both come back and visit!"

CHAPTER 14

Mr. Wilson was sleeping more and more lately, and hard to wake. It was like his bed exerted a lunar gravity, and for days he shuffled and sighed through rooms and conversations as though wading against its tidal pull. So that night it was a relief to find him once again his usual self, talking and joking at dinner. In fact, he was even *more* his usual self than he usually was, as though trying to make up for the past week. He seemed to have full use of the alphabet anyway, so Emily asked him about her eardrops. She'd been putting the same pink goop into her ears for years.

"I'm almost out," she told him. "I don't have to see the doctor, do I? You can just get more at the pharmacy?" Neither sibling was fond of their doctor. The mere mention of her gave Erno a chill.

She was the staff physician at Goodco, and Erno and Emily could see her for free, so they'd never seen anyone else. Unless you counted the school nurse. And it was hard to count the school nurse, whose solution for everything was to have you lie down behind a curtain while she called your parents.

"You won't have to go to the doctor anymore," Mr. Wilson answered with a sudden plunge in disposition. "Don't worry about it."

"But the eardrops—"

"Forget about the eardrops," he said abruptly, quieter. "You don't need them anymore." He rose from the table and moved to clear his plate.

"Just like that?" said Erno. "And she won't get dizzy?"

Mr. Wilson turned. His hands went up, palms out, like a mime trapped in a box. Just another invisible obstacle the kids couldn't see. In a way, he *was* trapped in a box—a box that diminished in livable space every day, every second, but so slowly that it had been impossible to react. What had once looked like the world now seemed like a coffin. But the kids didn't understand this. They couldn't see the great dark cloud in his mind. "She won't get dizzy. Don't worry," he told them, and began loading the dishwasher.

"It's okay. I'm okay," Emily said quickly. "My ears don't even hurt or anything. I can't even *remember* the last time they hurt."

"There. See?" Mr. Wilson said. "Trust your sister. She's the smart one."

Bang, the comment landed like a firecracker on the dining room table. Erno floundered in the terrible silence that followed, though Mr. Wilson went on busing the table as though he'd said nothing out of the ordinary. Emily shook her head at Erno, a ridiculous gesture.

He pushed back his chair and left the room. Emily followed.

"I don't know why he said that," she told him, stumbling up the stairs in pursuit.

"Sure you do."

"It's not true. We both get straight As."

"Oh, please." Erno stopped so abruptly that Emily ran into him. "You only get As because there aren't four extra letters at the beginning of the alphabet. Mr. Wilson doesn't care about grades. He only cares about the games."

"You've solved lots of them first. There was that one with the matchsticks . . . and the one with the algebra problems—"

"*Right,*" Erno said, "like I really could have beaten you at *math problems*? I know you let me win one game every year for my birthday."

Emily tried to look indignant, but it was obviously true.

"That's obviously not true," she said. She was getting jittery, and her eyes were rimmed with tears.

"It is," Erno replied. "I know it is. Every year I win one game in November, and that's it. Hey, I guess that means

I was going to win this one too."

He was upsetting her. She was looking stiff and a little spastic, and Erno knew what usually followed that. He instinctively glanced about to make sure she wasn't too near the top of the stairs, or anything on which she might hit her head if she fell. "Okay," he said, "calm down."

Emily said nothing, just swayed in the hallway, then flinched. A framed picture of the kids' trip to Menlo Park dropped suddenly from the wall and cracked. Emily seemed to gag, then cough, and stared cross-eyed at the small pink butterfly she had apparently just produced from her mouth. It rose off her tongue, propelled by the hot puff of her cough, and flitted over the banister to the floor below.

Erno followed its flight, so he missed it when her eyelids fluttered like pink butterflies and her doll-body tumbled to the floor.

"You made a butterfly," Erno said, scarcely a moment after her eyes reopened. "Out of your mouth. It flew downstairs, and I lost it."

"Can you help me up?"

Erno took her hand and helped her to her room, where they both sat down on the bed.

"It must have flown in when we weren't looking," said Emily, "and then I coughed it back out."

"I guess." Erno kicked his heels against the box spring.

147

"Emily? Instead of letting me win, why don't we just work on it together? I'm tired of competing against you. You're smarter. I'm not mad at Mr. Wilson or anything. I just don't want to do it anymore."

Emily stared for a moment. "Erno and Emily," she finally said.

Erno blinked. "Yeah . . . that's what I'm saying: Erno and Emily, the unbeatable team. Brains and brawn. Well, not brawn exactly, but I promise I'll start lifting weights—"

"No," said Emily. "That's the solution so far. To the game. *E*, *R*, the word *no*, the word *and*, and the letters *M-L-E*."

"*M-L-E*," Erno repeated. "Emily. I swear I would have figured that out. Well, wait—is that it? Is that the whole answer?"

"No. I think it's just a salutation—like it's the beginning of a letter. At the moment Dad's avoiding commas. Erno?"

"Yeah?"

"I had a dream just now," Emily answered, shivering. "When I was on the floor. Something terrible is going to happen."

"What? Why? What was the dream?"

Emily looked at him, and her face was scared but vague, as though she wasn't sure of herself.

"I . . . it was just an empty room. Empty except for a

chair in the middle. As plain a chair as you can think of, in an empty room."

"Okay."

"And, I thought, That's strange, because I knew in some way that I was dreaming and that an empty room with a chair was a strange thing to dream about."

Her body shook again.

"It was actually boring, you know? I was bored just looking at that chair. But dreams are never boring."

Erno huffed. "Sure they are. A few nights ago I had a dream I was walking around the school at night. Nothing happened; I just walked around. That's pretty boring."

"But it wasn't boring at the time," said Emily. "Right? It only seems boring now."

Erno frowned, trying to remember. "I guess so. That's weird."

"It's not weird. Being bored means whatever you're doing isn't holding your interest. Your attention wanders. But when you're dreaming, the dream is the *only* thing you're thinking about. Your mind can't wander 'cause the dream will just wander along with it. That's what I think, anyway."

"Go back to your dream," said Erno.

"Okay. I watched the room for a while, waiting for something to happen, but it didn't change for the longest time. Then, suddenly, I walked into the room."

Erno frowned. "Weren't you already in the room?"

"No. I was just watching it. And then I watched myself walk into the room. It was me, or . . . someone who looked just like me. And then the girl that looked just like me sat in the chair, facing me, and said . . . and said, very calmly,

'Something terrible is going to happen.'

"And then I woke up."

Erno felt like mentioning that this wasn't really that scary a dream, but after considering it a moment, he conceded that yes, actually, it was *kind* of scary.

"I think it's true," Emily said. "I think something terrible is going to happen."

"You mean you think this dream was some kind of . . . fortune-telling? A premonition?"

Emily shook her head and got up to kick off her shoes. As her feet slid into her slippers, she said, "No. No, I don't believe in that sort of thing."

"But you said—"

"I don't think I was telling the future or anything. It sounds crazy, I'm sure, and stupid, but I think the dream was my subconscious mind trying to tell my conscious mind something it already knows. I don't think it was really a dream at all. I already know what's going to happen, and it's so terrifying, I'm too afraid to even think about it."

Erno thought he ought to have something comforting to say about this, but, in all honesty, the thought of some great terror barreling down on them sounded about right. It sounded consistent. Every encouraging word that came to mind seemed falsely sweet and ugly, like supermarket birthday cake. It *would* be their birthday, he remembered, in a handful of hours. Happy Birthday to them.

"Please don't tell Dad I fell," said Emily. "I don't want to go see the doctor."

"Yeah. She's creepy."

"I don't even know her name," said Emily. "I asked her once, and she said Doctor."

Erno huffed. "Well, maybe you won't have to see her for a while. Maybe neither one of us will."

"I hope so."

Erno hoped so, too, because he didn't know that the doctor would be making a house call the next day.

There were two birthday cards stuck to the refrigerator with fruit-shaped magnets. They'd arrived from Goodco a week ago. They were, in fact, identical to the birthday cards Goodco had sent the year before, and the year before that. HAPPY BIRTHDAY TO A MEMBER OF THE GOODCO

FAMILY! read the front, which also featured cartoon art of Clover, Kookie, Agent SuperCar, the Snox Rabbit, and Chip, Sparkle, and Pip. The inside said MAY YOU ALWAYS STAY CRISPY IN MILK!, which Erno assumed was some kind of metaphor. That morning the siblings found that the words *Happy Birthday* had been cut out from each card with a knife. Mr. Wilson must have done it during the night, because he hadn't yet emerged from his bedroom upstairs.

When he still hadn't appeared for lunch, Erno and Emily set out to pick up their birthday cake alone. And on the way to the supermarket, they saw that *Happy* had been scribbled off a street sign on Happy Valley Avenue. They noticed a bedsheet half covering the billboard for the Happy Hunter Steakhouse. A bald man in a tie and shirtsleeves screamed at his employees outside a mattress store on Logres Avenue, demanding to know "Who would do this," and "What kind of person thinks this is funny" and "How will people know that Mattress King is having a Birthday Blowout Bash if some joker's painted a black rectangle over the word *Birthday*."

The huge neon sign at Happy Jack's Discount Furniture had a broken *Happy*, a rock still lodged conspicuously between the two *p*'s.

Emily looked at Erno, stunned. "I can't believe Dad vandalized a sign," she said.

At the supermarket, the bakery counter lady opened the white box so the twins could inspect their cake, which read HAPPY BIRTHDAY ERNANDO EMILE. They said it was fine and paid.

"I've decided what I want for my birthday," said Emily on the way back. "I want you to promise never to hate me." She was watching him out of the corner of her eye, as if he might disappoint her, as if he might refuse.

He didn't hate her, of course, and he thought perhaps that could be *his* thing. Emily's thing could be about being the smartest, and Erno's thing could be not hating her for it.

"Okay," he said. "Happy birthday. I promise never to hate you."

Emily smiled.

After a few seconds Erno added, "I also got you a gift certificate."

On the way home there were five different pay phones, and each of the first four rang as the twins passed. Erno supposed the phone company must be testing them or something, but still he had to suppress an urge to shout "I'll get it!" and answer one. He might have, as a joke to cheer Emily, but then he noticed the way she flinched at each and every ring.

They walked past the tennis courts and the Wall Street

Taco Exchange, and the fifth pay phone drew near. Emily walked stiffly, increasingly tense, and the phone rang. Here there was a man standing nearby waiting for the bus. He walked over to the pay phone and lifted the receiver.

"Hello?" the man said. "This is a pay phone. You must have dialed the wrong . . . . what? Yeah, there are some kids here."

The man looked over at the twins, and Emily began to walk faster.

"Hey," the man said, the receiver against his chest. "Is one of you named Erno?"

". . . Yeah . . ."

"Phone for you."

Erno stood there, uncertain. He watched Emily, who had now broken into a run, vanishing over the hill.

"Emily! Wait!"

The man with the phone thrust it forward. "C'mon, kid," he said. "I'm not your secretary."

Erno set down his birthday cake on the sidewalk and took the phone, and put the receiver to his ear. "H-hello?"

"Good-bye," said a familiar voice. Then the line went dead with a click.

CHAPTER 15

Erno ran the rest of the way home, too, the cake forgotten. He ran down three streets and up the concrete steps to their house, crunched through the dead leaves, and crossed the porch and dashed through the front door, which was standing open, and stopped suddenly in the foyer in front of a great piece of butcher paper tacked to the wall, the same thing Emily must have seen when she had first arrived. It read:

ERNO AND EMILY,
HAPPY BIRTHDAY.
GOOD-BYE.

Erno mouthed the last word and frowned. He had barely the time to take it in before he heard a great deal of creaking floorboards in the living room and a woman's voice.

"Come in, Erno."

Then a groaning noise made Erno whirl around, and he was startled to see a six-foot-tall, pink-marshmallow man pushing the door shut behind him. Given a moment, he realized it was only a regular man, dressed from head to toe in the same sort of rubber suit he'd seen Mr. Wilson wear at the Goodco factory. It was the color of stomach medicine. It was the color of ear medicine, come to think of it. The man stared out at Erno through a clear plastic oval and grabbed his arm with a white glove.

"Hey! Leggo. Emily! Where are you?"

"She's here," said the woman around the corner, and when Erno was hustled into the living room, he saw that it was their doctor. She was a tall woman in a deep blue outfit with a jacket like origami, and she was surrounded by four more men in identical pink suits.

Erno had always been strangely worried by the doctor's appearance. Her dark and sloping eyes, her striking, predatory face. Her brow was topped by precision bangs and curtained with straight, waist-length hair of such dissolving blackness that it resembled liquid, like ink. If you watched carefully you would swear her hair did not seem to quite sync with the movements of her body, or the air, but rather shivered at the ends as if caught in the hot vapors of her temper. And you *did* watch the doctor carefully, or else you stared at your feet.

Emily was trembling and staring at her feet in a chair in the center of the room. There was an empty chair beside her.

"Have a seat, Erno," the doctor said, "and tell us where your father is."

Erno didn't move right away, so he was pushed into place by the pink man behind him.

"You're our doctor," he said slowly. "From Goodco."

"Very good, Erno," she said. "Shows you've been paying attention. I *am* your doctor. But I am also your father's supervisor, and I demand to know where he is."

Erno just stared, wordlessly, at the strangeness of it all. The doctor changed tactics. She crouched down beside them, and her voice became suddenly soft, lilting, the sort of voice adults think will soothe children. This voice could have narrated a cartoon about ponies.

"See, the thing is, Erno, we need your help! And you and your, ah . . . sister have already been sooo helpful to us all these years. Yes, you have!"

Emily, who out of fear had not so much as looked at Erno when he arrived, now whispered something she may have never said before.

"I don't understand."

The doctor smiled in an unpleasant way. "Oh, I rather doubt that, dear," she said, and a pink-suit man chuckled.

"You see," the doctor continued, "for several years we've

been testing out a special chemical on you: Milk-7. We'd like to put it in our cereals. It's a very, very special chemical that makes you smarter! And now we are finishing our tests, and we need your father's notes. They . . . seem to have disappeared, like magic! As has your father."

Erno said, "Um, ma'am . . ."

"Oh, 'ma'am' is so formal," the woman said. "Call me something else. Vivian is nice. Would you like to call me Vivian?"

"Is that your name?" Erno asked.

"No."

"Ah. Um, so . . . .Mr. Wilson . . . .worked for you?"

"In Research and Development, yes."

"And he's been giving Emily and me—"

"Oh no, no," she said. "Not you. Just Emily. You were in the control group."

Emily shuddered.

"Okay," Erno said slowly, "so . . . Emily's been given that . . . Milk—"

"Oh, don't call it Milk-7," said the woman who wasn't named Vivian. "That sounds so clinical, doesn't it? We call it IntelliJuice™."

One of the pink men cleared his throat. "Actually, I believe Marketing is now calling it ThinkDrink™."

Not-Vivian smiled a thin smile.

"ThinkDrink™ then. Fine. Regardless, soon it will be

just one of the tasty chemicals that go into making Agent SuperCar™ Cereal so Naturally Good™."

Erno fidgeted in his chair and frowned. "I thought *corn* was what made Agent SuperCar™ cereal so 'Naturally Good.'"

Not-Vivian looked alarmed, as though Erno had said something you clearly could not make a cereal out of. Sofa cushions. Astronauts.

"Corn?" she said, looking back at the crowd of marsh-mallow men. "Are they putting *corn* in there now?"

"Of course there's corn," said Erno. "It says so on the front of the box. In our cupboard. 'Made with Corn.'"

One of the men went to fetch the box. Erno glanced at Emily, slumped heavily in her chair. She would have looked like a rag doll if it wasn't for the glassy terror in her eyes. The man returned.

"Ah, here we are," said Not-Vivian, holding the cereal box. She pointed at a label on the front. "Made with Gorn. *Gorn*. That's a G."

Erno stared.

"And if people like ThinkDrink™ in Agent SuperCar™ Cereal," she continued, "well, then we'll introduce it into the whole family of Goodco cereals: Puftees™, Burlap Crisp™, Honey Frosted Snox™, Cud™. . . . Imagine . . . breakfast cereals that make you smarter! What parent wouldn't buy them for their child, despite the regrettable side effects."

Emily said something too softly to hear.

"What was that, dear?" said Not-Vivian. "Speak up."

"I said, 'Where's our dad?'"

Not-Vivian stood up. She looked so tall suddenly.

"We . . . don't know. He was *supposed* to have brought the two of you in to the labs today. He never arrived, and, needless to say, neither did you. And his cell phone is no longer in service. But he *will* be found. His data will be found," said Not-Vivian in a voice that was suddenly cold and low. Then, just as suddenly, she was a pony cartoon again, albeit a cartoon about very bad ponies. "Until then you two will come with us! We'll do all sorts of fun tests. No . . . not tests. Games! We'll see how well you exercise in the Exercise Room and watch you interact in the Play Room. . . . That sounds nice, doesn't it? And then there's the Sleep Observation Lab (that's not a very good name, is it; we'll call that the Nap Room), and the Needle Room—"

Erno flinched. "Needle Room?"

"Yes, but that's not really a good name for it, either. It isn't so much a *room* as it is a tank that we'll keep you in—"

Emily flipped. She shrieked and kicked Not-Vivian in

161

the shin, then ran for the front door. Erno followed, but they were both quickly cornered and grabbed up by the men in pink suits. Emily continued to wail and kick, but her captor held her with arms outstretched like a bag of garbage. Erno looked around frantically for something, anything that might help him; and then suddenly, there it was. There *he* was, his head nearly touching the ceiling, though no one had heard him come in.

Erno should have remembered that it was Wednesday, the day Biggs came.

CHAPTER 16

There was a brittle silence. Biggs stood in the corner, hunched over the tall Tiffany lamp, and its orange glow made a hideous mask of his wooden face. His great blue shadow sprang up the wall and folded itself crookedly onto the ceiling. The five pink-rubber men turned and looked at Biggs, and Erno thought there was a breathless, respectful quiet as each man maybe reckoned there were *too* such things as monsters.

The man holding Emily set her down quickly, as though he had been caught playing with someone else's toy. "I . . . I wasn't," he said weakly, "I wouldn't have . . ."

Biggs roared, and it wasn't a man's roar. He picked up a marshmallow man and hit another marshmallow man with him. He tossed a third into the chesterfield sofa. The doctor ran for the door, but not before Emily kicked her in the knee. She hobbled out with three pink men behind

163

her. Another pink man stood behind Biggs, beating on his back with both fists like it was a punching bag. Biggs eventually responded by picking up the man around the middle.

"Lemme go! Lemme GO!" the man squealed, so Biggs laid him on the floor and put a bookcase on top of him. Then he turned and faced the final man, the pink man still holding Erno.

"Put him down," said Biggs. It was more like his old, dull voice, but with a hint of menace.

The man set Erno down slowly, and Erno ran to Emily, who had squeezed herself into a corner.

"You can't take these kids from us," the man said. "We *own* them."

Biggs snared his leg and dangled him upside down.

"*Who* owns them?" Biggs said directly into the scuba mask face, his hot breath fogging up the plastic.

"G-Goodco," the man stammered.

"Goodco," Biggs repeated slowly. "Goodco. I love your cereals."

"Um. Thanks?"

Biggs carried the pink man to the front door. "Don't mention it," he said, and threw him outside.

When Biggs returned to the living room, Erno and Emily still stood in the corner, uncertain what to do.

"You okay?" Biggs asked.

They nodded.

Biggs dropped to his knees. "MY BABIES!" he bawled, and scooped Erno and Emily to his chest, hugging them tight. "What if they'd *took* you?"

Pressed together against Biggs's sturdy chest, the twins looked at each other in surprise. This was more emotion than they'd ever seen Biggs show before. This was more emotion than they'd ever seen anyone show before.

"It's . . . It's okay. We're okay," said Erno.

Biggs began to weep fat, sticky tears.

"Don't know what I'd do," said Biggs, his breath coming in hot bursts. "Never let you out of my sight."

"We're fine, really. You rescued us."

This went on for some minutes before Biggs set them free and sat on the floor.

"Was so scared," he said, scratching at his ear.

"You didn't seem very scared," said Erno.

"Um . . . Biggs," said Emily, pointing past them.

Biggs looked. "Oh, yeah," he said, and lifted the bookcase. The last pink man crawled out from under it and ran out the front door.

"Dad's gone," Emily told Biggs.

"I know. Saw the note."

"Where did he go?"

"Dunno."

Emily nodded, like everything was suddenly very clear.

Erno remained confused.

"Waitaminute. Mr. Wilson's really gone? Like, *gone* gone?"

Emily nodded again. "Yes. I'm . . . sorry I didn't work it out sooner. He's sick, I think. I'm not sure why, exactly, but . . . I'll figure it out. In the meantime, we'd better leave. Those G-Goodco people might come back." She was beginning to tremble again. Erno squeezed her hand, and she stopped. ·

Biggs nodded and scratched his nose. "You'll come stay with me," he said, and got to his sizable feet.

The twins packed quickly and met back at the base of the stairs. Erno wondered what Biggs's house might be like. High ceilings, he suspected.

As if reading his mind, Biggs said, "Muh house is comfortable. You'll like it."

They walked out the front doorway. Biggs scratched under his chin. "Unless of course you don't.

"It's at the top of a tall tree," he added hopefully. "Kids like climbing trees."

Erno thought this was a strange thing to say, but he grinned politely and carried on grinning for the next thirty minutes until he found out that Biggs wasn't joking.

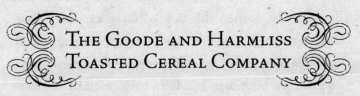

THE GOODE AND HARMLISS TOASTED CEREAL COMPANY

was founded in 1858 for the purpose of manufacturing quality breakfast cereals and attaining dominion over all the peoples of the Earth. Nathan Orbison Goode and Jack T. Harmliss started the company in their hometown of Goodborough, New Jersey, eight months after meeting on the campus of the University of Pennsylvania in Philadelphia.

Nathan Goode was of the *Mayflower* Goodes[1], a privileged son attending business classes at Penn. There he met Jack Harmliss, a penniless thug who eked out a living collecting money from privileged sons in exchange for not robbing them. When Harmliss presented Goode with

---

1   A wealthy family with millions in orthodontic hardware. They owned most of Goodborough, and indeed the town was named for the legendary family patriarch Zachariah Terribull Goode, who had made a name for himself fashioning complicated headgear for the punishment of indecent women. Dentists coveted these devices as well, and soon the Goode Ortho-dontical Emporium was born.

his (un)usual sales pitch in a darkened alley one night, Goode recognized in him a brilliant and original young entrepreneur.

Several drinks later they were fast friends, and found that they shared many passions. Both Goode and Harmliss bemoaned the lack of tasty, easy-to-prepare breakfast foods, and both had a secret longing for all-encompassing power over the peoples of the earth. More surprisingly, both men had been tormented by the same recurring dream since childhood: a radiant pink dragon, immensely powerful and yet trapped in darkness.

Goode would write of one of these dreams in 1882. Note the mention of the company's top-selling cereal at that time:

> I dreamed it again last night, and it colors my day. The awesome, blazing dragon gazed down on me like a disapproving mother, and bellowed that I should lose weight and put more tallow in the Toasted Sugar Beets.

The cereal is three-fifths tallow already! Any
more and I shall have to stick wicks in the boxes
and sell them as candles. What madness is this?

Madness or no, the added tallow would make Toasted
Sugar Beets the best-selling food of any kind in America,
topping even such staples as milk and salt.

That their cereal company was vastly successful is a
matter of common knowledge. Far less known is the
influence of the secret organization within the company
that they founded: the Good and Harmless Freemen of
America, or Freemen for short. The list of deeds attrib-
uted to this group is long and almost certainly exagger-
ated. It is doubtful, for example, that they were actually
responsible for the Great Fire in Chicago, the stock market
crash of 1929, or the extinction of the dodo. Some enthu-
siasts have suggested in recent years that the Freemen are
behind the Bigfoot "controversy," but such claims are usually given as little attention as they deserve.

Suspicions linger, however, about the society's power
in national and international politics. Freeman support is
unquestioningly sought by political candidates, and it is
said that they have handpicked every American president
from Ulysses S. Grant through the present day.

The symbology of the Freemen is complicated but consistent. Most will recognize the pink dragon as the Goode

and Harmliss Toasted Cereal Company (now Goodco) logo or as one of the marshmallow shapes in Weird-O's "red octagons, orange moons, pink dragons, green Gs, and purple pentagrams," and indeed, each of these shapes plays its own role in Freemen literature and lodge decor. Many other symbols would turn up as cereal mascots in the 1940s and '50s. There are the Triplets, who protect the Flame of Knowledge (Chip, Sparkle, and Pip—the Puftees Pixies); Lepus the Hare, who holds the Chalice of Spirits (the Snox Rabbit from Honey Frosted Snox); and El Chupacoco, who grasps the Fishing Rod of Insanity (Kookie the coconut vampire from KoKoLumps)[2].

---

2   Older readers may also remember Clover the Angry Leprechaun, who was discontinued from boxes of Burlap Crisp in 1962.

CHAPTER 17

Harvey *was* in Avalon Park. He'd made his way there slowly over the course of a few days and hunkered down in a damp and thickly shaded glen. He'd dug himself a hole to sit in. He was sitting in it now.

For the first time in his long life, sitting in a dank hole in the ground felt a lot like sitting in a dank hole in the ground. And now nature was calling.

He'd heard the Goodco guards use this expression on occasion. "Nature calls," one would say, and he'd step out of the room to do his business. Harvey had scoffed at this—Nature did not call these children of men. He supposed she probably had called them in the distant past—called them again and again, left messages, but eventually gave up trying. Nature should want nothing to do with the human being.

But now, in his dank hole, Harvey realized two things

about himself that made Nature seem very far away: that he had just, without thinking, made an analogy about telephone answering machines, and that he was once again about to walk halfway across the park to visit those Porta-Potties by the merry-go-round. Fifty years of confinement meant that he wouldn't have given a second thought to doing his business on a toilet in front of two armed guards; but he could no longer, gods help him, do it in the woods.

Harvey crawled to the entrance of his burrow and looked out at the stars. His nose joggled at the smell of a hot dog, somewhere. A revolting whisper of chemical pork.

"Thtupid humans and their thtupid hot dogs," he muttered, and pulled himself out of his hole. Then he crept, wanting a hot dog, to the edge of the park.

Biggs drove the kids to the border of Avalon Park, where he'd purchased a parking space. Biggs owned an old Citroën 2CV, a ridiculous little car made in France. It was like a curvy little clown shoe, all rust with a black top and fenders and a very earnest-looking grille. It was small by American standards, and with Biggs inside it looked like an optical illusion. Emily sat up front on the passenger side while Erno squeezed himself into the back horizontally.

Biggs's home, his *tree*, was a ten-minute walk into the

park grounds. Erno trained his eyes skyward, trying to catch a glimpse of a real house somewhere up among the leaves, but he never saw a thing, even when they came to a stop at the base of a huge oak.

"Here we are," said Biggs, looking up.

"It's . . . it's amazing," said Emily. "You can't see it at all."

"Thank you."

Erno tried not to stare, but Biggs had kicked off his custom-made shoes, and Erno could see his feet. His *feet*. They were like sides of cooked beef. Their knobby, curling toes splayed outward, too long, and the hair! Like little toupees.

"Um," said Erno, trying to prioritize all the questions he wanted eventually to ask, "how do we get up?"

"I usually just climb," Biggs answered, scratching his cheek.

"I'm afraid of heights," said Emily suddenly.

"What?" Erno replied. "You are? I didn't know that."

"I didn't know either until just now."

"Hmm," said Biggs. "That's bad."

"I can't go. I CAN'T GO! It's so *high*."

"I could carry you," said Biggs. "I could carry you both."

Emily let them know, by way of trembling, just what she thought of this idea.

"I think it's best, Emily," said Erno. "You won't have to even look. Here!"

173

Erno removed a scarf from his bag and tied it around Emily's head.

"There. You're blindfolded. You won't even know what's happening."

Emily's trembling quieted, then shuddered to a stop. "Okay."

Biggs lifted Emily up in one arm, and Erno climbed onto his back as though he were getting a simple piggy-back ride.

"I'll only be able to use one hand," Biggs said, "so I'll be slower than usual."

Erno hadn't the chance to comment before Biggs leaped into the air. He scrambled up the trunk like a squirrel and jumped from branch to branch like an ape. This was slow?

Emily shrieked. She was beginning to hyperventilate.

"It's okay!" shouted Erno. The air whooshed around them as they dipped and lurched ever upward. "He's really good at this!"

"Keep talking to me! Don't stop talking!"

"Um . . ."

"Talk! Tell me a story! Sing me a song!"

"Uh, okay . . . um . . . Rock-a-bye, baby, in the treetop. When the wind blows . . . Oh, um—"

"Erno!"

"WEEE AAALL LIIIVE IN A YELLOW SUBMARINE! A YELL— Oh, we're here."

They were. The tree house had appeared so suddenly that Erno saw it only a moment before he could touch it. It was like a great egg or cocoon, as big as a sailboat, shaped from curved branches and clever shingles that looked like dead leaves.

It's a nest. It's just a big nest, thought Erno; and he began to imagine what life would be like here, huddled among the harsh twigs, probably eating bugs and going to the bathroom God knows where.

"You go in first," Biggs told Erno, "and help your sister."

"Go . . . in? I . . . I don't see a door."

"Oh. Yeah," said Biggs, and he pulled at one of the branches, indistinguishable from all the rest. A round door, cut neat as you like, swung out from the twig-egg. Inside was a sort of hall leading to the house beyond.

This looks pretty clean, thought Erno as he took Emily's hand to guide her inside. Biggs joined them.

"Do we . . . do we light a candle?" asked Erno, realizing immediately what a dumb suggestion this was. Light a fire in a tree house?

"Naw," Biggs answered. "I'll just turn on the lights."

He flipped a switch behind Erno's head, and the foyer was illuminated by a warm amber glow from a glass globe overhead. More lights winked on around the corner, and a stereo on the same circuit started playing something bossa nova.

"Is it safe?" asked Emily, still blindfolded.

"It's . . . safe," Erno whispered to Emily. "The shag carpeting is a little thick, so watch out for that."

Biggs had to attend to Emily as Erno stumbled through the foyer, bewildered.

The next room (and, apart from the kitchen, the *only* room) was very hard on the eyes. It was hard because this room, with its smooth curves and (fake!) wood-paneled walls seemed to have no connection to the rough tangle of limbs and twigs that formed the outside of the house. It was hard on the eyes because beanbag chairs and aquariums are not things one expects to find in a tree. It was hard on the eyes because the green carpet didn't really go with the orange boomerang coffee table.

"Would've vacuumed," said Biggs, "if I'd known there'd be visitors."

"'S okay," said Erno. "'S fantastic."

Emily, eyes wide-open, brushed past Erno to look out a tiny window.

"It's slanted upward," she said, "so you can see the sky, but people below can't see in." Then she scrambled over to a metal post hanging down from the ceiling with two eyepieces like binoculars. "Is this a periscope?"

"Yup," Biggs agreed, scratching his jaw.

"Sooo," Erno said to Emily, "you're not afraid of heights anymore?"

"Oh, probably," she answered with a wave. "But I can't *tell* I'm high up. I can't even tell I'm in a tree."

Biggs grinned and walked into an adjoining room, the kitchen. "I'll make dinner. Get comfortable. Y'have to lay your sleeping bags out in there, 's only the one room."

"Where do *you* sleep?" asked Erno, seeing no bed.

"In the corner, standing up."

"Ah."

Emily was busily unpacking her things. When she came upon her pajamas, she took them behind a Japanese screen made of thick rice paper. Erno went to sit by the screen.

"Biggs lives in a tree," he said, as though he was the only one who'd noticed this.

"Yes," Emily answered. "I thought he might."

"You thought he . . . ? You did not!"

Emily poked her face around the screen. She hadn't even a hint of a smile.

"Sure. I figured it was something like that. I mean, his listed address is a post office box, and, you know, he's always scratching."

"What? Scratching? What does that have to do with anything? He just has dry skin."

"Hmm. That, or he's Bigfoot."

"Bigfoot."

"Yes. Or *a* Bigfoot. I don't really know."

Erno waited for Emily to laugh. She didn't, so he said "What?" again, so high his voice cracked.

Emily emerged from behind the screen, dressed in her pajamas, and sank into a beanbag chair.

"Biggs," she said. "Bigfoot. Get it?"

"Oh, come *on*. Just because his name is Biggs—"

"It's more than that. He's huge. His feet are even bigger. He's always scratching because he shaves his fur. He never makes any noise when he walks. He can smell things happening across the street!"

Erno didn't like how much sense she was making. "How long have you believed this?" he asked.

"I dunno. Since we were six or seven."

Erno threw his hands in the air. "I can't believe you never told me!"

Emily crossed her arms. "I *did* tell you! Like, five years ago I told you! You laughed so hard milk came out your nose!"

Erno winced, then looked down at the shag rug.

"Oh. Yeah. Well, I figured you were kidding."

"Yeah," said Emily. "I thought you might've. Anyway, I realized it was such a crazy idea that I'd better just keep it to myself."

"Have you ever asked Biggs?"

"What, if he's Bigfoot?"

"Yeah."

"Of course not!" Emily whispered, eyes wide with shock. "It might be *rude.*"

"Dinner!" Biggs shouted from the kitchen, and they both jumped.

Dinner was good. This was no surprise: Biggs had always been an excellent cook. There was trouble, however, in suddenly knowing that it might be Bigfoot who made you dinner, that it was Bigfoot who passed the broccoli, that it could be Bigfoot now, shouting, "Who wants SUNDAES?"

Biggs was clearly happier than normal. Perhaps he was pleased to have the Utz kids in his home, and to be able to see them more than usual, though he seemed occasionally to catch himself smiling too hard, or laughing too loud, and stopped. Perhaps in these moments Biggs remembered the misfortune that had brought them all here. But he could barely contain himself now, scooping out the ice cream, microwaving the chocolate fudge, sprinkling the crushed peanuts. And when he presented the kids with their desserts, Erno thought, *Bigfoot fixed me a sundae,* and didn't know whether to laugh or scream. *Bigfoot fixed me a* sundae. *The Loch Ness Monster cleaned my room. The Abominable Snowman knitted me a cardigan.*

"I have to go to the bathroom," he said as Bigfoot

cleared the table. Erno was a little anxious about this conversation. He'd seen every inch of the tree house—there was an outdoor shower just off the kitchen, but there wasn't any restroom.

Biggs paused, the dishwater suddenly still. "You can't hold it?"

"H . . . Hold it? Until when?"

"Morning."

Erno coughed. What happened in the morning? Maybe at midnight the car turned back into a toilet.

"You don't have a bathroom," Emily said. "You work somewhere during the day and you . . . go there."

Biggs nodded. "Library."

"You're a librarian?" asked Erno. "I figured you cleaned other houses . . . took care of other kids."

"Just you."

"Well, I have to go too," said Emily. "And I can't hold it until tomorrow. Did you see those Porta-Potties by the merry-go-round?"

There were two Porta-Potties, each an antiseptic blue closet on a particularly lush patch of grass by the quiet carousel. And one of the doors was locked, which was odd. It was the middle of the night—was a vagrant in there? So Erno waited with Biggs as Emily took her turn.

The merry-go-round looked haunted when it was dark and still. Each of the horses, the unicorn, the giant rabbit and rooster and dragon, were frozen with their necks back, their jaws open in surprise. Petrified. Or maybe they just preferred to breathe through their mouths—in spite of the Porta-Potties, a fair number of people seemed to be using the carousel for a toilet.

Biggs sidled up. "Have something for you," he said, and offered a small envelope. It was still sealed and bore the inscription GIVE ONLY TO ERNO in Mr. Wilson's familiar hand. "Found it on muh fridge this morning. Stuck there with a magnet shaped like a pie. Thought it was part of a new game."

"That's . . . weird."

"Yuh. Don't even *own* a pie magnet."

"No, I mean . . . nobody was supposed to know where you lived, right? How'd Mr. Wilson find your tree house, much less get inside?"

Biggs shrugged. "Known him a long time. From before he was made your foster dad. Might've guessed where I live."

"Where did you meet him?"

"Goodco factory. Was taking the tour. He pulled me out of line, wanted to know all about me. But . . . don't like to talk all that much."

Erno smiled a little at this.

"Asked if I liked kids," Biggs continued. "Knew some babies needed a nanny. Said yes."

Erno opened the envelope. Inside was a single sheet of folded notepaper, and a poem:

> *Ashes to ashes and dust to dust*
> *We push and pull to fill the void*
> *If change is just, then change we must*
> *I would not see my work destroyed*

> *P.S. Your doctor's a hag—*
> *Papa's got a brand-new bag.*

> *P.P.S. Don't show this to Emily.*

Erno stuffed the poem into his pocket and sighed. "He left a copy for Emily, I guess?"

"No."

Erno frowned. *No?* It couldn't be a new game if he was the only one playing it. Maybe it was something else entirely.

Emily emerged, and Erno took her place inside the same potty. The other one was still shut tight—he wondered if somebody could be sleeping in there.

On their return to the tree house Erno noticed Biggs glance over his shoulder a lot. Erno glanced back as well, but couldn't figure what the big man was looking at—there was nothing behind them but a carousel and two Porta-Potties, both of their doors slightly ajar.

IN 1991 CONGRESS LAUNCHED A SPECIAL INVESTIGATION into claims that Goodco was conducting secret experiments on human subjects. These experiments were purported to involve chemical additives that had not been approved by the Food and Drug Administration. These rumors were supported by public statements made by then Goodco vice president Paul Flanders in the fall of 1990 that the breakfast cereals of the future would "make kids smarter, and better-looking. It's very exciting," he continued. "We already have a kind of imitation corn that makes mice glow in the dark." When questioned by the media, Paul Flanders attempted to clarify his statements: "They . . . they don't glow *much*," he told reporters. "It's not like you could read by them or anything." Later at a formal news conference, Flanders claimed that the whole thing had been a joke, and also that he was retiring from his position at Goodco to spend more time with his family. And indeed he was with his family when they all perished in a hydrofoil accident in March of 1992.

If there was any truth to Flanders's statements, it probably wasn't Goodco's first attempt at a chemical additive. According to anonymous sources, Goodco experimented in the sixties with a mixture that would "Make You Grow Up Big and Strong." And it did make its subjects Big, and Strong, and a few other things besides (see Appendix XII, *Humboldt County v. Goodco*). The advertising department attempted to make the side effects sound like virtues:

"Goodco cereals!" went one pitch. "They'll make you Big and Strong and Put Hair on Your Chest!"

"Goodco! The cure for baldness is here . . . in a fun-to-eat cereal!"

But it was eventually agreed that while people want thick, luxurious hair on their heads, they don't necessarily want it all those other places (see *fig. 4.13*), and so the idea was scrapped.

As was the 1991 Congressional investigation, after the lead investigator himself remarked, on camera and while making a rude gesture, that he considered all accusations against Goodco to be "bollocks." He then abruptly resigned from public office and moved to a goat farm in Pennsylvania.

CHAPTER 18

Erno slept fitfully. In his dreams he worked the assembly line at Goodco, watching a shuddering steel bin fart puffed corn through a spray of artificial sweetener.

He was the only person in the factory. There wasn't supposed to be anyone else there.

In his dream the corn chute clogged. It continued to tremble angrily as Erno reached his hand up into the nozzle to pull free a small dead rabbit. Its eyes were shut tight, its fur dirty with bits of cereal and . . . something else. He set it aside and reached into the bin for another. Then a third rabbit, and a fourth—it was a bad clog. Then he heard a noise.

There wasn't supposed to be anyone else there. Someone or something was sneaking around the factory.

This part of the factory looked like Erno's house. Which was in a tree. Something was creeping through the tree, creeping through his house. Then he heard a voice, and he woke.

It took Erno a moment to remember where he was: in a sleeping bag next to Emily, in a living room in a tree house. As he remembered, he realized he could still hear the voice from his dream. It was Biggs's low bass, rumbling across the floor. Maybe the big man was having a weird dream, too.

Erno unsheathed himself from the sleeping bag and followed the voice to the kitchen, at which point it fell abruptly silent. Erno entered the dim kitchen to find Biggs watching him from the back door. Alone.

"Can't sleep?"

"I had a weird dream," Erno told him. "Were you talking to someone?"

Biggs might have turned his head just slightly and averted his eyes. It was dark. "To an invisible rabbit-man," he finally answered.

Erno smiled. "Heh. Okay. Well, I'm going back to bed," he said, and he did.

The night passed. It was always difficult for Erno to sleep well in a strange place, and this place was stranger than most. More difficult still is trying to sleep when there's a bird pecking your forehead.

"Oh, you scared it," said Emily when Erno lurched

188

awake. He saw a sparrow flit away and join a crowd of other birds snapping at a pile of seed in the foyer. The front door was cracked open, and Emily was sitting nearby, eating cereal.

"There are birds in the house," said Erno, his head full of sleep. "There are birds in the house. Does . . . does Biggs know you let them in?"

"I didn't. Biggs feeds the birds every morning."

"Because if he doesn't they peck him in the head?"

"No, silly," Emily said with a full mouth. "It was only pecking your forehead to get at the little pile of birdseed I put there."

Erno frowned. "You . . ."

Emily giggled, and Erno tried not to smile.

"If you weren't two minutes older, I'd beat you up."

"You could never beat me up," said Emily. "I know seven pressure points on the human body that will make a person fall asleep. I know two others that I think will cure rabies, but I haven't been able to test them."

Erno got to his feet. "Really?" he said. "You should have used them on Carla Owens. Why didn't you try them on the Goodco people?"

Emily looked anxious. "Most of the Goodco people were wearing those thick suits. It wouldn't have worked. And . . . besides. I can't think of stuff like that when . . ."

She trailed off, but Erno understood. They were

like members of a boy band: Emily was the smart one; Erno was the brave one. And the cute one, of course. He changed the subject.

"Is that Puftees?" he asked, pointing at her bowl. "I can't believe you're eating a Goodco cereal after all they've done!"

"It's all Biggs has for breakfast! Seriously, go check! He wasn't kidding when he told that pink-suit guy that he liked them."

Erno looked around. "Where is Biggs, anyway?"

"Out back," Emily answered. "And when he left, he took a razor with him."

"Okay."

"A *razor*," she repeated.

Erno rolled his eyes. "Oh, what, the Bigfoot thing? He just has to shave! His face!"

"Maybe, but when he took a new razor from the hall closet, I got a peek inside."

"So?"

"So go look."

Erno stepped over to the foyer, scattering birds as he did so, and cracked the closet door. Then he opened it wide. "It's just a . . . a . . . *whole lot* of razors," he said. He surveyed each shelf. There were assorted toiletries, spare towels, a vacuum, and about fifty bags of disposable razors. It really was a lot of razors.

"I guess that is a little weird," he added.

They couldn't go to the authorities—that much they agreed on. The chief of police was a direct descendant of Jack T. Harmliss, one of Goodco's founders, and his wife was vice president of Crunch Development. Every kid in Goodborough learned this in school. And most of the police force were probably Freemen as well—members of a 175-year-old secret club that included every rich and important person in town.

Come morning Emily wanted instead to go back to their house. She was certain Mr. Wilson would be looking for them there. So she sulked when she was outvoted, despite clearly being smart enough to understand what a bad idea it was.

"I think we should get some word to Scott," said Erno. "Let him know we're okay." He'd been avoiding Denton and Louis and Roger these past couple of weeks, so he imagined that Scott might be the only person to notice if the Utz kids went missing, much less care.

"Oh, sure," Emily snarled. "We can't go to our house because it's being watched. We can't go to the police because they're Freemen. But we should totally pay Scott a visit—they'll never find us there. We can ask his mom how work's going at Goodco."

"Goodco people might know who your friends are," Biggs agreed.

"And if they *do*, then Scott might be in trouble, and it's our fault. Shouldn't we check?"

Biggs looked glum. "Dangerous," he said.

"Probably not. I don't think they're that on the ball. If they'd been watching us that closely, they'd know where Mr. Wilson was."

Biggs scratched his chin.

"You didn't hear what that doctor woman said," Erno continued. "They thought Mr. Wilson was taking care of the whole thing. They trusted him to just bring us in to Goodco himself."

"That doesn't make sense," said Emily, her cheeks growing pink. "Dad never would have gone along with it. He must not have known."

On the subject of their foster father, and on this alone, Erno could claim to be the smart one. It wasn't nearly as satisfying as he thought it would be. "Mr. Wilson *was* the one who gave you the pink chemical. The IntelliJuice, or whatever."

"ThinkDrink. And he thought it was ear medicine."

Erno studied Emily for a moment, then nodded. "Yeah. You're probably right. You're *always* right. But . . . I still want to check on Scott. He's either safe—in which case we should let him know *we're* safe—or he's not, and he needs our help."

● ◑ ★

So it was agreed. Emily thought she might even be able to use Scott's computer to research Goodco. The tree house was a remarkable piece of work, but it didn't have any conveniences that had been invented after 1970.

Emily was already blindfolded and waiting at the front door when Biggs and Erno joined her. "We'll be back before dark," Biggs said loudly, which was odd because he so rarely raised his voice, much less spoke when he didn't absolutely have to. Then he gathered them up for another life-affirming drop to the ground, and ten minutes later they were at the car.

While he lay like luggage in the back of the Citroën, Erno thought about Mr. Wilson's new riddle. Particularly that last line:

P.P.S. Don't show this to Emily.

At this point Erno was inclined to do the exact opposite of anything Mr. Wilson asked of him, but he remembered the look Emily got each time the man was mentioned. What would it do to her to know he was still toying with them like this? It seemed now like his sister had always been running a maze, wending her way toward the rumor of some warm and nourishing reward while Mr. Wilson took careful notes from above. It turned Erno's stomach to think of it.

So why was he even considering the riddle? He could feel it in his pocket, as awkward as a two-dollar bill.

The car stopped, and Erno sat up as best he could. They were parked at the end of the street, having all agreed that they should watch and wait a bit before barreling up to Scott's front door. Goodco had a fleet of white vans, so they looked for this first.

"Not that they'd use a white van if they were being sneaky," said Emily. "Sneaky would be a lime-green Volkswagen. Nobody would suspect the assassins in the lime-green Volkswagen." She was right. Neither of the kids had seen many movies or TV shows, but bad guys always seemed to drive white vans or black town cars. They probably all shopped at the same evil dealership. Even Agent SuperCar's enemies drove around in white vans. White vans that turned into robot polar bears, but still.

"Biggs," said Erno. "Do you have any scrap paper in here?"

Biggs did. Every time he parked his car someone put a flyer for carpet cleaning on it, and he had a small collection of these in the glove box.

Emily twisted around to face him. "What do you need that for?"

"I thought I ought to write out some message to Scott, in case we have to leave in a hurry. I thought maybe I could write it out in a code or something, so the Goodco people won't know what it means."

"A code," Emily smiled. "Sounds like something Dad would do."

Erno forced himself to smile back.

After ten minutes Erno had scribbled all over four flyers for carpet cleaning, one for a weight-loss program, and yet another for tax services—that last one got him thinking. He started over.

"Emily, am I using the word *conspired* right?"

"'Conspired,'" said Emily. "Worked together to bring about a particular result."

"Thanks."

Another few minutes and he finally had a draft he felt comfortable leaving on Scott's doorstep. If it came to that. He'd enjoyed it: crafting a clue of his own instead of tripping over someone else's two or three times a month. He was still admiring his handiwork when Emily's crisp whisper brought him back to the here and now.

"Look," she was telling Biggs. "There he is again."

"What is it?" asked Erno.

"There's a guy. In that black car with the Pennsylvania plates. It's been here longer than we have, only I didn't notice there was someone sitting inside it until just a second ago."

Erno squinted at the back of the black car, the black *town* car, and saw the driver's head turn.

"I think he's watching Scott's house too," said Emily, back to a whisper.

Biggs looked like he was trying to make himself small, which was like watching someone fold an origami crane out of a refrigerator carton. The three of them stared at the man in the car, and the man in the car stared at the house.

Silence.

"Nobody's doing anything," said Erno after a long stretch of nobody doing anything.

"What do you want us to do?"

"I dunno. We could go ask him why he's here. We could question him about Goodco. Biggs could roll his car over."

"Those are all terrible ideas."

"Never rolled over anything bigger than a Jeep," said Biggs.

"Wait! Look."

The shiny black door of the town car opened, and a man in a black suit and dark sunglasses stepped out. He was lean, not so tall, and he clenched a plume of bloodred roses in his fist.

"Maybe he's dating Scott's mom," whispered Emily.

"Maybe he's just pretending to date her so he can kill everyone."

"He's probably just a dinner guest."

"At eleven in the morning?"

"It's Thanksgiving."

Erno blinked. "It is?"

The man in black crossed the street.

"We have to do *something*."

"Okay."

Erno kicked through the tiny rear door of the Citroën and tore off down the sidewalk as the man in black drew up to Scott's front stoop. Did the assassin hesitate? Did his finger waver at the doorbell as he contemplated his grim business? Erno bounded up to the stoop, slapped away the bouquet of roses (which were certainly hiding a gun, or a knife), and planted himself between the man and Scott's front door.

"What the—" The man flinched. He removed his sunglasses, and Erno got a good look at the face of Reggie Dwight as Biggs hustled up the steps with Emily in his arms.

Have you ever been close to a movie star? We're so used to seeing them through a screen or a pane of glass that we expect them to always be that way, like zoo animals. Then, suddenly, there's this giraffe standing in front of you, and you can't decide whether you should talk to it or run. But when Emily touched the man behind his ear, he fell asleep in a heap on the doorstep and didn't look so famous anymore.

"Oh, shoot," Emily said, looking down. "It's Scott's dad."

"It's Reggie Dwight," Erno corrected. "Wait . . ."

"Reggie Dwight is Scott and Polly's dad," Emily whispered loudly.

"He's . . . seriously?" said Erno.

"I was never a hundred percent positive, but it just made sense, you know? I tried to tell you, but you laughed so hard you choked on a cherry pit."

"You gotta stop telling me these kinds of things when I'm eating."

Reggie Dwight twitched and made a grunty noise.

"What should we do?"

"Kids," said Biggs. "Van."

It was at the top of the hill—a white van sliding like a fat specter around the corner.

And so they rang the doorbell and ran. Erno left his note to Scott tucked inside Reggie's jacket. It read:

> The accountant's student came to be
> the chairman of his company.
> We're high above where friends conspired
> to send him after he retired.

It was a riddle, sure—a clue like Mr. Wilson would have left. But it wasn't a game. It had never been a game.

CHAPTER 19

The doorbell rang. And a moment later Mom yelped "Oh my goodness—John!" in such a way that Scott thought he ought to go to the front door after all.

They'd known for only two hours that his father would be coming for Thanksgiving dinner. He'd called from New York, apologized for the last minuteness of it, didn't seem to even realize that it was an American holiday. The surprise had scarcely begun to fade when Scott joined his mother and discovered the man himself sleeping on their doorstep beside a jumble of stems and rose petals.

"Help me get him inside," said Mom. Scott lifted his dad's head while Mom dragged him by his expensive wing tips.

"What happened?" asked Polly when they joined her in the living room. "Is he drunk?"

"Your father doesn't drink, sweetie."

The three of them hoisted him to the lip of the sofa and rolled him onto his stomach. He gave a contented sigh.

"*Tch*," said Mom, examining the back of his suit jacket. "I should have vacuumed."

"What's wrong with him?"

"I don't know, baby. Give me a second."

"He's dressed like he's at a funeral," said Scott. "That's flattering."

"It's just how he is—how he's always been. Either he's wearing pink with orange feathers onstage or he looks like he's the CIA. He's not good with gray areas."

John smacked his lips and said, "Look who's talking." He opened his eyes cautiously and turned on his side. "What happened?"

"We were hoping you could tell us."

The movement dislodged a folded sheet of paper from the inside of John's jacket. It read FOR SCOTT ONLY in pencil. "Whoop," John murmured. "Mail for you."

Scott unfolded the riddle and read it.

"Was about to ring the doorbell," said John. "Boy came an' slapped my flowers and then I fell 'sleep."

Mom glanced at the note. "Is this one of Erno's family games?"

"I don't know."

Mom sighed. "Dinner's in an hour. Scott, you want to take your dad upstairs and help him get cleaned up?"

Scott did *not* particularly want to do this, actually, but he recognized it as one of those rhetorical questions.

"This is where you all live?" asked John as they ascended the stairs. "It's small."

"This is just our Thanksgiving house," Scott muttered. "We have a house for every day of the year."

"What was that?"

"Nothing."

Scott sat on the toilet lid as his father checked himself over in the mirror.

"I didn't mean anything . . . untoward," said John. "I'm glad to be here. I've been wanting to visit, but . . . it never seemed like the right time."

But then you punched the Queen of England, and your schedule cleared right up, thought Scott. He felt like he was always thinking mean thoughts like this. They scared him sometimes.

"Would you excuse me?"

Scott left the bathroom and turned into his own adjoining bedroom, and lightly closed the door behind him.

"That your da?" asked Mick. He was nestled in the bedclothes reading comic books.

"It's him," Scott whispered. "You'll have to be even more careful until he leaves. Right? I mean, we already know my mom can't see you, so I probably get it from Dad."

"He's not leavin'," said Mick. He folded a page of the comic back to mark his place, and Scott winced. This was *Abraham SuperLincoln #344*, and the first appearance of Penny Arcadian, but he thought better than to try to explain its historical significance to an elf.

"What do you mean, 'He's not leaving'?"

"Your ma's about to go off on her jaunt down south, isn't she?"

"To Antarctica. Goodco's sending her. But this woman from the Goodco day care will be looking after us. It's all set up already."

"Don't think so," said Mick, and he looked thoughtful. "Didn't suppose I had any glamour left for a foretellin'. Maybe I don't, an' it's just good ol'-fashioned wisdom. But I think your da will be stayin' on for a while."

Scott was shaking his head. "No. No, he wouldn't want to. I . . . I don't want him to," he said. It came out sounding a little like a question.

Mick shrugged. "He punched the Crown o' England— he can't be *all* bad."

Scott frowned and slipped back into the hall, where he almost knocked his father down.

"Is that Polly's room?" asked John.

"No. It's mine."

"I thought I heard you talking to someone."

"I was," Scott said. "To my imaginary friend." It was a

comfortable deception, since he wasn't entirely sure he was even lying.

"I had one of those when I was your age. Well, Polly's age maybe. Maybe younger."

"Uh-huh."

"It was this little gnome or something that I'd see now and again. I'd try to talk to him, but he'd always run away."

"You had an imaginary friend who wouldn't talk to you," said Scott as they returned to the stairs. "Did you have low self-esteem or something?"

John snorted. Scott wondered, of course, if his dad's childhood friend had been only as imaginary as the little man currently ruining his comic book collection. John had grown up in England, after all—he must have had at least as many opportunities to spot the Fay as Scott had here in New Jersey.

"So . . . how long are you staying?"

They descended the stairs before John answered. "Actually, your mother and I want to talk to you kids about that."

At dinner Mom asked Scott to say grace, which was ridiculous. They never said grace, except maybe when Grandma Adams visited. To be specific, Mom asked Scott to "say a few words," so Scott found himself saying more than a few words about the Pilgrims, and how they had to flee from England, and how awful England was back then because there wasn't any freedom and you couldn't just punch the queen whenever you felt like it; and now Scott could feel his face get hot and his mouth dry, so when his mom cleared her throat in kind of a serious way he said "Amen" midsentence and started dishing out mashed potatoes.

The turkey was dry, flavorless. Difficult to finish. And a halfway-decent metaphor for the dinner itself. Scott wouldn't have minded hearing Polly prattle on as she usually did on every conceivable subject, but she was apparently having one of her well-earned quiet moods. She always had one hand or the other hidden, and Scott knew she'd be clutching her little prince figurine like a rabbit's foot under the table.

After dinner Mom had the idea that the four of them should take a walk around the neighborhood and maybe drop in on the Utzes.

"We can wish them a happy Thanksgiving," she said, and didn't say anything about asking them to explain what exactly had happened earlier on the porch. Scott supposed the subject would just come up naturally. And during their walk his parents explained that they'd been talking and that John would be staying with them while Mom was doing research in Antarctica. This had the effect of thawing the last of Polly's shyness, and she began firing off comments and questions like she was making up for lost time.

The Utz house was dark and shuttered. Mom and John and Polly waited on the sidewalk as Scott rang the bell and peeked through the gaps at the edges of the windows.

"Maybe they left for the weekend," called Mom, and maybe they had—but when? There were two newspapers and an unclaimed package on the porch. Scott thought of the episode with John this morning, and of the riddle in his pocket.

Something was wrong.

THE GOOD AND HARMLESS FREEMEN OF AMERICA, or Freemen for short, share a history that is shrouded in mystery and contradiction. If you ask the Freemen themselves, they will tell you that the organization is a direct continuation of the Round Table of King Arthur. Since there is historical confusion regarding whether King Arthur or any of his knights were real persons or simply the stuff of legend, this claim is difficult to verify.

The Freemen certainly don't suggest any connection to Camelot through their iconography, which is mostly concerned with vague mysticism and breakfast cereal. Their most visible symbol, the Sickle and Spoon, symbolizes the harvesting of cereal and its consumption.[1] Freemen consider

1   In recent years the Sickle has become more symbolic than the Freemen Founders could ever have imagined: natural cereal grains have been almost entirely replaced in Goodco products by vat-grown imitation grain meals such as Gorn, Weet, Noats, and Gorn-Free, the Gornless Gorn substitute.

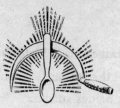

the night sky to be the Inverted Bowl of Heaven, which is filled with the cereal of the gods (stars) and of course the Milky Way. The Grand Hall of any well-established Freemen lodge will have a domed ceiling painted to resemble the cosmos. The floor will be decorated with any manner of icons and symbols.[2] From floor to ceiling will stretch two freestanding columns fashioned to resemble bundles of tall wheat and topped with capitals like ornate bowls. These represent the finished and unfinished cereal, which is also symbolic of each member's journey from an unfinished Initiate to a fully realized (and therefore fully free) Freeman. In some lodges each column will also be crowned by a globe: one painted to represent the Earth, the other utterly black. The meaning behind these globes is one of the Freemen's most closely guarded secrets, and made known only to those who reach the highest level of membership.

The Freemen have 987 levels of membership, the first three of which are achieved merely by filling out an application. The 8th level is granted upon full acceptance

---

2   The most common include the "Eye of the Dragon" (pink, usually surrounded by blue flame), a red octagon (which marks the beginning and end of a journey), a cow with a beehive for a hat (representing Nature's bounty), an apron (service to a higher purpose), and a large, radiant G (for Goodco).

into the local lodge, the 13th following Initiation, the 21st at the end of the Initiate's second week, and the 89th the first time he brings snacks.[3]

At the 89th level the Initiate will become a First Squire. At the 144th level he makes Second Squire, and at the 233rd he attains the rank of Knight Errant. At 377 he is a Knight of the Round, at 610 a Launcelot, and at 987 a Knight of the Siege Perilous. When a member crosses each of these important milestones, he is celebrated with a pageant and mystery play. Each play is intended to reveal some new secret of existence that has heretofore been hidden and to explain some fresh facet of the Freemen's ultimate purpose.

The Freemen believe that something has been lost. The Freemen believe that man is no longer whole. They hold that humanity's connection to the supernatural has been severed and that we can no longer feel the rough hands of our Creator: a Great Cultivator who has raised us, reaped us, and now wants us all to Awake to a New Morning in the Inverted Bowl of Heaven, once again reunited with the marshmallow magic of the universe.

---

3   The Initiate will not be permitted to bring snacks before his third month of membership. The snacks must include a nondairy option for those who have trouble with milk.

CHAPTER 20

Scott's mom had been packing for two weeks, but the following morning was still a panic. She'd prepared for her trip *too* early, and now she could no longer recall what she'd packed and what she hadn't, so the contents of each of her bags had to be taken apart and cataloged and put back together again. Polly followed Mom from room to room making helpful suggestions. Scott and John, meanwhile, stood stiffly in the living room and let the rest of the house bob around them.

A Goodco commercial was playing on the television. The Snox Rabbit, with his spreadsheets and supercomputers, was trying once more to discover the secret ingredient that made Honey Frosted Snox so delicious (all kids knew it was Honeycomb Magic; the Food and Drug Administration understood it to be monosodium glutamate). The Snox Rabbit pulled his ears in frustration. It made Scott want to brag, "I've met that guy," but he was concerned with how that would sound.

The four of them drove to the Philadelphia airport, where they learned one of Mom's bags was too heavy and so each suitcase was reopened and its contents redistributed while Mom handed over her identification and learned she'd been placed on the terrorist watch list because the name Doe sounded fake.

Eventually they rushed her to the edge of security, and she turned to face her kids. Scott was holding a small armful of things she'd willingly removed from the heaviest bag if it meant she would be allowed to check it through to New Zealand. She kissed him, and then Polly.

"I didn't mean to leave like this," she told them. "When you think of me in the coming weeks, try to remember me as a sane person."

John took the pile of clothes and books from Scott. "Can we send these to you? At the base?"

"I am not even worried about those things right now. At this point if we just manage to put the right person on the plane, I'll consider the morning a success."

She kissed Scott and Polly again and fumbled with her passport and boarding pass at the first security checkpoint. Then she was waving to them from the winding line, and five minutes later she was gone.

The other people in the airport made it impossible to forget that John was there. Despite his sunglasses and baseball cap they stared and pointed and whispered in each other's ears. *Look at him there*, thought Scott, *holding Mom's things. I didn't need help holding Mom's things.* He moved to take them back.

"That's okay," said John. "I've . . . well, all right."

On the way home John demonstrated that he hadn't driven a car in kind of a long time. *The wrong person got on the plane after all,* thought Scott, because he was feeling dramatic and sorry for himself.

In the front seat, Polly whispered occasionally to her little prince figurine and tramped him to and fro along the armrest. The little prince discovered the magical lever that lowered the Crystal Portal of the Wind, and so Scott was gusted intermittently from the passenger window as Polly worked it down and up again.

"Please stop," said Scott.

"Is that *your* imaginary friend?" John asked Polly, nodding at the prince.

"He's not imaginary," said Polly, and she confirmed this by way of stabbing John in the arm with its tiny sword.

"*Ow.*"

They crossed over the Walt Whitman Bridge and back into New Jersey.

"So your mom will spend all day getting to New Zealand," John said after a stretch of silence, "and then she stays there for a couple days?"

"That's where they give her her big red coat," Polly explained. "And she takes a class on how to behave in Antarctica."

"How to behave?"

"Yeah. Like: Don't take anything from the ice. Don't leave anything behind. No touching the penguins. Stuff like that."

"I have to admit," said John, "I don't really understand why a breakfast cereal company needs a physicist. Or why they need her in Antarctica."

Scott huffed. Though in truth he didn't really understand it, either.

"Goodco funds all kinds of research that isn't about breakfast," said Polly. "Like, as a charity."

"Well. Then I guess I'm glad I'm filming a commercial for them tomorrow."

"Are you doing it at the factory?" asked Polly, and then she trilled with sudden excitement. "*Are you filming it at our house?*"

John grinned with his movie star teeth. "I don't think that's been decided. I'm still waiting to hear word. They wanted to do the commercial in California, you know. I convinced them to let me film it here so I could see you two."

Scott didn't have to look to know his father was watching him in the rearview mirror. The whole situation made him feel sick to his stomach.

Well, something was making him sick, anyway. It was possibly John's driving.

Home again, Scott raced ahead of his father and sister and let himself in. Once upstairs he shut his bedroom door behind him.

"Ma get off okay?" asked Mick from under the bed.

"Barely. Why are you under the bed?"

"Like it down here. 'S dark. Musty."

"Are you ready to go look for Harvey some more? I've thought of a way you can repay me for my help."

Mick crawled into the open and blinked. "How's that?"

"You can help me look for Erno and Emily, too. I think something's happened to them. Erno left me this note." He handed the riddle to Mick, who climbed atop the bed to read it.

"'S gibberish," pronounced the elf after a minute.

"I don't think it is," said Scott.

"Well I don't know much abou' businessmen types, or where they retire. Don't a lot o' people go to Florida?"

"Listen—if I'm right and Erno is in trouble, then I

think he left me a riddle only because he was afraid the wrong person might read his note. He would leave me something only I could solve."

"Yeah?"

"'The accountant's student came to be the chairman of his company.' A couple weeks ago we met an accountant named Merle Lynn."

"Merlin? That old fraud?"

"Merle Lynn. He was just this guy. But the wizard Merlin's student was King Arthur, wasn't he?"

"So they said," Mick mused. "There was a lot of excitement abou' that boy. We thought he might be a good king to the Fay. One of our queens tried to help him out, but he wasn't so different from all the rest in the end."

"King Arthur was real?"

"As real as you an' me," said Mick. "Well, as real as you, anyway. Don' want to speak ill o' Queen Nimue, but I think it was a mistake givin' him that sword. Starts everything off on th' wrong foot, that does. You know what makes a nice gift for a new king? Houseplant."

"Sure. Anyway, Arthur became chairman of *his* company, if you call his company the Knights of the Round Table. Or England. So where did King Arthur retire?"

Mick's eyes brightened, and he smiled up at Scott. "Avalon."

CHAPTER 21

Erno studied Mr. Wilson's riddle and lifted his legs whenever Biggs came near. The big man pushed the vacuum over the carpet where Erno's feet had been, pulled it back again, pushed and pulled around the room. He really was such a fussy giant. He'd vacuumed twice since they'd arrived. But then again, the kids were probably getting more crumbs in his carpet than he was accustomed to.

Erno still intended to keep the riddle to himself, for now. Emily was just out the back door taking a shower, but at least there was no possibility of her walking into the living room unexpectedly: she was having her shower while blindfolded and tied to the porch railing.

Erno whispered,

> "Ashes to ashes and dust to dust
> We push and pull to fill the void

If change is just, then change we must
I would not see my work destroyed

"P.S. Your doctor's a hag—
Papa's got a brand-new bag."

"What work, I wonder," he continued to whisper, not that a whisper was necessary. The drone of the vacuum cleaner was loud enough to overwhelm more conversational tones or even, for example, the distant shouts of a girl who was finished with her shower but still tied to the porch railing. Erno skimmed the poem again and glanced at Biggs. He waved for the big man's attention.

Biggs flicked a switch, and the vacuum groaned its last. "Yuh?"

Erno nodded at the vacuum bag, which deflated as the machine exhaled. "What happens when you fill that thing with . . . ashes and dust?"

Biggs scratched his cheek. "Gotta change the bag."

Then, from out back: "*BIGGS!*"

The big man was startled—you could tell because his expression almost changed. He rushed through the kitchen, grabbing a towel and a thick bathrobe on the way. Erno stuffed the riddle back into his pack and removed the book he'd been reading. A minute later Emily entered the room, looking like a wet movie star in her big, white, furry bathrobe.

"Been shouting for five minutes," she grumbled. "We need a new system. I really think we should take a serious look at the system as it stands right now."

"Biggs was cleaning. Hey—what's another word for *void?*"

"*Vacuum, emptiness, nothingness, vacuity, abyss—*"

"Thanks, that's enough."

"Why'd you need to know?"

"No reason."

Biggs had to go to work at the library, and Emily wanted to tag along and research Goodco.

"You'll be okay?" Biggs asked as they prepared to leave him behind. "Won't get bored?"

"I won't get bored." Erno was certain.

They left, on foot, and after counting to fifty, Erno leaped to open the foyer closet and wheel out the vacuum cleaner. He stared at all its parts for a moment, then unzipped the bag and found a smaller paper bag inside. He pulled at this, but it wouldn't come free, so he pulled harder and fell onto his backside with the bag and a thick burst of gray, clumpy fluff. It got all over the floor; it stuck to his face and hair. Erno snorted a couple of times to clear his nostrils and examined the paper bag.

It had a circular hole, reinforced with cardboard where it had been attached to the vacuum's throat. He peered into it. Was there a shape inside, a shape that couldn't possibly have been sucked in through the vacuum's mouth?

After a minute he tweezed it out through the circular opening with his fingertips: a long cardboard mailing tube, furry with dust. There were plastic caps in each end, and he pried one of these out and pulled at the contents.

It was another yellow scroll tied with a pink ribbon. What really surprised Erno, though, was what huddled at the bottom of the tube, below the scroll: money. A great wad of bills—hundred-dollar bills—bound by a strip of pink paper. Ben Franklin's thick face gazed up at Erno from each bill, looking bored and disappointed, a look that said, *You should really put me in the bank, you know—a penny saved is a penny earned and all that—but you won't, I know you won't; nobody listens to old Ben Franklin.* Erno counted the crisp notes hastily and then wondered as he finished why Mr. Wilson had hidden ten thousand dollars inside a vacuum cleaner.

Next he untied the scroll, heart sinking as he expected yet another riddle. But this sheet of yellow paper had a small gold key taped to its center and a handwritten message:

Where Emily threw up a rainbow.

Well, there was only one place where Erno could remember Emily doing *that*.

Biggs kept a bicycle for warm weather. It took all the strength Erno had to lower it noisily down the trunk of the tree, dangled from a length of wet rope, so that when he descended he could only manage to slide on his palms and arches.

He was going to get in trouble. There was no way he could get into the tree house by himself, much less hoist a bike back up there. But he'd keep his errand a secret. Despite being much smaller than Biggs, he could still ride the man's bicycle if he didn't mind bumping his crotch against the crossbar from time to time. Of course he *did* mind bumping his crotch against the crossbar from time to time.

Once, four years ago, Emily had traveled alone by train to the National Mathlympics in Washington DC. All the other mathletes were middle schoolers, and Emily was only nine; but she'd been training with seventh and eighth graders after school because the fourth grade had ceased to challenge her. She wasn't team captain, but this was only because of her complete lack of leadership qualities, and because the older kids would never have consented to being fronted by a nine-year-old. But Emily was hands-down the star mathlete—she'd just never traveled alone before is all.

She had looked pale that morning. More than usual even.

So Mr. Wilson (who had been so much more enthusiastic about his foster children back then, Erno remembered) cooked Emily a huge good-luck breakfast with sausage *and* bacon *and* French toast *and* fried eggs. Mr. Wilson also believed in something called "breakfast dessert," which Erno generally found redundant. He'd just eaten French toast, after all, which is basically just a pile of doughnuts. So when asked, Erno said he thought he'd skip breakfast dessert today. Emily selected a bag of miniature fruity marshmallows. Pink, green, yellow, orange. She comforted herself by eating these all the way to the train station—and inside the train station, and while waiting for her tickets to print at the kiosk. Then she spilled both the bag and the contents of her stomach on the way to the train platform. Erno thought he could probably remember the exact spot.

It wasn't until he neared his destination that Erno realized what a sick joke of a hiding place this was. The train station was a Greek-looking stone box in the center of Goodborough, and its columned facade faced the tallest building in town: the Freemen's Temple. If the temple had an architectural style, it would be called Early American Evil. It looked like it had been assembled on an Indian burial ground from the mismatching pieces of seven or eight evil castles. Somewhere a hundred years ago a

bunch of vampires must have returned home at sunset and wondered where all their gargoyles had gone.

Erno fiddled with the U-lock in front of the station and shot suspicious looks over his shoulder as if the entire Freemen society might sneak up after he left to steal Biggs's bicycle. He felt exposed. As soon as he could, he slipped into the train station and walked briskly away from the entrance.

The station was high ceilinged, marble tiled, full of people, bags, and carts that sold flowers and coffee and cinnamon buns. Erno weaved through obstacles toward the hall that led to the NJ Transit train platforms. And when he found what he believed to be the exact spot where Emily had lost her marshmallows four years ago, he half expected it to feel significant: colder than the rest of the hallway maybe, or haunted by the distant wails of embarrassed vomiting. But it was just a spot. A spot next to a wall of coin-operated lockers.

Some of the lockers had keys inside their locks, and these did not look like the mysterious key from the vacuum cleaner bag. But Erno inserted that key into the closest locker, and when it fit, he turned. The door sprung open and revealed another cardboard cylinder and a small note that read *Good work, Erno*.

Despite himself Erno's heart took flight at these simple words, then retreated sheepishly back into his chest.

There were a lot of papers here. The rolled-up stack inside was thick, and difficult to squeeze from the tube. Once out, the pink pages stretched and uncurled in Erno's arms. These were the notes Not-Vivian had wanted so badly to find, thought Erno, skimming the first page. They had to be. The paragraphs were dotted with references to Milk-7, and mentions of E1 and E2. Erno flipped through the contents. The notes were organized like a journal, but with the odd drawing here or diagram there. Things that made no immediate sense to him. But he was struck with a sobering thought: Mr. Wilson had stuffed ten thousand dollars into a vacuum cleaner, but what he'd *really* hidden well were these notes.

CHAPTER 22

There was a polite knock at the door, so Scott knew it was John, wanting to talk again. Polly would not have knocked so tentatively. Or at all.

Mick crawled back under the bed. "Yeah?" said Scott.

It wasn't the Reggie Dwight of historical dramas and action movies that opened the door. Reggie Dwight the movie star was commanding and calm. He would dash in on a horse. Or a pair of skis. Reggie Dwight would drop from the ceiling in a tuxedo brandishing some lean German pistol. John Doe sputtered in wearing a white tee and swishy beige pants.

"That was Goodco," said John.

"What was Goodco?"

"The telephone call. A minute ago."

"I didn't hear it ring."

"It doesn't," John sighed, "really matter. They want me

at the factory tomorrow morning, early. For the commercial shoot. They're going to send a car. I think it would be all right if you kids came along."

Scott fidgeted. "Do I have to?"

John looked at him silently, then scratched the back of his neck. "Polly wants to go. I venture to say she is desperate to go. She may do something cartoonish, like explode or whistle like a kettle if she can't."

Scott nodded. "You should take her."

"Yes. Well, I can't leave you home alone . . . can I? A ten-year-old?"

"I'm eleven."

John winced. "Oh, heck. I'm sorry—"

Polly appeared in the doorframe. She had fixed herself a plate of frosting.

"We get to go see the commercial!" she sang, hopping.

John smiled warmly at her. She beamed up at him. "It's not going to be as exciting as you think," he told her. Then, "Are you eating frosting?"

"Not exciting: Sounds great," Scott grumbled. He hadn't intended to grumble. The comment sounded light, playful in his head. Less grumbly. John glowered, and Scott added, "Why are you in your pajamas already?"

"They're not pajamas. They're yoga bottoms. And this isn't about my bottoms—"

"Erno and Emily wanted to know if I could sleep over

tonight," Scott said quickly as the thought struck him. "That would be perfect, right? Then you wouldn't have to worry about me tomorrow."

John nodded slowly. "Erno and Emily? Are they the friends we tried to visit last night?"

"They're back. Erno says sorry about the flowers. He thought they were . . . something else. I didn't really get it."

Polly was looking daggers at him. Hurt, confused daggers. She could tell he was trying to get away with something but was perhaps puzzled by his lifetime record of never trying to get away with anything.

"All right," said John. "When you've packed your kit, I'll take you."

"I can walk," Scott insisted.

"You're allowed?"

Polly was still staring. "He's allowed," she said.

"'Twas one o' the magic places," Mick told Scott as they exited the bus at the edge of Avalon Park. "The Isle o' Avalon. You'd know it as Glastonbury." Mick glanced up at Scott's blank face. "All right, maybe yeh wouldn't. But yeh might know it as the place where the Lady o' the Lake lived."

Scott had heard of her, at least. "She gave King Arthur his sword, Excalibur."

"Aye. Queen Nimue, the Lady o' the Lake. She lived on

that rich island where it was always apples an' twilight. She raised Lancelot, too."

"Lancelot the knight? Really?"

"Really. Lancelot du Lac. He was French, but he grew up beneath the water. That's what *du lac* means—'of the lake.'"

"*Beneath* the water?"

"Lotta caves down there."

They came to a stop in the parking lots next to the Avalon Park Authority offices. Nearby, families were grilling and throwing Frisbees in spite of the autumn air.

"Want to get inside the backpack?"

"I really don't."

Mick was now operating under the theory that Americans were generally too afraid of personal embarrassment to make much ado over a two-foot-tall elf-man. Even those who *could* see him would look quickly away for fear they might appear to be staring. Even those who stared wouldn't mention it to others for fear of saying the wrong thing.

"Your man James Bond should'a been a dwarf," Mick said. "He could stroll right into the secret lair an' all the bad guys'd pretend not to notice him."

"I don't think you're supposed to say *dwarf*," said Scott. "So what now?"

They stared at the vast, expansive park. What now, indeed.

"'We're high above where friends conspired to send him

after he retired,'" said Scott, and he self-consciously scanned the sky for a hot-air balloon. "They can't possibly be hiding in a tree, can they?"

"I didn't want to be the first to say it."

"This is a lot of trees."

They instinctively headed for the center of the park. If someone were trying to hide, it would be there. The trees were half bare and littered with brittle leaves. Scott and Mick crunched along a fenced and winding path until, in silent agreement, they hopped the fence and crossed a mossy glen.

"We're going to get deer ticks," said Scott, just because nobody had said anything for thirty minutes.

After another thirty minutes they decided arbitrarily that they had reached the geographical center of the park and began to trace a scribbly spiral outward, all the while watching the boughs of the passing trees. After two hours Scott was ready to call it hopeless when he noticed Mick was whistling beside him.

"You're in a good mood today."

"One o' us oughta be. Yeh feelin' bad abou' lying to your da?"

"It wasn't a lie. I *am* going to Erno and Emily's. If we can find . . . wherever it is they're staying. Erno *did* invite us, with that riddle."

"All right."

After a respectful silence Mick started whistling again.

"Just don't know why you're whistling—we're terrible at this."

"We're doin' fine. Besides, it occurs to me today that I am a free elf. I'm outside in Pan's hairy arms, gettin' pleasantly lost in a park that just happens to be named for one of the great elfin places. A park that hides both the children an' the rabbit-man we're hunting."

"We don't know that—"

"'Tis good luck, it is. It's things comin' together. It's significant."

"Maybe."

"No maybe. We're going to turn a corner soon an' find our pooka. We're going to look up, an' there'll be our tree. Like that one."

Scott looked up because Mick was looking up, but he didn't see anything.

"Which one?"

"That one there, with all the dead wood like a great bloody nest."

It was some distance off: a huge oak with thinning leaves. But it was densely packed with loose branches, and Scott had to admit it would make a good (if dangerous) place to hide. He squinted at it for a few moments before he noticed that Mick had walked on ahead, and he hustled to catch up.

"Y'know," said Mick, "that tree reminds me of a story."

"Oh good."

"This was back in the old days. 'Twas coming on summer, an' a little finch was late to lay her eggs, so she flitted from tree to tree, askin' permission to build her nest. Each time she stopped she waited for the tree to think it through (which took its time—a tree has heavy thoughts, an' no way to deliver them but on the backs o' termites and ants), an' each time the answer was no."

"Uh-huh."

"An' eventually she happened upon a crater, a great bowl in a black mountain where nothing grew. This crater was filled with the bones o' dead trees: a great tangle o' kindling an' branches an' boughs an' trunks. Some hard as iron, some made dark an' soft by fire. So this lady finch

says to herself, 'It may be no tree, but sure an' it's a safe place to make my nest.' An' back and forth she goes with straw an' twigs, an' soon there's a tiny wee egg, an egg in a snug little nest, a nest restin' in the center o' that vast woodpile, the pile inside the crater at the heart o' the black mountain where nothing grew."

"We're here," said Scott. He stopped at the base of the tree and peered up into the canopy.

"Not finished. So the finch mother looks down an' laments, 'Just one lonesome egg, an' now a storm moves in.' Ev'ry chaffinch has a rain song—"

"Every what?"

"Chaffinch. 'S a kind of finch. So. Every chaffinch has a rain song, an' she sings hers then while the whole crater goes gloomy with wind an' shadow, an' then that shadow gets thicker, yet smaller, an' the finch looks up to see not a cloud at all but the monstrous body of the Great Dragon Saxbriton comin' in for a landing."

Scott circled the trunk, searching for a way to investigate. But the lowest braches, barely nubs, were ten feet off the ground. Erno and Emily couldn't climb this.

"The poor mother bird tears out o' there; and Saxbriton, unwitting, settles down in her colossal nest atop the solitary egg o' the finch.

"In the coming days the crater is visited by one o' the Good Folk, a charmin' elf-man of Ireland."

"Was it you?" asked Scott.

"What? No."

"Oh. It seemed like it was going to be one of those kinds of stories."

"It isn't," said Mick, and he sat down on a mossy stone to gaze up at the treetop. "The old elf weens that he's discovered the lair o' the Great Dragon Saxbriton, whose terrible furnace of a belly makes the air hazy with heat an' sulfur an' magic. Then the dragon rises, an' takes flight, an' the elf sees she's left behind a tiny egg in the center of her nest.

"It's difficult, but he scrambles over the twigs an' timber, and soon he's lookin' down at the egg o' the largest dragon in all the isles. It's smaller than he would have expected, but greenish an' speckled with purple an' rose. Some say the Fair Folk have no hearts, but somethin' thumped hard in his chest as the elf snatched the dragon's egg an' raced down the side o' the mountain.

"He came first upon Finn, a giant of some renown. The elf showed Finn his prize and said, 'The dragon's egg!' but Finn was dubious. "Tis awful small,' said the giant in his rumblin' thunderous voice. 'Great things come from small packages,' groused the elf, an' he went on his way.

"Next he happened upon Oberon himself, consort to Queen Titania an' commander o' the troopin' fairies. 'Look here,' the elf told his king. 'The egg of Saxbriton!' But Oberon sneered an' tilted his horn'd head. "Tis plain for a dragon's egg,' said His Majesty, but the old elf huffed. "Tis its insides what counts.' And he took the dragon's egg to his own mound, an' kept it warm under the earth, an' sang it an original song abou' loyalty to the one who hatched you an' the smiting of his enemies."

Scott called "Hello!" to the sky. The day was overcast and silvery, as though the sun itself had been pulled cobweb-thin and spread like gauze over the earth. Now that they weren't walking anymore he was getting cold.

"When the egg twitched an' made to hatch, the old elf gathered Oberon an' Finn and all the fairies great an' small to watch an' share in his triumph. An' hatch the egg did, its fuzzy tenant laid bare. All was quiet; all were still. 'Behold!' bellowed the old elf. 'The son o' the Great Dragon Saxbriton, BORN MAGICALLY IN THE FORM OF A FINCH!'"

"Heh," said Scott. Mick nodded.

"But the elf knew it was a lie. The other fairies knew it too, an' their laughter still rang in the elf's ears long after they'd gone," said Mick, and he looked down at his hands.

"He fed an' cared for that baby bird, whom he named Finchbriton, but his heart (if he had a heart) was not in it. So when Finchbriton was fledged, the elf took him from the mound an' placed him up in a birch tree an' left him. But the bird followed him home. Everywhere he went

Finchbriton followed, to the fairies' amusement an' the old elf's consternation."

Scott eventually elected to climb a smaller tree nearby just to get on higher ground. "Keep going," he said when Mick seemed to pause. "I can hear you."

"One day the elf had his fill o' the taunts an' the laughter, an' he walked Finchbriton into Morrigan's Wood. You won't find its like today. They said it had grown up around the site of an ancient battle, one tree for each fallen soul, an' crows still picked at the bark an' the cork of these trees an' dark sap flowed from the knotholes. The elf took Finchbriton into this forest in a wooden cage and left 'im.

"But as he returned home, his heart (if he had a heart) turned inside him, an' he ran back for the cage, callin' 'Finchbriton! Finchbriton, where are yeh?' An' from time to time he thought he heard the trill o' his little bird, but he could not find him, an' by nightfall both elf an' bird were lost.

"There were wolves in that Ireland. An' the wolves of Morrígan's Wood were large an' silent as death. The old elf did not even know he was hunted 'til they were upon him, a whole pack o' them. The leader, a great brute, showed his startlin' teeth an' padded forward on long legs to take the old elf's throat. But then the night was brilliant as day. Finchbriton was there, breathin' blue fire, an' in a trice the wolves were singed an' whimpering all the way back to their den.

"Finchbriton led them home, whistling bright flame. The elf supposed he had a heart after all, an' it felt like a naked new bird in his rib cage. An' the finch an' he were never parted," said Mick, his voice low and not so boisterous as before. "An' that's the end."

A high breeze made the upper branches shiver but left the two of them undisturbed. Scott paused in his tree and watched Mick, some twelve feet below.

"Are you okay?"

"Tolerable. Just rememberin'."

"So . . . was he really a dragon in the shape of a finch?"

"Nah, he was a finch."

"And . . . he could breathe fire just because a dragon sat on him—?"

"*I dunno*," Mick snapped. "Who can say? Go an' spend a fortnight under a great dragon's unmentionables an' report back; we'll compare notes."

Scott didn't know what to say to Mick. The story seemed to have taken something out of him.

"Sorry," Mick muttered finally.

"What will you do when you find Harvey?" asked Scott. "Will you try to go home?"

"Home . . . ," said Mick. "'Tis no home for such as us."

"Why? I mean, you're both from Ireland, aren't you?"

"Different Ireland. Different isles. I don't think I'm in my own world at all."

"Oh, right. You said that before. So fairies and people live in different worlds."

"It wasn't always so," said Mick. "Somethin's changed."

"What do you mean?"

"Who are you talking to?" asked a voice. A new voice. Scott's balance failed him, and he held fast to the oak's slender branches.

"Erno! We were looking for you."

"We?"

"I. I was just . . . talking to myself."

Erno was standing stiffly beside a large mountain bike. He grinned up at Scott. "There's a lot of that going around. You should talk to Biggs about it."

"Is that Biggs's tree house?" asked Scott as he climbed back down toward the ground. Getting down was so much trickier than getting up. "I tried shouting hello up to it, but nobody answered."

"Well, 'hello' doesn't work. What you should have shouted was 'HAPPY ARBOR DAY, PRESIDENT FILLMORE!' That works."

"I never would have thought to shout that."

"Yeah, that's kind of the point."

Mick got to his feet and moved when it became clear that Erno was going to trip over him otherwise. "Told yeh things was coming together," he told Scott.

Scott nodded, and tumbled kind of unceremoniously to earth. And now that he and Erno were on level ground he felt suddenly awkward. He'd been worried about his friends, and he almost bubbled over with relief to know they were okay. He thought maybe he and Erno should hug, or shake hands, but what he really wanted was for some useful surprise to distract them until the moment passed. Then an eight-foot-tall man dropped to the ground wearing only a bath towel.

CHAPTER 23

"Where *were you?*" Biggs asked Erno. He didn't even give Scott a glance. "So worried."

"Sorry. I'm sorry," said Erno. "I just saw Scott through the periscope, looking for us. So I rode out to find him." Erno shot Scott a look. "It took longer than I thought it would."

More lies. Scott sighed.

After a moment Biggs nodded. "Sorry I took so long," he said. "Was in the shower. 'Lo, Scott," he finished, and then looked rather squarely at Mick as though waiting to be introduced.

"Um," said Scott.

"All right, grab an armful of wet housekeeper," said Erno as he hopped on Biggs's back. Scott gave Mick a meaningful look, and the little man climbed into his backpack.

They fell, in fits and starts, into the sky. Scott regretted the cherry water ice he'd eaten earlier as a syrupy bile rose in his throat. Biggs soon deposited Scott on a strong branch and revealed the way inside his strangely homey nest egg. Then he went back for his bike. Erno ran in ahead to announce Scott, and soon Emily came squealing to meet him in the foyer with nearly homicidal enthusiasm. Had she hugged him with any more momentum they might both have tumbled backward through the still-open door and dropped a hundred feet to their adorable deaths.

"Hi," Scott said, blushing.

"I knew you'd find us," said Emily. "You won't believe what's happened."

Biggs returned and excused himself to go finish his shower. Emily led Scott into Biggs's living room, which contained Erno and some 50s modern furniture and a rabbit-man perched atop a bookcase reading *Half Magic*.

Harvey looked over the edge of his book at Scott. "*You?*" he coughed. Scott set his backpack down and unzipped the top. Harvey goggled. "Mick?"

"Harv!"

Scott found it hard to concentrate on Erno and Emily's story while the elf and pooka had their noisy, backslapping reunion. Mick produced his little flask, and the two of them passed it back and forth.

"What do you keep looking at?" asked Erno.

"Nothing. Sorry. That's awful, what Goodco was doing. And Mr. Wilson was a part of it?"

"No," said Emily.

Erno didn't answer, though you could kind of tell he wanted to.

Biggs returned wearing a white shirt and a tweed vest and slacks. He watched Mick and Harvey on the bookcase, then noticed Scott watching him.

"You can see them?" asked Biggs and Scott in unison.

"See them what?" asked Erno.

"The big guy ith touched," Harvey told Mick. "Goodco did a number on him in the thixties."

Biggs sat heavily in the corner chair. His glacial face cracked, just a little.

"Didn't know they were real," he said. "The things I see. Not really real."

"What are we talking about?" said Erno. "Scott?"

Scott glanced at Mick. Mick said, "Harvey, I think these are all good people. Yeh have any glamour left?"

"Thome."

"Enough for us both?"

"No. No way. That'th too much."

Mick jerked his head toward the Utz kids. "Not if yeh know their True Names."

Harvey seemed to be considering this, then he gave a resigned little shrug. "Erno and Emily Utth," he said as his

242

ears shivered, and Erno fell straight off the couch.

"Easter Bunny!" Erno shouted, pointing. "Little . . . munchkin!"

"Thtupid kid."

"What?" said Emily.

"Wait—you!" Erno said to Mick. "You're that angry leprechaun!"

"Angry clurichaun, actually," Mick growled.

"They're magical . . . refugees," said Scott. "They're from another world or something. Goodco has been holding them prisoner and stealing their magic."

"Have they been here this whole time?" Erno asked, breathless.

"No, no—Mick came with me."

"Met Harvey by the Porta-Potties," said Biggs. "Said he needed a place to hide."

"Why didn't you tell us?" Erno asked him while crawling back onto the couch.

"Thought it was all in muh head."

"I used to think they were auras," Scott explained.

"WHAT ARE YOU ALL TALKING ABOUT?!" wailed Emily. "Are you making fun of me?"

Everyone fell silent and stared at her. Mick climbed down to the floor.

"No one's making fun of you," Scott said quietly. "Why do you think we are?"

"You all . . . planned this somehow," Emily muttered. "You said, 'Let's pretend there are invisible people in the room to scare Emily.'"

Mick stepped over to the sofa. "Yeh still can't see me, lass? Or hear me?"

Emily gave no indication she could.

"Emily . . . ," said Erno. "There's a leprechaun next to you. And a . . . rabbit-man on top of the bookshelf."

Emily was looking like a balloon in search of a pin. "No such thing," she whispered as she pressed backward into the crook of the sofa.

"What'th with her?"

Mick looked up and over his shoulder. "She doesn't believe in us, Harv."

Harvey slumped. "That'th all right. I don't believe in me, either."

"Maybe Emily Utz isn't her True Name?"

"Sure it is," said Erno. "What do you mean?"

"A True Name isn't just what yeh call yourself," said Mick. "'Tis who yeh think yeh really are. It's the name that feels like home."

"So what difference does it make, anyway?" asked Scott. He was frightened for Emily, who was big-eyed and jerking her head back and forth like a sparrow.

"If yeh know a fellow's True Name, it gives yeh . . . influence. Your magics will work better on that person."

Erno glanced at Emily. "Try . . . try Emily Wilson."

"Thatth not it," said Harvey from the bookcase. "Thereth thomething elth up with her. Can't you thmell it? She thtinkth of magic."

Scott frowned as Emily started vibrating like a cell phone. And were the lights actually dimming? "Magic should make it easier for her to see you, shouldn't it? Not harder."

"STOP IT! STOP IT! IT'S NOT FUNNY!"

No one was laughing. Emily squirmed in her seat as Biggs rushed to take her in his arms. The lamps went out, there was a sharp crack and a flash of pink, and when the lights flickered on again the tree house was pierced in two dozen places with bony twigs. They jutted through the walls, ceiling, and floor at odd angles.

Mick hustled to the front door, and a stale hush hung in the air until he returned.

"It's tree branches," he reported. "Grew right in from the outside."

Erno touched one of the thin branches. "Did . . . did Emily do this?" he asked.

Biggs was swaddling Emily in his arms, rocking his weight from foot to foot. She appeared to have fallen dead asleep.

"Maybe we should go," Scott whispered to Mick.

"Aye."

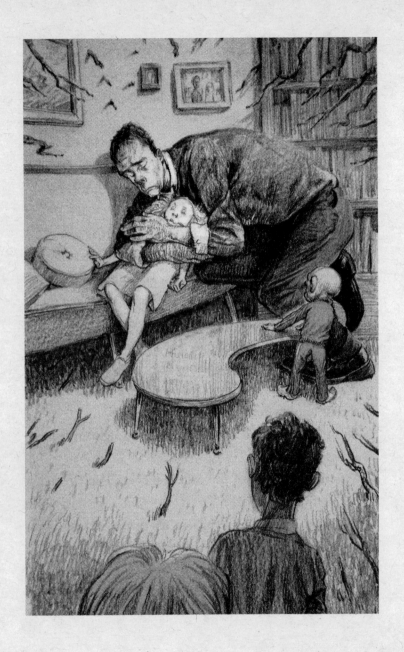

Harvey proceeded to climb down from the bookcase. "Lookth like you're gonna have a pooka in your baythment after all," he told Scott. "Should have jutht helped me from the thtart."

"Wait," said Scott. "Whoa. He can't stay at my house."

"He's right, Harv. Scott here has a little sister and a da' what can probably see us."

"What?" Harvey sputtered, his ears stock-straight.

Mick tried to calm him. "Yeh know how adult humans can be. Been hard enough just keeping *me* out o' sight, an' I can fit in a backpack."

"Inhothpitable mithcreants! Thcoundrelth! Dithcourteouth reprobateth!"

Scott glanced at Mick. "Is he still making words?"

"Promised you could stay here," Biggs told Harvey with his quiet thunder. "Still can. Just have to not upset Emily so."

Harvey seemed to be preparing some fresh snark, then thought better of it. He and Erno followed Scott and Mick to the door.

"What did Mr. Wilson *do* to her?" said Scott.

"I don't know yet," Erno answered. "I'm gonna find out."

"That was strong stuff, that was," said Mick. "Wild magic. No cause, no justification."

"So . . . she's got some weird powers now," said Erno, "and she doesn't know how to control them. You guys are

247

magic, right? You can teach her."

Mick shook his head. "I couldn't have done what your sister just did on my *best* day. Not without a very good reason."

"Is this another one of your rules?" asked Scott. "Like having to be good to get your glamour back? Seems like magic shouldn't *have* rules."

"Magic is all abou' rules. If we didn't have rules we'd be gods. Even back when I had my glamour I couldn't just do whatever I wanted. But I got what I deserved. Lemme tell yeh a story."

Scott sighed, and settled against the front door.

"This is back in the Old Days, in the Old World," said Mick, "an' a hermit catches one o' the Good Folk in his radish patch an' demands him some fairy treasure. So the old elf shows the hermit exactly which plant hides the gold. Why does he do this? 'Cause he has to, don't he? That's the arrangement; them's the rules. Now, the hermit doesn't have a shovel, so he ties a red garter around the radish greens an' heads back to his cave t' fetch one. An' when he comes back, what does he find?"

"That the elf has taken off the garter," said Scott.

"No! He comes back to find that *every* radish plant's got a garter now. Every last radish, an' a few thistles besides."

"And *this* elf was you?"

"No. He was a friend o' a friend. The point is, that elf

couldn't just remove the garter. The hermit had caught him fair an' square. But he could be tricky. We were *made* to be tricky."

"I alwayth thought your Bugth Bunny mutht be a pooka," said Harvey quietly. "He jutht wantth to live hith life. He'th a thimple thort. But when thomeone mithtreatth him, he can do impothible thingth. Tie a shotgun in a bow, drop an anvil out of the thky. Pull dynamite out of nowhere—he can do anything, if he hath a good enough reathon."

Mick smiled at the rabbit-man. "How'd yeh escape, Harv?"

"It wath Thamhain," Harvey answered. "I did one of the guardth a favor."

"Thowin?" said Scott. He didn't know that word. And he wouldn't have recognized it even if he'd seen it— Samhain was an Irish word, and like so many Irish words, it didn't sound (SOW-in) anything like it looked.

"*Sam*hain. November Day," Mick said. "The first o' the month."

"We pooka get a little more glamourouth on Thamhain. And thometimeth we give true anthwers, if people athk the right quethtionth. Don't know how thome Goodco guard knew about that."

"Wikipedia," suggested Erno.

"He wanted to know if hith girl would marry him. I thaid yeth."

"Was it true?" asked Scott.

"Gueth tho, or he wouldn't have let me out. Lucky me it wath a fifty-fifty quethtion."

Biggs was still cradling Emily, and possibly singing something atonally.

"How do we get down again?" asked Scott.

Erno grinned. "Rope."

Scott lowered them down, and he and Mick walked vaguely back toward the bus stop. It was dark, and Scott wondered what to say at home. That he'd changed his mind about the sleepover? That he and Erno had had a fight? He supposed he could tell John that Emily had one of her spells. *Spells*. It was almost funny except that it wasn't.

"Told you," said Mick. "Things comin' together. We set off lookin' for the Utz kids an' find a tree full o' everybody. That's magic, too."

"It's like a story."

"Same thing. The universe don't like plot. Story is magic's way o' telling the universe to sod off."

"That's good then, right?" said Scott. After this episode with Emily, he was ready for some optimism. "Magic wants us all to live happily ever after."

"Not necessarily," Mick answered. "Magic likes a good tragedy, too."

CHAPTER 24

"Can people see you now?" Scott asked Mick as they sat on a bench, waiting for the bus. "Because of the glamour Harvey gave you, I mean?"

"Nah. That was only good for the children. Or the lad, at any rate."

"Why didn't it work on Emily? Could you smell magic on her like Harvey could?"

Mick shook his head. "Harvey's got a considerable nose. An' Emily's something I've never seen before. If she's full o' magic like Harv says, she's keeping it way down in her root cellar where I can't see it at all."

"Maybe she's a changeling," Scott muttered. "It's . . . it's not like she and Erno exactly look like brother and sister."

"Meant t' ask you about that. One o' them adopted?"

"No. I mean . . . they're supposed to be twins," said

Scott, and Mick huffed. "I've tried to bring it up with Erno, but I've never gotten very far."

"Well, if she was just a changeling, she'd be able to see me an' Harvey an' all the other things that don't belong in this world."

Down the street a windowless white van was pulling into the parking lot next to the Park Authority Building. Scott was on alert for white vans, for all the good it did. Now that he was paying attention it seemed like they were *everywhere*. So far they'd only meant plumbers or flower deliveries. This one had a long ladder hitched to the side.

"Okay," he said to Mick. "Well, if you don't belong in this world, then where?"

"Maybe nowhere. Listen, I'll tell yeh a story."

Another story. Mick was getting nothing if not more talkative.

"This was abou' a thousand years ago," the old elf began. "I don't remember much before it happened, an' sure an' I don't remember everything since. But I remember this: one day, a thousand years ago, the sun rose twice."

In the lands of King Anguish of Ireland, the sun lingered just beyond horizon's door as though smitten with all creation, and reluctant to say good night. This was the twilight time, and the favorite time of the Fay. The old elf-man Fergus Ór (for if he had always existed, then he had always been old) emerged from his mound, clean as a turnip. He stood and whistled, and before long the fire-bird, Finchbriton, joined him. Then Fergus packed his pipe, and Finchbriton took his perch, and each smoked a while in his own way.

"Quiet this evening," Fergus said, and the little bird trilled in response. "Well, I ween it's because so many good Christian men an' boys are off helpin' our friend Arthur," Fergus explained.

Finchbriton warbled humbly.

"No cause to be embarrassed; yeh weren't to know. I only mean Arthur. He's King o' the Britons, he is," said Fergus. "But I amn't much of a Briton meself, an' you're a bit of a bird, if yeh don't mind me sayin' so."

"Who's a bit of a bird?" asked a passing bean-sidhe, who stopped and watched Fergus from a thicket of dead trees. She was pallid and clothed in diaphanous tatters; and Fergus thought she could be beautiful if only she fixed her hair, or at least combed the worms out of it.

"Just my friend here," said Fergus, and he pointed to Finchbriton with the stem of his pipe. "Only don't tell him; he thinks he's a dragon."

"You and that bird," the bean-sidhe sneered.

"Me an' this bird," Fergus agreed. "That's it exactly.

What brings you by, Mona? Not business, I hope."

"Not business," said the bean-sidhe with notable regret. "I should be in the east, at Camlann. A great battle rages."

"Still? It's not Arthur an' Nimue's boy again, is it?"

"Arthur and Lancelot are again of one accord. Today they fight Mordred, Arthur's bastard son."

"Well, aren't you the gossip."

And then a strange sun rose in the east. To begin with, there was only a glow, like the first light of morning.

"Well now," whispered Fergus, as much to himself as to the bird or the bean-sidhe. "What do yeh make o' that?"

The bean-sidhe turned to the east and clutched at the trees. Her hair writhed.

"A sign! A new day begins, and Arthur hath prevailed! Or died!"

This strange sun breached the hills, looking jagged and broken through the trees. It grew larger, closer, not a sun but a dome, or else a great sphere of light that was half above the ground, half below. Finchbriton flew to Fergus's shoulder and whistled low.

It came at them, this curved radiant wall, and passed on through. Then they were inside the

light, and the light was magic. Pure magic, like neither elf nor bird had experienced before. The trees
held their branches still, while every blade of grass
quivered and the stars fell like cherry blossoms all
around. Fergus burst out laughing: round peals of
laughter like church bells. Finchbriton sang out loud
and clear and set the tops of trees ablaze, while the
bean-sidhe keened and wailed and fell to her knees.

Everything blurred, and it occurred to Fergus
through his tears that he was seeing double. Then
perhaps his brain guttered a bit, and he dropped to
the earth.

"Seein' double," Mick repeated. "That's what really
stayed with me after I woke up again."

"Finchbriton?" asked Scott. "You said that elf wasn't
you."

"Yeah. I lied."

The buses didn't run much at night. Scott breathed on
his hands to warm them and watched another white van
pull up and park next to the first. Mick played with the
zipper on his jacket and slumped back against the bench,
which was papered with an ad for Aspercreme. Then he
took another little drink from his flask.

"What is that stuff, anyway?" asked Scott.

"Perfume."

"Perfume?"

"It's fine for fairies," said Mick, sounding defensive. "You shouldn't drink it, though—very bad for boys an' such."

"Were you just giving me the 'not until you're older' speech?"

"Heh. Yeah. Not till you're twenty-one hundred."

"So what was it? The big sphere of light? What happened?"

"Didn't know what it was then, still don't. Suddenly there's no sun or moon anymore, but it's always twilight, so that's all right. 'Ceptin' the air still seemed to crackle with magic. Too much glamour, an' unfamiliar glamour, too. Like the magics o' the whole world had come to roost in Britain an' Ireland. Then word got around that France wasn't there anymore, either."

"Not there?"

"Most of it, anyway. Gone. Iceland too, and Saxony. An' all other points north, south, east, an' west. All gone, except for Britain an' Ireland, Ireland an' Britain. Let's call the two o' them Pretannica—the Greeks did."

"Pretannica," Scott repeated. The magical world. Sounded like one of those thick fantasy books with a lot of complicated maps inside.

"Pretannica's there; everythin' else's missin'. Yeh travel too far an' you'd find an ever-thickening fog o' enchantment that could not be crossed. Which drove the humans nutty as conkers. Suddenly a farmer who'd never been so much as ten miles from home pined to see all the riches o' Araby. They tried to get through the fog, they never came back."

"That's scary."

"Sure. Can't say I thought of it much at first, though. Ireland was my home, an' I'd never really believed the rest o' the world existed, anyway. I'd always lived in a bubble. It was maybe a hundred years before anyone realized the bubble was closing in."

"You mean getting smaller?" asked Scott. He imagined his desk globe, and half a Ping Pong ball covering the British Isles.

"Right. The bubble was contracting. Slowly, but still. Now the Good Folk take notice. We figure it's all the humans' fault somehow. We remember the Battle o' Camlann, even if they mostly don't. Father an' son killed one another on the battlefield, an unnatural act. Maybe this was punishment. People believed in things like that back then."

"You said Arthur retired. He died in battle?"

"Well, some said he died; some said he was only badly wounded an' taken to Avalon to rest up an' return. I wasn't there."

There were three white vans now, though thus far Scott hadn't noticed anyone get out. He realized they must be

Park Authority vans, the way they were lining up in front of the building like that.

"So how did you fairies fix things? Make the world as it was before?"

"We didn't. The Good Folk aren't much for makin' plans. We're a flighty bunch." Mick sat up. "Rumors start spreadin', though, abou' the Fay disappearin'. The superstitious fairies (an' we're all a little superstitious) revive all the old stories abou' elves going to hell to pay a tithe to the devil, but truth is, it's not just the Fay disappearin'. It's all manner o' magical creatures. They're slippin' away, three or four a year. Then one morning it happens to me, an' I'm in New Jersey."

Afterward, when the reporters from the *Goodborough Telegraph* asked Mary Coleman just how her baby daughter had come to be replaced by a tiny bald Irishman, she told them that two burly kidnappers had made the switch right before her eyes. When *Harper's Weekly* asked her to recount the same story three days later, it was four kidnappers with pistols and a getaway carriage. But in truth she'd only looked away from where her baby lay for a moment, and when she turned back, there was a wrinkled little man in the pram, looking every bit as surprised as Mary.

"Dear Ann!" Mary screeched. "What's become of you?!"

"What?" said Fergus Ór.

"You're not my baby! What have you done with my baby?!"

"I've nothin' to do with your baby, lass, an' I—"

"Kidnapper! An Irishman! Help! Help!"

Fergus could see where this was going. He struggled up out of the soft quilted poufs of the cradle and tumbled over the side of the carriage to the street. He was in a narrow cobblestone lane, slick with rain and lined with shops. It was day. There was true sunlight here, such like he hadn't felt for centuries. It made him squint. Through his squint he saw people, all of them staring back at him.

"He stole my little girl!" the woman was telling them. "He's Irish!"

They were approaching from all sides. Men in long coats and top hats, a barefooted boy. A peddler pushing a cart hung with knives and holding a long whetstone like a cudgel. Fergus pivoted about, looking for an alley, but there were no alleys. Then he composed himself—grabby human hands were something else he hadn't felt for centuries, and he wouldn't feel any today either if he kept his head. He let the glamour slide off him as he ducked to avoid the swing of a walking stick and leaped to escape the lunge of the peddler, and heard the sharp crack of the one connecting with the other. He tore off down the street, the cobblestones so punishing against his feet, and left the men and boys to discuss in high voices just what had become of him.

Within a week the *Telegraph* warned that substantial numbers of hungry Irishmen might now be posing as infants, looking to be fed. It was a popular story and gave rise to the slang term "paddy wagon," which initially referred to a baby carriage but later became synonymous with the police van. A chapbook published later that year intimated that the little man may well have been a changeling—an Old World fairy left in place of a stolen child—but of course this theory was widely regarded as hogwash.

Fergus wended his way north to the edge of town, feeling naked without his glamour. More than once a dog, unable to see him but still haunted by apparitions of smell and sound, would whimper or bark in his direction. Once only, in a poor shantytown at the edge of the thin woods, he thought twin girls might be watching him pass; but he didn't stop to make conversation. He walked briskly through the camp, came to a river and a bridge, checked for trolls, and came away disappointed.

In the centuries since the Gloria (or the Morning Glory, or the Marvel—that world-changing-sphere of light and magic had inspired as many names as it had questions), the forests of Pretannica had grown tangled and primeval. So the woods here looked comparatively precious, almost cute. Like a crowd of reedy, earnest children. When Fergus realized the forest was getting no thicker, he paused to rest, and to reach out with his senses. He raised a glamour and felt about for some magic. Anything. Even before the Gloria, the air of Pretannica had always held some faint trace of magic. It infused the air like humidity—the sort of thing you'd only notice when it was suddenly gone. This forest was a desert, and Fergus began to panic.

After half a day of walking it was sunset, and Fergus could feel that familiar light unwind him a little. He searched again for magics and sensed something slight but not so far away. *A kinsman*, he thought, and put on his best glamour. Enchantment was not just for the humans, after all; with his glamour, Fergus appeared a full two inches taller, and magnificently wrinkled, like a cabbage. He slid down a mossy hill toward a dying oak, its roots laid bare by erosion. And huddled beneath that rib cage of dry roots was the fairy.

"Well met, cousin," said Fergus before the creature lunged.

It fell upon Fergus and pressed him to the ground,
its chapped hooves grinding the dirt on either side of
the old elf's head. It had a long face like a horse. But
not exactly like a horse. It had a pair of large, limp
bat's wings that dangled uselessly from its shoulders.

"Cousin!" Fergus panted. "I meant no offense!
Grant mercy on your poor Irish relation!"

The fairy flared his nostrils and breathed a sul-
furous wind that made Fergus's eyes water. Then it
withdrew and sat back on its haunches.

"Cousin," the fairy repeated hoarsely. Fergus
scrambled back a bit on his hands and heels and
stopped when his rump hit a stone.

The fairy sat like a man, with its spindly legs
crossed in front. Both hands and feet were hoofed,
and horns grew like briar from its temples.

Was it some strange kelpie? No, it wasn't dripping anything, especially. It was a pooka, Fergus
realized, though he'd never seen one so anatomically
confused. *Best not to mention it,* he thought. "Cousin,
where am I?"

"New Jersey."

Fergus frowned. "There's a *new* Jersey now?" He
supposed there should be—the old Jersey had been

swallowed five hundred years ago by the Gloria wall.

It was an odd characteristic of the Fay that, though none of them could claim to have seen a true fairy birth, they were all nonetheless connected like a family. No one remembered back far enough to say just how this had started. There was an old human's tale that claimed the fairies had become enchanted by the notion of human families and decided to imitate them. But (the story said) they'd gotten it wrong: they made an ancient-looking boggart the son of a beautiful elf who was the very picture of youth, or perhaps a bone-eating giant was now uncle to a swarm of electric little sprites. The Fay had no comment except to note that the humans' tales tended to flatter the humans.

So the two fairies compared family trees and determined that they were indeed third cousins, on their mothers' sides. It was dark when Fergus asked, "What d'yeh call yourself, friend?"

"The Jersey Devil," said the Jersey Devil.

"That's . . . nice," said Fergus, forcing a smile.

The fairy's wings shivered and then once again lay still. "You're in a new world. You've crossed an ocean and something far greater than an ocean to get here. You're just arrived?"

"'This mornin,'" Fergus answered. "Blimey, I'm one o' the disappeared now, amn't I?"

The Jersey Devil stood up on its hind legs and, with visible strain, spread its rank wings. Fergus could see moonlight through the skin. "Run as far as you can from this place. There is a . . . grain mill nearby. They trap our kind. They take our magic, I know not why. I escaped, but I am drained, and my glamour is addled."

"It'll be restored, friend," Fergus whispered. "Yeh need only live honorably—"

"It does not come back, here."

The pooka was still standing, still spreading its wings, though it trembled with the effort.

"This earth does not love us. Run, or out of kindness I will kill you myself and drink your blood, and with stolen glamour I will set upon the men of the grain mill and make their hearts to brast. *Run or perish!*" hissed the Jersey Devil.

"So I ran," said Mick. "Holed up in Washington during the war. Ran some more after Lincoln died. Tried to stow away to Ireland, an' that's when they caught me. The first time."

Mick heaved a great sigh.

"I think it's like . . . ," he added, then faltered. "Like the whole universe got cracked. Like an egg with two yolks. An' the yolks, the worlds inside, they got split apart, an' this yolk's a lot bigger than the other." Mick chewed on his lip. "It's not one o' my better metaphors."

Scott didn't know what to say, so they were quiet a minute.

"Maybe the buses don't run this late," he spoke finally, and stood up to examine the sign beside the bench. That's when he saw them: eleven white vans in the parking lot, two blocks away, and a twelfth just pulling up. "Um."

Mick looked up. But he was short, and there was a hedge. "What is it?" he whispered. "I can't see."

In a rapid drill of clunking doors and pattering feet, seventy men emerged with rifles and black jumpsuits and glinting eyes. Among them was a small detachment of men in pink rubber suits carrying what looked like an aluminum crate between them. And two more men not dressed like the others.

"Haskoll and Papa," Scott whispered. He had never felt so sure of anything.

Mick was standing atop the bench. "Maybe they don' know exactly where they're goin'," he said. "Maybe we can get to the tree first."

Papa was giving the assembly some orders, but he was

interrupted by Haskoll. Scott couldn't make out any of it.

Five of the men mounted four-wheel ATVs. The rest saluted Haskoll. Then they all trooped off around the Park Authority building, and Scott and Mick sprinted back into the trees.

CHAPTER 25

Here are some of the things that lined up in Erno's favor tonight:

- He learned that Emily is a very sound sleeper on evenings when she's been magically spazzy.
- Even if you trip over her.
- He found that Biggs is a very sound sleeper too and will not wake if you
  - bang your knee into the coffee table
  - trip over Emily again
  - drop a tube full of your foster father's notes onto the kitchen tile
  - and noisily pull back a dinette chair so you can sit down and read them.

E1 and E2. E1 and E2. Were they chemicals? No, not

chemicals. But they were mentioned all throughout the notes, on every page.

E1 shows increasing signs of agoraphobia and anxiety disorder.

Later,

E2 exhibits normal socialization skills and no verifiable neuroses.

Too many of the words were unfamiliar. Erno couldn't tell if E1 and E2 were people or lab rabbits. Or rabbit-people.

Then his eyes strayed over a highlighted paragraph:

In short, E2 is, in many respects, an average and acceptably adjusted boy.

Boy, thought Erno.

He is outgoing, athletic, and inquisitive. E2 consistently tests among the 99th percentile nationally and has an IQ of 135 (with a two-point margin of error). He would seem gifted in any company other than E1. Her

*IQ, as previously stated, is too high to be measured in any
conventional sense.*

"Oh," Erno whispered. "E1 and E2. Emily and Erno."

*Despite both children's intelligence, however, neither
seems to suspect, much less understand, that they are not
actually siblings. Regarding E1 in particular, we must
infer that she's constructed strong walls in her mind to protect herself from knowledge she does not wish to possess.*

"Jeez." Erno sighed. "Give me *some* credit. I know we're
not brother and sister."

He read on, occasionally pausing to read and reread
the same sentence, trying to spin meaning from some of
the longer, tangled words. What he gathered, though,
was that there seemed to be something seriously wrong
with Emily. She was smart, of course, wickedly smart, but
the notes suggested that the Milk-7 was hurting her too.
Poisoning her mind. That was what he thought it said,
anyway. Maybe it was why she cried all the time. One
thing seemed clear: Emily thought she'd been taking it to
stop her dizzy spells, but the Milk was probably giving
her the spells in the first place. There was a whole paper
about it.

Erno began to tremble with anger. Mr. Wilson had done this. To his own foster daughter he had done this. Erno flipped carelessly through the notes, treating them roughly, thinking about what he'd do and say if Mr. Wilson were there.

He stopped at a strange page. The handwriting was different, looser. He checked it against the other pages. *No,* he thought, *it's Mr. Wilson's writing.* There was the same funny letter *g.* But this new page was more relaxed, like he was writing a diary rather than a book report. It said:

> *October 19—I'm forty today. That also means I've been taking the Milk for ten years.*

Erno frowned and whispered, "He was taking it, too?"

There was even an unfinished verse in the margins, possibly the clue to some new game he'd been devising.

> *There's a sort of sorting shorthand*
> *both for magic beast and fairy.*
> *All the sly land on the island,*
> *all the dumb land in the*

"Gary," suggested a voice. Erno flinched. "Interethting reading?" added Harvey, who was leaning over his shoulder.

Erno rolled up the notes. "You can't sleep, either?"

"I take little napth through the day. Are there uthually tho many people in the park at night?"

"What do you mean? What people?"

"I heard voiceth."

Erno couldn't hear anything. He swung his legs around and walked past Harvey to the tree house periscope. He pressed his eyes up to the eyepieces: two cold rings against his face. Outside, the night sky was bleeding light.

"Are those flares?" Erno whispered.

"Which way?" called Scott. He and Mick had found the tree before by accident, and things weren't quite coming together this time.

"This way! This way!" answered the little man.

Above them, flares flickered and fell like slow stars. The air buzzed with the roar of ATVs. The roar grew louder, and Scott and Mick dived into a clump of ferns just before an ATV rider with a big helmet-mounted lamp thundered by in a blaze of light.

"This is too dangerous for you," Scott hissed. "You should get in the backpack."

"Nah. That'd just slow us down."

They emerged and took off running again.

"What we need is one o' them motor-bikes," Mick said in a plainly hyphenated fashion.

"I've asked for something like that every year for three Christmases."

"Good *luck*. I can't even get Kris Kringle to pay back the twenty quid he owes me."

Scott ran for another few beats. "You're friends with *Santa Claus?*"

"*Former* friends. Next time he's in jail he can find someone *else* to bail him out."

The sound of another ATV grew closer. Mick grabbed Scott's sleeve and brought him to a stop. "Hold up," he said. "Christmas's come early this year."

When this second ATV rider rounded a copse of trees, he saw, in the pink of his helmet-mounted arc light, a squinting old man with a tiny head. He screeched to a halt and peered through the pink lenses of his big black goggles.

"You!" he barked as he dismounted. "Stay there! Keep those hands where I can see them!"

The normal-sized man with the tiny wrinkled head raised his arms. "These hands?" he asked.

The rider was all in black, with some kind of thick and undoubtedly bulletproof vest and an oily black gun slung over his shoulder. He reached back to touch this gun as if drawing some shallow sense of strength and security from it, which of course he was. He also had a small stone around his neck on a tether, a coldstone, and this

was busily giving off purple sparks. But in the glare of his headlamp, the rider hadn't noticed.

This old man was strangely built, like he hadn't enough head but had entirely too much neck. "The park isn't safe tonight," the rider told him. "You should return to your home."

"Mind turnin' that off, lad?" the old man asked.

"Sorry," said the rider, and he reached up to switch off the pink light of the helmet.

"Yeh have somethin' in your eye," the old man added.

"I . . . huh?"

The rider pulled the goggles up and over his helmet. And then he winced when he saw that, while the old man was still standing before him, his head had just now disappeared.

"Oh," said the rider, and then Mick leaped off Scott's shoulders and punched the man with his hard little walnut fists. The rider stumbled backward and sprawled over the fenders of his ATV.

The whole thing came off like a gag in a cartoon, albeit a cartoon with punching. Lots of punching.

"See," said Mick to the rider, who was now unconscious and prostrate on the ground, "I says, 'Yeh have somethin' in your eye.' An' then you says, 'What have I got in my eye?' An' then I says, 'My fist.' Yeh did it wrong."

"'That was . . . kind of violent," said Scott as he fixed his shirt and jacket.

"You shoulda seen me in the ol' days," Mick heaved as he sat down on the rider's back. "Coulda tied his gun in a bow. Coulda dropped an anvil on him. Think yeh can drive his motor-bike? I can't reach the handlebars."

Erno shook Biggs awake, then Emily. She gave a tiny mewl and got to her feet.

"What's going on?" she whispered with her palms over her eyes. Above them the small windows flickered with light. All around, distant shouts.

Biggs strode forward in his XXXL monogrammed pajamas (*B.B.*) and scooped Emily up to his shoulders. "Smoke," he said.

It took Erno a few seconds before he could smell it too, and by then anyone could see it seeping in through cracks, around the edges of windows, or collecting like evil thoughts around the hundred holes left by Emily's wild magic.

"Have to get out," Biggs added.

Erno darted from the living room to the kitchen and back. "I can't see Harvey," he announced, then coughed. "He's invisible again."

Biggs scanned the tree house through the thickening haze. Emily was coughing now, too.

"MY CAR KEYS." The big man held Emily close and bellowed as he turned. "*RABBIT-MAN, WHERE ARE MY CAR KEYS?*"

Scott and Mick jolted forward on the ATV. They lurched and rattled. The hand controls were really sensitive.

"Yeh drive like a spastic," said Mick from the back-pack.

"Maybe you should drive then," Scott answered, his voice muffled by the big black helmet. "Oh right, you can't because you're the size of a football."

They were silent for a moment as they hurtled toward some distant glow.

"'M bigger'n a football," Mick muttered.

They bucked over roots and stones, and all the while that strange light in the distance shimmered and grew.

"Oh no," Scott whispered. He had just begun to feel the heat of it. And then the trees parted, and Biggs's oak was burning from the top down like a colossal torch. The tree house was engulfed and snapping angrily. The ashes of Biggs's life rose in the blistering air.

There were a lot of people here, dressed in black with black guns, casting black shadows.

"We're too late," Mick said. "Turn back. If they're alive we can't help 'em. Stop. Scott?"

Scott finally brought the ATV to a stop and turned it

haltingly in the opposite direction. "I don't know where to go."

"Just away," said Mick. "We'll think o' somethin'."

They had been fleeing for perhaps a minute when Scott felt something strike his helmet. For one thrilling moment he thought he was being shot at.

"Woah," said Mick. "Stop a second. Someone's throwin' rocks."

Scott slowed. "Someone's throwing rocks, and you want to stop?"

"Behind us. Look! It's Harvey."

Scott stopped and looked. It *was* Harvey, or someone who looked like Harvey. So it was pretty safe to assume it was Harvey.

"They're coming!" Harvey shouted. "Thayve me!"

"Where are the rest?" asked Mick as he leaped down from the backpack and the rabbit-man neared. "The big man an' the kids?"

"I don't know," said Harvey, his ears twitching about. His trousers were sooty and his tie torn. "It wath all very confuthing. Caoth. There wathn't anything I could do to help. They're probably fine. We should go."

Then, in one thrilling moment, they *were* being shot at. There was someone, a fair distance away but closing fast on another ATV, pistol blazing. As they stumbled over one another to mount up, Scott could just barely make out a voice over the drone of the engine, a familiar voice shouting between gunshots.

"Hey, Scotty!" *Bang.* "Hold up, I want to ask you something!" *Bang bang.* The last shot cracked a stone just three feet away as Scott urged the ATV into motion again.

"That's Haskoll, isn't it?" asked Mick from the backpack.

"Who'th Hathkoll?" asked Harvey from the seat just behind Scott. If Scott could have comfortably answered, he would have first asked the pooka to hold on to something other than his neck.

Scott weaved in and out of the underbrush, slalomed through trees. Occasionally the report of Haskoll's pistol and the destruction of some nearby piece of tree trunk informed them that he hadn't run out of bullets yet.

An earpiece inside the helmet Scott was wearing crackled to life. "Heeyy, buddy. Just wanted to keep you apprised of the situation: up to now I've been missing on purpose, because Goodco wanted your friends alive. But I just got a kill order. To kill you. Doesn't that sound all double-oh-seven? 'Kill order.' What a world."

Scott turned a hard left and almost flipped the ATV.

"Jeez," said Harvey. "Kid driveth like a thpathtic."

"He knows."

"See," said Haskoll inside Scott's helmet, "seems the bigwig just decided your pals are more trouble than they're worth. And Goodco has never really had a problem with killing children. But if you've ever read the side of one of their cereal boxes you know that already, amiright, Scotty?"

Two shots rang out, and Scott thought he could feel them pass closer. Or maybe he was just imagining it.

"Oh," said Haskoll, "and FYI: I'm not going to run out of bullets. This is a magic gun. Seriously. Bigwig has a history of handing out magic weapons. Crazy, right? I call it 'Glamdring.' *Blam!*"

Haskoll had actually said '*blam*,' but he'd fired at the same time, and Scott felt a thud shudder up through the seat of his pants. Then there was another bang from the ATV itself, which presently shimmied and stalled, and struck a log Scott had been struggling to avoid. All three passengers were bucked over the handlebars and into a bed of ferns.

Their ATV was on fire, and blooming with thick, dark smoke. They disentangled themselves in a panic as they listened to the approaching buzz of Haskoll's vehicle. So there was no surprise when they turned to find him just stopping, some thirty feet off, and aiming Glamdring in their direction. He was wearing jeans with flip-flops and a T-shirt with a picture of a unicorn wearing a hoodie.

This is the man who's going to kill me, Scott thought. It was an odd thought, as though he'd been expecting an entirely different sort of man to kill him.

"'Kay, just in case Scotty hasn't filled you in," said Haskoll, and he waggled his pistol. "Magic gun, kill order. Bigwig doesn't care whether I bring you two in dead or alive, so you can make this all go more smoothly if you step away from Scotty and sit tight a minute."

Meaning he's just going to kill me, thought Scott with a pukey sort of rage boiling up inside him. Later (and there would be a later) he would think about how he'd been furious not because he was going to die, but because there were people such as Haskoll in the world. That they could live and breathe and were permitted to walk around looking to the naked eye as if they were perfectly ordinary human beings. *There should be fancy goggles with coal-black lenses that would show you what this man really looked like,* Scott thought.

Haskoll was going about the one-handed business of producing a cigarette and lighting it with a shiny metal lighter. Mick was still standing close to Scott, though Harvey had stepped some distance away. His long ears were rigidly straight, and Scott thought he could hear the pooka muttering, ". . . Won't go back, won't never go back . . ."

They all shivered in the breeze.

"That's sweet," said Haskoll around the edge of his cigarette. "The leprechaun is standing by you, Scotty."

"Clurichaun," Mick mumbled automatically.

"Friends are so important," Haskoll continued. "More important than the *air we breathe*. But can I say, and I'm just being honest, that as far as human shields go, the Mayor of Munchkinland there is neither human nor a shield—"

"GAAH! Jeez!" Scott snarled suddenly. Even Mick jumped. "Could you possibly just go ahead and kill me?! You're not seriously so evil that you're actually going to make me listen to you *talk* first, are you?"

"Whoah! Hey, Scotty's grown a pair—"

"Shut up. Okay? My name is Scott. Or Scottish, or . . ." Scott took a breath. "Look, just because you've won doesn't mean you're clever, or funny. You're just a horrible jerk with a gun. And an idiot. And you dress like an idiot. If you have a magic gun, you call it *Ex-Calibre*, okay? It's obvious. You stole Glamdring from *The Hobbit*."

"'Ex-Calibre,'" Haskoll repeated. "Huh."

"And seriously . . . friends are more important than air? Do you even listen to yourself? You talk like a birthday card. Some awful birthday card with flowers on the front."

Possibly the greatest insult of all was that Haskoll wasn't even looking at him anymore. His attention had been stolen by Harvey, whom Scott was dimly aware had begun to flinch and quiver as he muttered. The rabbit-man was having a kind of fit, and his pink eyes flashed with something other than moonlight.

"So . . . you know, in closing: you're stupid," Scott added. "Can't we just get this over with?"

"Yeah . . . ," Haskoll agreed, his eyes still on Harvey. "Yeah, maybe we should." He pulled a walkie-talkie from the ATV to his mouth and said, "This is Haskoll. Converge on my GPS. I have two for transport back to HQ." Then he leveled his weapon at Scott's chest.

"WON'T NEVER GO BACK!" Harvey screeched.

"Why don't you shut the—" Haskoll began, and that's when he was crushed by something heavy from above.

It was a metal . . . something . . . the size of a refrigerator. It might conceivably have been cylindrical a second before but was now looking kind of cubist. It had landed with a powerful crunch and a thump that rippled through the ground to where Scott and Mick stood. It was smoking. It had Haskoll and an ATV under it.

An owl hooted, somewhere.

"What . . . *is* that?" said Scott.

Mick stepped forward. "I think it's a piece o' airplane."

Scott winced at the sky. "Hopefully not a really important piece of airplane."

"WON'T NEVER GO BACK!" Harvey said again. He was hoarse and panting. The light in his eyes had dimmed.

"Do you . . . think they can still converge on his GPS?" asked Scott.

"Hmm," said Mick. "Either way, we better hoof it. Harvey?"

"Yeth," said the rabbit-man. He was looking suddenly tired.

"Time to go."

CHAPTER 26

The metal crate in which they were being carried was just big enough that Erno could turn to look out the narrow opening beside his head, then back again to check on Emily. She seemed unhappy but calm, oddly resigned. As if she'd always expected to end up in a cage eventually. As though she'd been backing into one her whole life.

"I'm sorry, Erno," she whispered suddenly.

"Sorry . . . for what? What did *you* do?"

"I knew this was going to happen. Something like this. I've known all along, but I wouldn't let myself believe it. Did you know," she continued, "that I did a little research about my ear infection a while back?"

Erno shook his head.

"All the books I checked said it should normally last about six months to a year. Six months to a year, and here I've had it since I was a baby."

Erno nodded, and wondered if she realized her pink ear medicine had been causing the trouble rather than treating it. "Did you ask Mr. Wilson about it?"

"He said I had a special kind of infection. Very rare. He said I'd probably need to use these drops for a long time. I didn't look into it after that," Emily said. "I just trusted Dad. I was only five."

Five, thought Erno.

"I just didn't think about it. I . . . didn't let myself," she whispered. "I've been like this for a long time. It's like, I suddenly remember that I've forgotten something. Something really important. But when I try to concentrate, to recall what the important thing is, it slips away. It slips away, and I forget that I ever remembered that I forgot it, for a while. But I'm facing it now. I'm facing it all, and it's like I already know everything. *Everything*. I know it's not true, of course, but that's what it feels like."

"You don't know everything," Erno tried to comfort her. "You . . . don't know what number I'm thinking of."

"Seven," said Emily.

Erno frowned.

"It's like my mind's a black hole," she continued. "All the knowledge of the world just rushes in."

"Wait," said Erno. "I'm thinking of another one. Between one and one hundred."

"Forty-three."

"That's . . . not it," Erno attempted to say casually.

"Don't lie."

"Okay," Erno admitted. "But how did you know?"

"You wanted a number near the middle because it seemed safer," Emily explained. "All those other numbers, like padding on either side. But not *too* near the middle. So something in the forties, because you subconsciously believe anything over fifty is aggressive, and you're not an aggressive person."

Erno huffed.

"You chose an odd number," Emily continued, "because odd numbers seem more 'random.' You—"

"Okay, new one!" Erno whispered hotly. "Sixteen!"

Emily paused, delicately.

"Erno, *I'm* supposed to guess, not—"

"Okay! Yes. I know that. So—you guess."

"It's still sixteen, isn't it."

Erno sighed. "Yes."

"The only thing I don't get is what happened in the tree house," Emily said with a little frown. "When I blacked out."

"The magic?"

She scoffed. "There's no such thing."

The guards carrying their crate trudged along out of the park, their gaits swaying the crate in a constant tide that was getting Erno a little queasy. He could only imagine what it was doing to Emily. Somewhere, close by, still more soldiers were carrying the unconscious body of Biggs. It had taken ten men to subdue him.

"There's something else I know," Emily continued, more softly than before. "I know that . . . we were brought together and . . . raised together for the sake of an experiment. To test the Milk-7. I know . . . I know we're not really brother and sister."

Erno turned away from the window. Emily was all folded up, tiny as she could be, her arms hugging her knees to her chest. He reached out and put his hand over hers.

"Sure we are." He smiled. "Don't be stupid."

"This is Biggs's car?" asked Scott. It didn't seem possible.

"I've theen him get out of it," said Harvey as he unlocked the door. "It'th like a pop-up book."

"An' you have the keys . . . why?" said Mick.

"I was clothetht to them. We planned to meet at the car. Gueth they didn't make it. So! I can drop you guyth thomewhere but then I'm driving thtraight through to Mexthico."

"Wait," said Scott, "no."

"Harvey," Mick began, "those kids need help. That big man who took yeh in needs help. Yeh said before that yeh could smell magic in Em'ly. I was thinkin' . . ."

Harvey spun around and threw his hands up. "What? That I could track her? Rethcue everyone? After that thtunt I pulled in the park, I'm lucky I thtill have enough glamour to light a candle!"

"Yeh owe these folks. They took yeh in. If you want that glamour back—"

"I gotta live an honorable life? Thweet Danu, are you joking? This ith where magic cometh to die, Mick! Have you theriouthly not figured thith out yet? Glamour doethn't return, here. I'm . . . I'm thorry yourth ith gone, but . . ."

They fell silent, and Mick bowed his head. *He thinks it's gone, too*, thought Scott. *Mick thinks his magic's gone for good.*

"There's livin' well for its own sake," Mick murmured. "An' doin' what's right. There's still that."

Harvey lifted his ears, looked suddenly resolute. "You've forgotten what we are. We're the angelth what didn't fall all the way. We're the mere anarchy loothed upon the world," he told Mick. "You've forgotten what *I* am, anyway. In four thouthand yearth I haven't never done no one a good deed he didn't regret."

"Forget it, Mick," Scott muttered. "He doesn't have to. He already saved my life."

"Lithen to thith one. Thith really the kid you want to hitch your wagon to, Mick? I liked him better when he wath about to die. Thomeone should point a gun at him every day of hith life."

"Shut it," said Mick. "Forget what yeh owe that family, but remember what yeh owe *me*. I broke yeh outta Goodco twice, in seventy-three an' in eighty-six. Take us where them kids're being held an' we're square, an' then it's off to Mexico with you."

Harvey's ears sagged again. Then he stepped aside and opened the car door like a valet. *"Andale, muchachos."*

The slit window offered Erno and Emily only notions of where they were, and where they might be going. Still, Emily said "Freemen's Temple" as their cage chattered across the floor of the pitch-black and rumbling cargo van, and when the doors opened, Erno thought she must be right. He saw bits and swatches of that Halloween building again, and their hutch was hauled by soldiers right up to its dark doors. The doors gave way, and then it was candlelight, bits of red and gold, two towering columns, men . . . in robes? Then hallways, more doors, and a floor in a great dark room where they came finally to rest.

A massive cluster of overhead lights came on at once with a sound like a cough, then grew slowly warmer and brighter as if the room itself were waking. They were on the cold marble of a sunken circular floor that was ringed by six rows of stadium seats—fussily decorated walnut wood seats with black velvet cushions and dark gold trim.

A gladiator arena, thought Erno.

"A surgery," said Emily. And then Erno realized she was right again: more than anything, the room resembled a painting in the Philadelphia art museum of a crowd of spectators watching doctors cut into a dead or sleeping patient. *The Gross Clinic,* it was called, and it was.

Four doors opened at compass points, and robed figures filed in. Black-hooded mantles, open in front over pink waistcoats, white aprons, and deep red pants. All men. They sat down silently, and in an orderly and practiced manner. Emily's chest rose and fell rapidly to the shallow breaths and fluttering heartbeat of the tiny animal she was.

"Freemen," said a voice somewhere. No one had stood, and the room was something of an echo chamber, so it was hard to determine who was speaking. "They say good things come to those who wait."

"Whoever *they* are," said another robe, and there was a murmur of good-natured laughter.

"Indeed," said another robe, possibly the first again. Now Erno saw him, descending the stadium stairs to stand by the cage. "They. *They* with their ancient wisdom. The mysterious *they* who pull the strings. I think, for the sake of argument, that we can agree that *they* are *we?*"

Another murmur, one of agreement. "Quite so," said an anonymous someone.

"They also say, I believe, that one cannot make an omelet without breaking a few eggs. I regret you can't see much through this cage, but if, on your way to tonight's ceremony, you choose to peek through its thin windows, you might pay your respects to these two unfortunate eggs we'll be breaking."

Erno was pretty sure he'd followed all that. He wished he hadn't.

"And let us have a round for our Augustus Wilson—"

Emily gasped.

"—who like Launcelot has faltered and fled but like Launcelot has returned to us once more. Gus?"

Mr. Wilson pulled back his hood and rose to acknowledge the light applause. Emily wasn't watching.

"It's really him," whispered Erno. "It's—"

"I know who it is," said Emily.

Harvey drove with wild abandon. Harvey drove as if cars, pedestrians, bicycles, and birds were all semi-imaginary figments to be dispersed with curses and constant honking. Harvey drove much like Scott expected him to, really. The fact that Harvey was doing all this with his rabbity head sticking out the window didn't attract so much attention as the fact that nobody else on the road could see him in the first place.

In fact, when the attention of the other drivers wasn't

focused on the sight of an apparently driverless car, it was focused almost entirely on the one passenger the drivers could see: Scott, who had somehow ended up in the backseat despite being the tallest if you didn't count Harvey's ears.

"I should be in the front seat," he proclaimed quietly.

"Yeh should call shotgun then," said Mick.

"Don't even understand how an elf knows about shotgun."

"MOVE IT!" shouted Harvey between sniffs of his nose. "Don't the halfwitth in thith town know reckleth driving when they thee it? OUTTA THE WAY, HAMHOCKTH!"

He'd lost Emily's trail, so they were circling the same block while Harvey tried to sniff it out again.

"You're not old enough for the front," Mick argued.

"*You're* not *big* enough," Scott answered. He mollified himself by imagining Mick wriggling in a big plastic car seat.

"There," the rabbit-man said finally, pulling in his head. His ears looked like they'd just come out of the dryer. "I think I have her again. Heading eatht."

"Thought we'd be headed toward Goodco headquarters," said Scott. "Or even the factory, but . . . you know where we might be going . . ."

"The Freemen's Temple by the train station?" Mick answered. "I was thinkin' it, too."

They made another couple turns and then the train station was in view. "Why don't yeh let us out there, Harvey," said Mick, so Harvey drove up to the passenger drop-off island west of the station as if Scott and Mick were just any boy and his imaginary friend, running late for a train.

"Hey," said Harvey as Mick and Scott stumbled from the car. "Hey. Mick."

Mick turned.

Harvey seemed, for once, pleasantly at a loss for words. "May the road rithe to meet you," he said finally.

Mick held Harvey's gaze for a moment, then grunted and turned away.

The station was nearly deserted this time of night. They walked around the edge and turned the corner, and then they could see it: the temple. All gargoyles and arches. The whole structure was a massive gargoyle, crouching over the boulevard.

"Last chance to go to the police," Scott breathed.

"We *are* goin' to the police," Mick answered, jutting his chin toward the temple. "They're just inside, waitin' for us."

Scott sighed. A last car turned in front of them and then the light was theirs.

"So how are we going to do this? How do we even get in?"

Mick grinned up at him. "Betcha they forgot to lock the door."

● ○ ★

There was a spirited conversation going on in the surgery. Most of the cloaked men had already left the room for the ceremony mentioned earlier, but a new man had joined them. Not a Freeman perhaps. He wasn't wearing a robe but rather seemed to be dressed for fishing or a safari. A Freeman was just answering some question of his that Erno hadn't heard.

"He's . . . it's . . ."

"I think 'it' will suffice," said the new man.

"It's being held in another part of the temple. Under constant guard. It's very strong."

"I have seen the beast in action, and I wholeheartedly agree," said the new man. "What a find. I will even take him in lieu of payment."

"They're talking about Biggs," Emily whispered.

"I know," said Erno. "I mean, I figured."

The new man circled their cage, squinting from a distance through the slits. His hands trembled slightly. But that may have been age rather than nerves, thought Erno. He was pretty old.

"As soon as Haskoll returns he will help me fully sedate and transport the specimen back to the lodge. It'll be nice to have one that a person can see without rose-colored glasses, wot?"

"But he's not really Bigfoot," a Freeman tried to explain.

"We think he might be this kid Goodco tested on in the sixties."

"Indeed. And then this 'kid' escaped from Goodco's West Coast facility and into the northern California woods, where its movements were recorded in the famous Patterson-Gimlin film. There may be no such animal as Bigfoot, gentlemen, but this fellow will do in a pinch, eh? I'm going to display him next to the wet bar."

All but one of the remaining Freemen took up this debate, which seemed to center on whether their leader would want the Bigfoot or not, and whether their leader's interests trumped the old man's. Throughout this, one Freeman stood apart. He just now came to crouch by the cage.

"Hello, kids," said Mr. Wilson.

Erno called him a name that he hadn't even realized he knew until that moment. Mr. Wilson cleared his throat.

"Hi, Dad," whispered Emily.

Erno sighed. "What are you going to do to us?"

"Me? Nothing. I'm not a part of this anymore, Erno."

"Oh, my mistake—you know what threw me off? The matching outfits."

"I tried to run away," Mr. Wilson whispered, and he looked over his shoulder at the others by the door. "I'll run away again. But they were right on my tail, and it was either come in or be captured."

"You're an American hero."

Emily was still backed into the corner of the cage, as far from Mr. Wilson's face as she could be. But still she touched Erno on the hand, a touch that chided, *Don't be mean.*

"I've been sick," said Mr. Wilson. "I haven't been myself—"

"Because you've been taking the Milk," Erno interjected. "And it changed you, right? Poisoned your mind like it's poisoned Emily's? Just clear something up for me, because I'm totally confused: does Jekyll turn into Hyde in this example or is it Hyde into Jekyll?"

Mr. Wilson looked down at the floor, then over his shoulder again. "I can't take back what I've done. But you kids should know that I care about you in my own way."

Emily made a little noise. She'd been crying, silently. "*Obviously,*" she whimpered. "I already *know* that."

Mr. Wilson smiled. "Course you do."

"Well, I guess I haven't figured out this new game yet," said Erno. "So tell me why I should believe anything you say."

"Because I've just unlocked your cage," Mr. Wilson replied, then he rose quickly and walked away.

CHAPTER 27

Scott and Mick were in. They'd followed a sign around the back of the temple that said DELIVERIES IN REAR, and had found a vacant loading dock and an unlocked door. Now they were hiding behind a stack of crates in a cinder block room piled high with boxes and cans. Their eyes adjusted to the scant moonlight slicing in through high windows.

"Freemen eat a lot of Maraschino cherries," whispered Scott.

"I imagine they throw most o' them away," Mick answered. "They're just garnish."

"How do you—?"

"This isn't my first time here. The Freemen have a house drink they call a Pink Dragon."

"Adults are so weird."

"It's people are weird. People are weirder'n anybody."

They moved carefully through the room toward a dimly lit doorway draped with long slats of plastic, passing palettes of lemon juice, boxes of cocktail onions, crates of liquor with butler names like Hennessy and Hendrick. Maybe all the Freemen would be drunk, thought Scott. He hadn't spent any time around drunk people and so assumed they'd be easier to deal with.

They reached the door and peered through the dirty plastic slats into a hallway. Halfway down there were two men in black, like the ones in the park, lacking only the motorcycle helmets. They were armed and wearing pink lenses and standing on either side of a big metal door. At the end of the hall was another door to who knows where. Mick pulled Scott back into the shadows.

"That's a big freezer, that is," Mick whispered. "*Somethin'* important inside."

"Oh my God. Erno and Emily. They're going to eat them."

"They're not gonna—"

"*They're going to grind them up and make cereal out of them.*"

Mick seemed to be considering this.

"Rumor has it they've been puttin' pixie in the Puftees since the mid-eighties," he admitted.

Scott gagged.

"Put it outta your head," said Mick. "Whatever's in that freezer, we wan' it. We'll deal with whatever it is once it's ours. Just gotta get those wardens outta the way. Yeh see their pink goggles? They're takin' no chances."

Scott swallowed and nodded. Then he had an idea.

He began, slowly and quietly, to move boxes and jars.

After some time Mick seemed to understand and joined in. He helped with the olive jars, then opened a bottle of vodka and started emptying it in a circle on the floor. Scott came over.

"What's that for?" he whispered.

"For the ring o' fire."

"The . . . what?"

Mick stared back. "I assumed we were trappin' 'em in a ring o' fire. What were *you* plannin'?"

Scott pointed to different parts of the setup and sort of mimed what he expected to happen.

Mick looked it all over, then nodded. "'Kay, but if it goes south I'm lightin' a ring o' fire. Found some matches by the back door."

Scott scanned the ceiling for sprinklers or smoke detectors and, seeing none, shrugged. "Ready?"

Mick nodded, and Scott crept up to the door to the hall again. Then he burst through the plastic slats.

"Oh no!" he cried theatrically. The guards turned and raised their rifles, and Scott felt a flutter of panic. What if they just shot him in the back before he could get through the slats again? But he turned and retreated anyway into the storeroom, hopped, stopped, and got out of the way. The first man emerged through the slats at a run, tripped over the box of vermouth they'd set on the floor, and fell face-first onto the vast bed of olive jars that lay there on their sides like rollers on an assembly line. He was swept forward across the face of this bed of jars and hit his head against the cinder block wall. Then Mick knocked a stack of liquor boxes on top of him for good measure.

But the second guard was not so reckless. He crouched at the slats and poked his head and weapon through, and aimed both squarely at Mick.

"Don't move!" he shouted. "Do *not* move. Where's that kid? Kid! Come out where I can see you or I shoot the midget."

Scott emerged from behind some crates with his hands up.

"All right," said the man. "Go stand by your friend." He kept his gun leveled as he backed cautiously over the scattered jars and boxes toward his partner.

"He okay?" asked Scott.

"Shut up!" He crouched next to the prostrate body of the other guard and pushed liquor boxes aside.

"Mick?" whispered Scott.

Mick lit a match and tossed it, and then both guards were encircled by a wall of limpid flame. A wall that was not anywhere near as tall as Scott expected it to be.

Still, in the confusion, he and Mick darted in opposite directions: Scott behind a forklift, Mick through the slats and into the hallway. The guard waved his weapon around, let his moment pass, and turned to heave his partner up off the floor.

Mick darted back out from the hallway into the storeroom and passed by where Scott was hiding. "Lad! Have yeh seen a knife anywheres?"

"Hey!" shouted the guard. He dropped his partner to the floor, raised his gun, squinted over the flames. But Mick was quick, and already out of his line of sight.

"I saw a box cutter on top of the cherries," Scott called back. "Mick! We could have done something cool with this forklift."

"Too late for that!" said Mick as he rushed back again. He had the box cutter in his hand.

"HEY!" repeated the guard, who had hoisted the other man over his shoulder a second time. Once more he dumped his partner and raised his weapon, but Mick was already gone. "You two are so dead." The liquor flames had widened and spread, but were by now burning pretty low. Eventually the guard realized there wasn't really any fire left to save his partner from and dropped him again. "You're lucky I almost never shoot kids," he shouted in Scott's direction, then stepped gingerly through the jars and olives and last licks of flame toward the hall.

There was an old beige phone with a long curly cord mounted on the wall next to the doorway. The guard took this off the hook and crouched down at Mick's level, separating the plastic slats with the barrel of his rifle so he could peek down the corridor. "This is Jacobs at the freezer," he said into the mouthpiece. Scott craned his neck over the forklift to see.

Then the slats clattered open and the man fell back, looked up, up some more, higher still at the massive, steaming-cold, slouching figure of Biggs. The big man was shivering, barely on his feet. Mick was doing his best to steady him, but thanks to the size difference, the elf looked more like a leg-humping dog than a viable means of support.

"Um," said the guard. He rose quickly, falling back, and dropped the beige receiver in favor of lifting his rifle to the level of Biggs's chest. Biggs stumbled forward, swung both arms upward like sledgehammers, and knocked the guard clean off his feet. The rifle went off with a powerful bang and chipped a divot of plaster off the ceiling. The guard collapsed in a heap, and then so did Biggs.

Scott ran to join them as Mick began slapping Biggs's face, trying to revive him. Scott picked up the telephone receiver where it lay.

"Never mind," he told it, and hung up.

CHAPTER 28

The surgery was empty now apart from three stragglers. Everyone else had gone off to watch some kind of initiation ceremony that was taking place in another part of the temple, or so Erno had gathered. He watched from his cage as a variety of bare metal carts were wheeled in and arranged around the room. Two appeared to be gurneys: cold steel beds with leather restraints for arms and legs. Two more were merely carts laden with scalpels, scissors, clamps, tiny saws (was that a corkscrew?), sponges, and a dozen other instruments whose purpose could not be deciphered from their shiny alien curves. Amid these was a glass jar with the word *ether* spelled on the side in flaking gold.

One of the remaining Freemen had changed into surgical scrubs and was just snapping a pair of rubber gloves over his hands. He had white hair and dark-framed glasses and a kindly grandpa look about him. "I suppose this is to be the only anesthetic?" he asked, waving at the ether. "I have an anesthesia machine at headquarters."

"Word has it that some person or persons have been snooping around HQ recently," a Freeman answered from the gallery. "Our Lady didn't want to risk bringing them there after hours."

"We know it's not ideal, Bill," said another Freeman. "Everyone's improvising. We've barely had a second to look through Wilson's notes."

The notes, thought Erno with a sinking feeling. He'd done his best to smuggle them out of the tree house, but they were in Goodco's hands now.

"*Wilson,*" a Freeman sneered. "His sudden change of heart has been a bit *too* sudden for my tastes."

"We're watching him."

Emily was rocking slightly, trying to calm herself. She had her arms pinned against her chest, and she plucked at the wires of her headgear. Erno scooched to her side, wrapped his arm around her. He wouldn't tell her everything was going to be all right. She was too smart for that. He would tell her a story. He would attempt the ridiculous task of taking her mind off of all of this.

"You know what this reminds me of?" he whispered. "Our first trip to Cereal Town. Do you remember?"

It seemed to take a moment for Emily to register that

he was talking to her. Her blurry-eyed stare came into focus, and she turned to look at Erno. "Wh-what?"

The surgeon moved the carts just so and organized his instruments, moving certain favorites up from lower shelves. There was a row of scalpels and other tools on the lowest shelf of a cart right next to the door of the cage. If Mr. Wilson had told the truth and that door was really unlocked, then Erno could reach through it and grab one of those scalpels. But he'd certainly be seen.

"You insisted on riding the Cereality ride," he reminded Emily. "Even though you get sick in the back-seat of a car, you had to go on Cereality." In Cereality, you and a friend were fastened into a big pink pod and got to experience life as a Goodco cereal puff. Through a mixture of actual movement and IMAX-style wrap-around screens, you had the sensation of tumbling out of the box and into a bowl, getting drenched with milk, being spooned up and into a colossal mouth, and then finally splashing down into an Olympic-sized stomach. Then your pod opened, and you left through a big door in the side of the stomach labeled EXIT, which wasn't very realistic but was a lot more wholesome than the way food usually leaves the body.

Emily was just staring at him. She'd stopped rocking.

They'd gotten trapped in that big cereal puff, just like they were trapped now in this crate. That was the only reason Erno had brought it up—that and the fact that it had, in time, become one of those reliably popular family stories that always got everyone laughing. But now Erno was remembering that day, that ride, the way Emily changed her mind after it was too late and screamed to be let off. How the ride plummeted and rocked, spun and lurched through the air and past monolithic teeth. He remembered how he'd tried to comfort her even then, though they were much younger. How this had always sort of been Erno's job. But Emily could not be comforted that day—she'd thrown a fit just as the lights went out and the whole ride stuttered to a halt with Erno and Emily's pod only halfway down the esophagus. They'd stayed that way for two hours while Cereal Town's rescue crew worked to get the ride moving again.

Emily had done it. Erno realized this now as he recalled all the flickering lights and the pink butterfly in Emily's mouth and the tree branches that grew right into Biggs's living room. Emily had broken a theme park ride with her mind.

And now here she was, giving herself over to Erno's story, hanging on his every word. He was going to have to do something dreadful. He wondered if Emily would ever forgive him.

"Do you . . . do you remember when they finally let us

out of that stupid ride? How good it felt to be outside?"

Emily might just have smiled then, barely. "Yeah."

"It's not going to be like that this time," Erno told her. "We're never going to get out of here alive."

Emily flinched backward, away from Erno, just as fearfully as if he'd slapped her face.

"Now then," said the surgeon as he turned to the other two Freemen. "Subject E1 has been taking the Milk-7 by auditory canal for ten years. Milk-7 being, as I'm sure you know, primarily crop-milk from the species *Draco mythologicus* in an alcohol-saline solution. It is, and I think you gentlemen understand my distaste of this word, *magic*. And in strong doses it appears to make the human subject altogether less magical."

"Yes," said another Freeman. "It's that bit I don't understand."

"The human body was never meant to be a vessel for magic. The human mind recoils at it, builds up defenses against it, like it's fighting a disease. As a result the subject gets smarter, more rigidly rational—"

The Freeman interrupted. "Also unpredictable, unstable, occasionally emotional—"

"Also that. And prone to physical frailty and dizzy spells. All symptoms I think we'll neglect to mention in the cereal commercials."

The taller of the two Freemen in the gallery chuckled. The other, a little boiled egg of a man, did not.

"So the girl has all this magic inside her," he said, "but still no magical . . . talents?"

"None whatsoever, according to Wilson's notes."

Emily was trembling. It hurt to look at her. So Erno looked instead at the cart covered with scalpels and tools, visible through a slit in the door, and reminded himself just how badly he needed some kind of diversion.

"They're going to do bad stuff to us," he whispered. "Both of us. And I think that old man is going to have Biggs stuffed. And you know . . . I think they're going to do something bad to Mr. Wil . . . to Dad, too. Did you hear them? They don't trust him. And why should they? They . . . know he loves us more than them."

The surgeon opened the jar marked *ether* and dipped a cloth into the colorless liquid inside. He said, "We believe magical residue builds up in the appendix, of all places."

"So *that's* what it's for," said the tall Freeman merrily.

"I'd prefer fewer jokes," said the egg. "Personally. I mean, E1 is a little girl, after all. I have a granddaughter her age."

The surgeon coughed.

"If you don't have the stomach for this, there's a pageant on downstairs," said the tall man. "Why don't you go and watch the dancing."

"Because I've been *asked* to attend, and to rush the girl's appendix to Our Lady once it's removed. You're just here because you want to watch."

"It's the girl's *and* the boy's appendixes, actually," said the surgeon. "She wants both now."

Emily's eyes appeared to be clouding over. Her lips were barely parted, and Erno could see a faint light coming from within: a pink light. But they needed more than butterflies now.

"Did you hear that?" he asked her. "They're going to cut us both open."

The little man frowned at the surgeon. "Both? Surely modern medicine already knows what a normal appendix looks like."

"There's some idea going around that E2 might have absorbed some magic simply by being around E1. Sounds a little hippy-dippy to me, but I have my orders. Now then. Appendectomies rarely result in the death of the patient, so we'll have to dispose of the subjects by other means—"

Emily's eyes shut tight. She sneezed, and the room went dark.

"What the—"

This was more like it. Erno tested the cage door. Mr. Wilson had told the truth: it swung open with a shrill creak that Erno could feel in his back teeth. He prayed that none of the men had noticed as he thrust his arm through the gap and grasped at the nearest cart for a weapon. His hand closed over something cold and smooth, and he snatched it back into the cage.

Dim orange emergency lights switched on.

"How on earth did we trip the breaker?" asked the surgeon, scanning the ceiling. "We're probably the only Freemen on this entire floor."

The egg-shaped Freeman stood and felt his way to the closest exit. "I'll go find the circuit box," he said, then he was gone.

The weak orange light barely illuminated the inside of the crate, so Erno squinted to get a better look at the prize he'd snatched. A hard, red, rubber triangle attached to a silver handle like a spoon's. Erno grimaced at the cart outside. An entire shelf covered in knives, and he'd managed to grab a reflex hammer.

The surgeon put his hands on his hips and shrugged. "Hm. Well, let's get the subjects on the gurneys before Maxwell returns. I don't expect he was going to be much help, anyway."

The tall Freeman joined the surgeon. "He's a sensitive soul," he said with a disdainful air. "Never stops talking about his ugly little grandchildren."

The surgeon dipped his cloth anew into the ether and kneeled by the cage. Erno crawled away from the door, but Emily stayed where she was—either frozen by fear or else now completely detached from what was going on around her. The tall man stood behind as the surgeon fiddled with the latch.

"Funny," said the surgeon. "Do you know this wasn't even locked?" Then he opened the cage door and stuck his head inside.

Erno slid forward, pulled the glasses off the surgeon's face, and thocked him in the eye with his reflex hammer.

"*OW!*" said the surgeon, and a few other things besides. In his confusion he raised his good hand to his eye, the hand with the cloth in it, and recoiled a little from the smell of ether. He looked dazed.

"What happened?" asked the tall man, crouching low.

On little more than instinct, Erno tugged the cloth from the surgeon's hand and pressed it firmly to the man's nose and mouth. He tried to back away, but soon shuddered and slumped forward. Half inside the crate, half out.

"Little devils," growled the tall man. The surgeon's body partly blocked the crate door, but there was still more than enough room for the tall man to reach inside and pull Emily roughly through the gap.

She struggled now in the arms of the tall man in the dim room, kicking and howling. Erno started to climb over the logy body of the surgeon, then thought better of it and first heaved the man farther into the cage. Then he climbed over and out the door, crammed the man's legs inside, and locked him in. He rose, light-headed and panting from the effort.

"Open that!" barked the tall man as he struggled to keep his hold on Emily. "Let him out this instant!"

Now Emily really had the shakes. The tall man looked down at her with some dawning recognition that Mr. Wilson's notes might not have been entirely accurate. He pinned Emily down on one of the gurneys and fumbled with the leather restraints. Her hair began to stand on end. Pink glow stick smudges appeared before her eyes, tracing out nonsense in a quickening hand.

Erno ran for the jar of ether, but the liquid ignited in his hands. He tossed the jar aside in a panic, and it shattered against the floor, spreading glass shards and a spatter of flames.

The tall man saw the flames, saw the weird light show, and quailed. He backed away from the gurney, from Emily, and into a cart full of tools. Here he grabbed a pair of lean scissors and held them over his head. Erno braced himself to rush in for a tackle when there was a bright flash, and the scissors clattered to the floor, and the tall man was still standing there but with a flower for a head.

He staggered, then reached up with quaking hands and tore at the petals. Atop his neck was an enormous pink rose in full bloom, its innermost petals quivering as if trying to speak. He reeled about as Erno watched in terror.

Then, just as suddenly as it had changed, it changed back. The tall man was intact, his horrified face maybe still lingering on whatever thoughts one thinks when one's head is a flower. He gaped at Erno, then Emily, and with a strangled cry he turned and ran, tumbled over a cart, and cracked his head on the marble floor.

The overhead lights came back on.

Erno investigated the tall man where he lay. He was still breathing, so Erno tied his hands and feet with some rubber tourniquet bands. Then he went to unbuckle the restraints that held Emily, now passed out, on the cold gurney. Then he turned to see the little egg-shaped Freeman standing in a doorway.

"What happened?" asked the Freeman as he descended the stairs. "Are they . . ."

"The one on the floor was a flower, but he's better now," said Erno, and he stepped between the advancing man and his sister. "The doctor's asleep in the cage."

Too late Erno realized that he should be looking for a new weapon. The little man got there first. He picked up a small mallet, like a metal gavel, from the nearest tray. He held it like a remote control in front of him and drew slowly closer. Erno cast about. The tall man's scissors were near his feet. He would go for those.

Then the little man kneeled down on the floor and turned the mallet around so that he was holding the head.

The chrome handle pointed at Erno's chest.

"Hit me hard," said the man. "Here," he added, indicating his temple.

Erno just stared.

"Make it look good."

"What?"

"I can't have them thinking I helped you," said the man. He looked up at the gurney. "She's just like Chloe, my daughter's girl."

Erno took the hammer. "Really?"

The little man shrugged and smiled. "They all are."

Erno wound back his arm and brought the hammer down in one swift motion.

"*AH! OWWW!*" groaned the little man. He curled up and clutched at his head. "Jeez, *ow ow ow ow ow.* That . . . that *really, really* hurt." He coughed and breathed heavily. Erno examined the man's temple.

"Do you want me to do it again?"

"NO! No, no, no. Man . . . why didn't that work? I thought it would knock me out."

"I only thought it 'cause you thought it."

"Jeez." He pushed back and sat down.

"Maybe you can just pretend to be unconscious," Erno suggested. "They'll believe you. Your head's even bleeding a little."

"Yeah, maybe. Hey, look who's up."

Emily had slid down from the gurney. She came around to stand between them.

"I'm sorry, Emily," said Erno. "I'm sorry I . . . I couldn't think of any other way—"

Emily cut him short with a look. Then she gave the same look to the little egg man.

"I'm sorry too, Emily," he said. Then she touched him behind the ear, and he fell asleep.

CHAPTER 29

Even between the two of them, Scott and Mick could only drag Biggs a few feet at a time. They had managed to pull him, in this fashion, through a large but empty kitchen, into a service elevator, out of the service elevator, and down a long and dimly lit hall across a piebald red carpet. Neither boy nor elf had yet admitted that they had no idea where they were going, that they were moving for the sake of movement. Every so often Mick paused to force some of the contents of a bottle of brandy down Biggs's throat.

"Is that really a good idea?" Scott asked finally. "I mean, he's already unconscious—"

"Best thing for a cold body, is brandy," said Mick. "Well, second to a roarin' fire. Or a blanket or some warm clothes. Or an electric heater or what have you. But if'n you haven't all those things? Brandy."

"Mmpf," said Biggs suddenly, and he sputtered and twitched. Mick tried to hold his head up. "Muh . . . muh babies. Where . . ."

"Erno and Emily?" asked Scott. "We . . . don't know. We're trying to find them."

This roused Biggs, and he struggled to get to his feet.

"Take it easy," Mick told him. "Your time in the freezer's made yeh logy. Or maybe they drugged yeh too. Did they drug yeh?"

"Dunno. What that noise?"

There *was* a noise. Scott hadn't even registered it. Was it applause? It might have been coming from below them. There were two doors in this hall, one labeled MEZZANINE A and the other MEZZANINE B. Scott tested the first and opened it a crack.

He looked down across a dark and nearly empty seating area. Here and there sat robed figures—some hooded, some with hoods drawn back to reveal wizened, spotty heads and feathery white hair. Two were in wheelchairs pushed up against the guardrail in front. Also at the front of the sloping mezzanine sat a man with headphones before a wide console studded with switches and controls. He touched one of these, and music swelled. He touched another, and lights rose in the auditorium below.

They were overlooking a vast hall with a proscenium

arch and stage at one end. It was curtained in black and pink and flanked by two tremendous pillars carved to look like wheat. Atop each of these was a bowl, and atop each bowl was a sphere—one painted to look like the Earth, one solid black.

There were more seats beneath him, Scott supposed, probably filled with Freemen. But he couldn't see for sure without stepping away from the back wall, out of the shadows, and risking detection by the old men in the mezzanine. What he *could* see was the stage with its amber glow, its intricately painted backdrops. It gave the impression of a sunlit glen peopled with trees and flowers.

Mick and Biggs were at his side now. "What is this?" Scott whispered. "Are they putting on a play?"

"It's an initiation, I expect," Mick whispered back. He seemed transfixed by the top right corner of the stage.

"This is lucky then. They're all probably watching the show. Meanwhile we can find Erno and Emily and get out of here. What are you looking at?"

"The dark globe," said Mick. "Look. 'Tis Pretannica: the magical world."

Scott looked again. Now he could see that he'd been mistaken—the globe wasn't solidly black after all but had a small round patch of blue and green where England might conceivably be.

"These folk know things," Mick added. "Think it might do to watch this li'l mystery play."

"No," Biggs rumbled. "Have to find the kids."

"Just for a wee bit," promised Mick.

While they'd been talking, a man's name had been called, and this man just now stepped onto the stage and squinted awkwardly into the harsh lights.

"SHAWN HIGGINBOTTOM," a disembodied voice boomed. "YOU ARE THIS NIGHT A KNIGHT OF THE ROUND, HAVING ACHIEVED THE THREE HUNDRED AND SEVENTY-SEVENTH LEVEL OF FREEDOM."

Thunderous applause.

"TAKE NOW THE SEAT OF HONOR BENEATH THE SICKLE AND THE SPOON, AND UNVEIL THINE EYES TO THE GRAND MYSTERIES OF THE UNIVERSE."

More applause, and Shawn Higginbottom left the stage by the same stairs. Then some prancing, staccato music started, and the grand universal mysteries were unveiled by way of a middle-aged man cavorting around the stage in green tights.

He'd just emerged from a slit in the forest backdrop, tipped his tricorn hat, and—*God help them*, thought Scott—he was going to sing.

> *"I am a leprechaun, spry and free—*
> *slipped through a rip in re-al-i-ty—*
> *lost and alone as an elf can be—*
> *poor little wee little me!"*

Scott nudged Mick. "You were *right*," he whispered. "It's a good thing we stayed."

Mick scowled at the leprechaun and made a furious sort of gurgling noise as two more men emerged dressed as the front and back ends of a pantomime unicorn.

> *"Lost little unicorn, woe is me!*
> *Interdimensional deportee!*
> *But lo! There are gentlemen behind yon tree—*
> *just who can those two men be?"*

Two new players entered in old-timey clothes, mustaches and sideburns, and wet-looking hair. Any kid in Goodborough could have told you who they were.

> *"I'm Jack Harmliss!*
> *I'm Nate Goode!*
> *Imagine meeting you in this tulgey wood!*
> *Come along with us and we'll give you food*
> *and make you a part of our happy brood!"*

All the players frolicked offstage together.

"Yeah," Mick huffed. "That's *just* how it happened."

Scott could sense Biggs getting fidgety behind them. "Come on," he said. "Let's go."

Just then the mood and tenor of everything changed. Cymbals crashed. The music turned very operatic, and the theater lights dimmed to a dusky red. The spectators in the mezzanine, even those in wheelchairs, inched forward just slightly in their seats. This was obviously the good bit.

Black-gloved hands reached through a tall slit in the fabric of the forest backdrop and pulled it wide. Harsh light poured through. A chorus of men's voices sang,

> *"Rich with the magic sheared and shorn*
> *from lep-re-chaun and u-ni-corn*
> *we open reality's wispy veil*
> *and bring that vale a whale!"*

Scott frowned. "What?"

From their vantage point at the rear of the mezzanine, they'd missed the slow procession through the hall below of pallbearers carrying, between them, a mock whale decked out like a parade float. But they saw it now: a long blue whale, fabric over a wooden frame, shimmering with flowers and bits of crepe and tin. There were no seats down on the floor, so a hundred standing Freemen stepped aside as it nosed its way up the steps to the stage.

"This play just got weird," Scott murmured.

> *"The invisible will shiver*
> *and will open up a sliver,*
> *and (delighted) we'll deliver*
> *up a whale into the vale!"*

"Not so weird as yeh think," whispered Mick. "When somethin' living goes through the opening 'tween worlds, somethin' of a similar size on th' other side has to take its place."

Scott thought. "That's . . . that's why you appeared in that baby carriage when you came here," he said. "Some poor baby ended up on the other side. In Pretannica."

"Right."

Scott thought some more. "Blue whales are the biggest animals that ever were. Bigger than dinosaurs."

Mick sighed. "Yep."

The opening in the backdrop was pulled wider, wider, and then the pallbearers with their make-believe whale passed through. Drums rolled like thunder. The man at the console was sliding lighting controls like a sugar-crazed toddler.

Scott glanced back at Biggs, but Biggs wasn't there.

Then something pink, something big, began to emerge from backstage.

CHAPTER 30

The little egg man snored on the cold marble.

"Emily," said Erno. "I'm really, really sorry—"

"Forget it."

"I *had* to say those things. To scare you. Do you understand?"

Emily sighed and looked around.

"I turned the lights off," she muttered. "I set a fire and turned a man's head into a flower."

"Yeah."

Emily shook her head as if someone had told a bad joke.

"I know it's usually my job to make you feel better," said Erno, "not worse, but—"

"Your *job?*"

"Not . . . not a job like I don't want to do it, I just mean—"

"Yes. Fine. I understand why you did it. Good plan. Can we escape already? I really have to go to the bathroom."

Erno had to go as well—it hadn't occurred to the Freemen to take them, or they just hadn't cared.

"When we're outside we can run to the train station," he said, and moved toward one of the room's four exits.

"No. Not that way. The Freemen left by three different doors, but nobody went through that one." She was right: at three compass points the rooms were appointed with tall, stately double doors. The fourth door was plain, unpolished, designed as though meant only for servants or inferiors. It wasn't even as tall as a normal door.

They stepped through it and into a stairwell.

"We're upstairs," Erno said, and then the memory—of being inside the cage, tilted then turning, tilted then turning—came back to him.

"We're on the third floor," said Emily. "Facing east. If we can get all the way down to the basement, we should. Buildings this old all had coal chutes. Might be more discreet than just trying to walk out the front door."

"You're doing good now," said Erno, and he smiled. But behind the smile he was gagging a little on sour disappointment. He deserved this—a bossy Emily was just the right punishment for the way he'd talked to her in the cage. But he hated himself for wanting her to fall apart again, just a little. If Emily was suddenly going to be so brave all the time, what did she need *him* for?

"I just have to keep it together a little while longer."

They hustled down the stairs listening for voices, other footsteps. On every landing there was a narrow window, taller but no wider than those that had been in their cage. They descended past the basement, hit bottom, and pushed cautiously through the only door.

It was a boiler room. Dark, hot. Lit like a dying fire. Floor to ceiling it was blackened concrete and stone, vaulted with a rib cage of dark metal girders. Five ancient gray boilers like massive skulls lined the floor, with bars for teeth and eyes that were shuttered by thick iron doors. A tangle of pipes wormed up through the ceiling.

"Let's go down to the basement, says Emily," Erno muttered. "It's not like it'll be the scariest room you've ever seen."

"*Shh.*"

They crept inside, Emily peering all around in search of the coal chute or any other way out. Erno couldn't stop looking at the boilers. They were all lit like jack-o'-lanterns, with red-orange fire behind their teeth. Except for the middle one, which glowed blue. And where the others' fires were warm and even, the middle fire was fitful and inconsistent: it went perfectly dark, then flared up, then went dark again. It didn't seem to be working right.

"There's the coal chute," said Emily. It was, unsurprisingly, above a large pile of coal. Erno motioned her over.

"Why is that one different?" he asked, pointing out the blue boiler.

"They must have retrofit it for natural gas," Emily said. "They should have fixed all five up that way. Coal is really—"

Erno would have to learn about coal another time, because just then they heard shuffling outside a second door on the other end of the room. They scrambled behind the nearest boiler, crouched down low, and felt its devilish fever against their cheeks and ears. A man entered the room. An astronaut.

No, that wasn't quite right. He was dressed from head to toe in silver foil, with a shiny bucket helmet with a reflective gold visor and a pair of gloves that were like oven mitts that went up to the elbows.

"I blame our upbringing," Erno whispered, more to himself than to Emily. "If we'd been allowed to watch scary movies, we'd have realized we're the stupid kids that get killed right away." Beside him, Emily's breathing quickened. She touched Erno's hand, and he felt an ugly sense of satisfaction.

The tinfoil man was carrying an odd box. It was like a gray lantern with a cakey brick texture. There was a metal door on one end and a hook in the top. And a coiled metal whatsit jutting out the bottom. He carried this thing over to the middle boiler and knelt on the floor.

"You behave now," he told the box, or the boiler, or possibly himself. Then he opened the barred doors at the base of the furnace and thrust in his gloved hand.

"What is he . . . ?" whispered Erno.

The tin man fished around inside the mouth of blue flame until he found what he was after, and this he withdrew and stuffed inside the lantern-box. It was small. Erno almost thought he'd seen what it was, but no—he *couldn't* have. He couldn't have seen what he thought he saw.

The man closed the boiler, rose, and walked back the way he'd come. "Showtime, you little firecracker," he said to himself, or to the thing in the box. But he might as well have been speaking to a spark, just now growing in Emily's chest, that wasn't going to let her leave the temple without some answers.

"Slow down," hissed Erno. "We have to be more *careful.*"

"I told you to go to the train station," Emily whispered as she scurried through the halls of the temple. "I didn't ask you to come."

"We were almost free."

"You heard the Freemen earlier. They're all in some ceremony. There's no one to stop us from going through their things. I want to know what's going on," Emily answered, and Erno cursed himself once more for losing Mr. Wilson's notes.

This corridor was paneled shoulder-high with oiled wood and wallpapered scarlet to the tin-tiled ceiling. It was lined with painted portraits of serious-looking men in robes and fez hats. The frames bore plates that said things like ASA STANDISH, GRAND AMBROSIUS 1893–1905. WHITEHEAD WILLETT, GRAND AMBROSIUS 1879–1893. If you ran by them fast enough it was like a flip-book of facial hair. At the end of the hall was a pair of ornate doors that looked promisingly important.

Erno tried one of the handles, then the other, but the doors were locked.

"Office of the Grand Ambrosius," Emily read off the door. "He's the leader of all the chapters. The top Freeman in the country." She glared at the locks as if all the answers she'd ever wanted were behind these doors. Her whole stupid life explained.

"It's just a simple tumbler lock," she said finally. "I could pick it with a hairpin."

"Do you have a hairpin?"

"No."

"Maybe I could shoot it off for you, eh?" said someone behind them.

The kids turned. At the other end of the hall was an old man with a gun. The same hunter they'd seen quibbling over custody of Biggs back in the surgery. He walked slowly toward them, in no hurry at all. Or rather, thought

Erno, like someone trying to come off as unhurried and self-possessed even as his blood raced inside him. The man's hands shook. His face appeared watery and fragile. But a nervous villain with a gun wasn't any more of a comfort than a confident one.

"I'd tell you to call me Papa," said the hunter, "but I'm told papas are a bit of a sore point for you two."

Erno stepped in front of Emily.

"Chivalrous," said Papa. "Good lad."

The gun looked like an antique, but a well-cared-for antique. It probably shot antique bullets and everything.

"They haven't given you your Bigfoot yet," Erno said, just as he realized it. That was good.

The hunter was only a handful of feet away now. Even with trembling hands he was unlikely to miss. "No. It seems they thought all their old test subjects from the sixties were dead, but now they've grasped that your nanny was one of them, and they want to hold him for observation."

"Probably want his appendix," Emily growled.

"Undoubtedly, though I shudder to think what they want it *for*. Regardless, they are playing hardball, as I believe you Yanks say. So I've come up here looking for something of theirs to take. Some bargaining chip. But you two will do splendidly, wot?"

"You're not a Freeman," asked Erno, stalling for time. "Who *are* you?"

"Last of the great white hunters. The Freemen and I used to be bitter rivals, you know: they wanted the fairy-tale creatures; I wanted the fairy-tale creatures. In recent years we've come to a gentleman's agreement: I hunt the occasional snipe for them, and they let me shoot the dumb animals after they've milked the magic out of them. But now they're getting greedy and making me resort to common kidnappery. It's unsportsmanlike."

It wasn't easy keeping his cool in the face of this man and his gun, but now Erno looked past him and relaxed a bit. "We're not going anywhere with you."

"You are, and consider this: it is my understanding that Goodco only *really* needs the girl. So, manners. Manners, and you'll come through this sound as a pound. And I'll see my Bigfoot again."

"Sooner than you think," said Erno.

"Eh? What?"

"He moves really quietly, you know."

Papa frowned, but the frown soon dissolved with understanding. "Oh balls," he said, and turned just in time to be socked in the face. He dropped at once.

"Biggs!" Emily cheered, and rushed forward to hug the big man. "How did you find us?"

"Tracked your scent."

Erno grimaced. "Mine or Emily's?"

"Yours. Smells like milk."

"It does not."

"Biggs," said Emily sweetly. "I'd like to see what's inside this door. Would you rip it off its hinges for us?"

CHAPTER 31

It advanced through the backdrop, the enormous pink head, the enormous pink neck of an enormous pink dragon. A dragon only slightly less intimidating for being constructed out of fabric, wood, carnations, and wire. The chorus sang,

> "Oh,
> Great Dragon Saxbriton, leave your lair—
> the door we tore in earth and air
> that lays the way 'tween Here and There
> awaits its blushing bride!"

Scott turned to Mick. "Saxbriton? Isn't that the dragon from your story?"

"Aye. Mightiest dragon in all the land."

"And she's pink? Just like the dragon in the Goodco

logo? How have you not mentioned this?"

Mick shrugged. "Lotta dragons 're pink. That is, lotta dragons 're red an' lotta dragons 're white, an' . . . *ahem* . . . when two dragons love each other very much—"

"I don't need the birds-and-the-bees talk, thank you."

> *"The dreary age of man adjourns.*
> *Our worlds are wed, and love returns!*
> *The sapphire fire of Faerie burns*
> *a path 'cross the divide!"*

"Sapphire fire?" whispered Mick.

At this, as if on cue, the puppet dragon lifted its head, parted its jaws, and released a plume of brilliant blue flame.

"Did yeh see it?" Mick jumped. "That blue fire!"

"It's a gas fire," Scott said sagely. The Doe family had a gas stove.

"No. No gas fire is so blue. Not *that* blue . . ."

Two new backdrops descended from the rafters. They were not as wide as the painted forest—just narrow strips, really, made to look like yellowed paper and hanging to either side of the dragon's head. Two hundred names were inscribed on these banners—a list of knights, it seemed. Sir William Marsters, Sir Patrick Stevenson, Sir Sanjay Applethwaite . . .

"My dad," Scott breathed. "My dad's name is written on the one on the right."

> *"Where are the knights, once brash and bold*
> *whom dragons fought in days of old?*
> *They're tired and fat! Their queen's a fake!*
> *They fall like dodoes in our wake—"*

Here there was a bit of stagecraft: the red lights brightened, were joined by blues and greens until the light was colorless—and now, in the colorless light, one could see red Xs over each and every name. Two hundred British knights crossed out as if their deaths were only items on a hideous to-do list. Again the pink dragon breathed fire.

"Sir Reginald Dwight," murmured Scott, testing the name. Assuring himself that he was not mistaken, because it was all too strange. "Why is my dad's name crossed out on that list?"

"Did yeh hear that?" said Mick, speaking over the cusp of Scott's question. "When the dragon blazes—a *whistlin'*. Did yeh hear the whistlin'?"

"No. I mean . . . was it part of the music? I think we should go. Did you see my dad's name?"

Now, the Big Finish. The lights flickered in nauseating fashion across billows of smoke and glittering confetti as though anticipating the grand entrance of some vest-wearing and puffy-shirted stage magician who would Rock Your World with Magic. And indeed, just such a puffy-shirted man walked on from the wings, though he was also sporting pointy ears and antlers and a crown of holly. And he was joined by another Freeman in drag, wiggling about with fake boobs and a big bustle. The leprechaun and unicorn were back and dancing—apparently delighted to have had all of their magic sucked out of them—and here, too, were a host of other elves, goblins, a "giant" on stilts, and a disquieting number of leotards. The dragon blazed again.

"What do you—"

"*Shhh!*" Mick hissed.

In front of it all a row of eight more Freemen entered on their knees. It took a moment for Scott to realize they were supposed to be kids—a Dennis the Menace-y cast of characters designed by someone whose attention to actual children had ended abruptly in 1950. Many bows and buckles, slingshots and huge lollies.

> "*The children, stuffed with cereal*
> *and magic most ethereal,*
> *rise up and give themselves*
> *as sacrifices to the elves!*"

The dragon roared flame a fourth time. Scott thought that maybe he could hear a whistling after all. "Sounds like a bird," he said.

"Sounds like rain," Mick growled, before dashing forward and leaping over the balcony.

CHAPTER 32

Eventually Erno gave up trying to read anything himself and just took to organizing piles of papers for Emily, who was breezing through reams of material at breakneck speed and apparently absorbing every word.

The office of the Grand Ambrosius was large and lush. Carpets piled upon carpets. Velvety wallpaper and a huge desk so old looking and solid that it might have been a fossil from an age when prehistoric desks roamed the Earth. Emily looked adorable sitting behind it. The file cabinet in the corner had opened after only one spirited pull from Biggs, and its contents were stacked in piles on the desktop and around on the floor.

"Look at this," said Emily, and she handed a report off to Erno. The first page was a list of names and occupations. Wallace Spears, the liberal Democrat member of Parliament for Berwick-upon-Tweed, for example. Gordon

Maris, jockey. Branson Murdoch, owner of NewsCast.

"Who are they?"

"Well, they're all Knights Bachelor. And most of them are dead."

"Bachelor?" Erno said uncertainly. "Does that mean they weren't married?"

"In this case it just means they're members of a particular order of knighthood. The lowest-ranked order, actually, but the oldest, too. But look about halfway down the first column."

"What am I—oh. Is that—"

"Yes," said Emily. "And I think it's a good thing his name isn't highlighted. A lot of those knights have disappeared, or died kind of young. A lot of accidents that might not have been accidents. A lot of natural causes that were probably anything but."

"We need to warn him."

"We will. Just let me finish this stack—"

"Should go," said Biggs. "Find Scott and Mick. Escape."

Both Utz kids looked up and spoke in unison, like twins do on TV:

"Scott and Mick are *here*?"

Mick's drop from the mezzanine had been a long one, but luckily he landed on a Freeman. He skipped nimbly from the top of one man's head to the heads of two or three shorter Freemen standing nearby and made it to the floor no worse for the wear apart from a slight limp. Meanwhile, the men recovered and spun about, bewildered, trying to identify whoever had the nerve to slap them on the heads like that. Scott saw all this from the mezzanine's front railing, and then realized that while few if any of the Freemen could see Mick, Scott had just given himself away to the dozen or so old men sitting behind him.

"Raise the alarm!" shouted an aged but still powerfully built man as he rose sharply. "One of them's escaped!"

"No . . . ," said another, his dry voice barely carrying over the music. "This is a different boy entirely."

"That's right." Scott nodded as he edged back toward the exit. "My dad's down below." Would this wash? He supposed the Freemen wouldn't have a Take Your Child to Work Day. "He said I could watch from up here."

More men were rising. The one who'd spoken first was crab-walking along his row of seats, and he scowled. He'd obviously been scowling all his life, and his face, like a mother's warning, had stuck that way. "Who's your dad then? *Hm?*" he asked. There was a lot of "Gotcha!" in his tone.

The music died. Grunts and shouts shot up over the railing, and Scott tried to peek casually over his shoulder as he racked his brain for the name of some classmate whose father would likely be a Freeman. Mick had made his way to the stage undetected but not without a certain amount of shoving, and came now to a stop just under the dragon's jaws.

"Denton Peters," Scott said finally, remembering that Denton's father had spoken on Career Day about being one of Goodco's lawyers. And didn't everyone call the boy Denton Peters the Third when they wanted to get under his skin? Scott congratulated himself on his quick thinking and wondered why none of the old men seemed to be as impressed with him as he was.

"Young Peters is only a Second Squire," creaked a frail and nearly translucent man in a wheelchair some twelve feet away. "He shouldn't be here tonight—"

"He's not," said the big Freeman with a yellow grin. "And neither is his son."

Onstage, Mick leaped high and hung from the dragon's lower jaw, crumpling its papier-mâché teeth. He fished his arm to the back of its throat and grasped at something. Something electric, it seemed, because the jaws sprayed sparks and Mick was thrown backward eight feet toward the front of the stage, where he creamed the unicorn.

"BENNETT!" a ringing voice called out. It must have belonged to one of the men wearing microphones onstage. "TURN UP THE BLACK LIGHTS! SOMETHING IS HERE!"

Then the man behind the console, who between his

duties and headphones had not yet noticed Scott at all, dialed down all of the lights except for a scattering of deeply purple bulbs that were arranged around the auditorium. The only other illumination came from the console itself, and from what little moonlight bled through a stained glass rosette in the ceiling. And from the teeth and white aprons of the Freemen themselves, which now glowed in a cosmic bowling kind of way. Scott mentally applauded himself for having chosen dark clothes.

"Watch him!" ordered one of the old men. "He'll slip away!"

Down below, the grunts and shouts of confusion suddenly jelled, gained purpose. Mick was as bright as a glow stick now, and any Freeman could see him shake off the electric shock and make another run at the dragon.

"What the devil's going on down there?" said the scowling man.

Scott ducked the grabby arms of a nearby Freeman and the swooping cane of another and darted front and center of the mezzanine, where he heaved hard against the wheeled chair of the man behind the console. The man, Bennett, was small and sagged like a half-melted snowman. He rolled some five or six feet, still tethered to the console by his headphones, and was yanked face-first off his chair.

Scott lost a moment gaping at the console, dazzled by

its multitude of sliders, buttons, knobs, and dials. Then he did what boys have always done when confronted with some electronic contraption they don't know how to use: he pushed everything at once.

The theater got very, very bright. Brighter than it was meant to, apparently, because then there was a hair-raising squawk and a pop, and everything went entirely dark. No black lights. Only the dim blush of the rosette skylight. And quiet. For a moment every Freeman was afraid of that dark, and silent. Scott felt his way along the balcony rail, gazed out toward the stage, and held his breath.

Then there was a hot flourish of blue like a flaming sword in the darkness. And with this a trill, a whistling. Weak orange emergency lights flickered on and gave a twilight radiance to the hall, and blue flame erupted again. The Freemen panicked, collided with one another, and otherwise behaved like the theatergoers at the end of *King Kong* when the gorilla decides he doesn't want his picture taken. And center stage was Mick, smiling, with a finch on his head.

"There's the boy!" an old Freeman shouted behind Scott. "It's his fault!"

"Grab him!" said another, and Scott turned to find Freemen all around him. Then, distantly, the bang of a door; blows and grunts growing closer, a flailing of robes and arms, and Scott *was* being grabbed by large, strong hands that lifted him and took him hurtling over the balcony.

CHAPTER 33

For a second or two all Scott could think about was gravity, but then they landed on the floor below the mezzanine—safely—and he had a look at the man who had grabbed him.

"Oh," he said.

"Hey," said Erno.

Biggs was carrying Scott under one arm like a folding chair, Emily under the other; Erno was hanging down his back. Biggs set Scott down and Erno dropped to the floor, but the big man seemed reluctant to give up Emily.

Many Freemen had fled and continued to flee to the exits, but some stalwarts had stayed. Thirty, maybe. More than enough to make Scott nervous. And what if those men from the freezer with the guns had gotten themselves untied? What if there were more like them?

Mick and Finchbriton were still onstage, and a dozen

351

or more Freemen were circling them, closing in. Including the Freeman in drag and, ironically, the one dressed up like a St. Patrick's Day decoration. If they couldn't see Mick without the black lights, they could apparently see the bird just fine.

"They were keepin' him inna metal box!" Mick shouted to Scott. "An' shockin' him like a dancin' chicken! Danu help me, Finchbriton, I didn't know yeh were here!"

Finchbriton flapped atop Mick's head like some preposterous hat.

"We have to just get out of here," Scott called to the others. "Before they figure out what to do with us."

"What's the rush?" asked the old elf. "Me an' the bird have a hundred an' fifty years o' small talk to catch up on with these gennlemen. We've been indisposed, yeh see."

"No, c'mon, guys—"

"I'm with the leprechaun," said Erno.

"Clurichaun," said Scott. But he could see the bloodlust in Erno's eyes. Here he was, among his captors, with a pet Bigfoot at his command. With the biggest big brother of all. And Biggs wasn't exactly shrinking from a fight, either. There were cloaked figures all around him, and the big man took his first swing. Which missed.

At this the throng of Freemen fell upon them. Biggs swung again, connecting spectacularly with a chin inside a dark hood. But soon he had two Freemen hanging from his good arm. Finchbriton let loose another jet of flame, which scattered a half dozen robes before catching the edge of the theater curtain. Licks of blue started climbing the proscenium. Then a Freeman produced a fire extinguisher from the inside of his robe and gave the bird (and Mick's head) a good foaming. Finchbriton was whisked across the stage and landed, ruffled and sputtering, on the floor.

Erno was rolling himself at the feet of approaching Freemen and sending them reeling. Biggs socked most of the rest. But not all. Eventually he was forced to set Emily down as more and more dark-robed shapes attached themselves to him like leeches—at the arms, the shoulders, the neck—trying to weigh him down and squeeze the fight out of him.

Scott felt useless. Eventually he ran to Emily's side.

"Is . . . is that Mick?" she asked him. She was looking right at the elf. Or possibly she was looking right at the pasting of extinguisher foam on his head that, to her eyes, probably appeared to be floating two feet above the stage. The Freemen certainly seemed to see it, and they were now rushing toward both elf and finch. They tackled Mick at roughly the same time as Erno was pinned and Biggs crumpled under a dog-pile of black bodies.

There were only a handful of unoccupied Freemen now. Maybe these, like Scott and Emily, were the most timid, the least athletic of those who hadn't simply panicked and run at the first sign of trouble. But they looked confident now with only a pair of sixth graders to contend with. They looked pretty pleased with themselves, actually.

"Any ideas?" Scott whispered to Emily.

Emily gave it some thought. "Stay low, aim for the crotch," she concluded.

Thank goodness we have a certified genius on our team, thought Scott. Then he fished his arm around and unhooked one of the zipper pulls from his backpack. He held the thing aloft, his thumb twitching over its red button.

"Don't come any closer," he told the Freemen, "or I'll do it."

The men stopped dead. The one in front winced at Scott's hand. "Do . . . do what?"

Activate my LED flashlight, thought Scott. "Trust me, you don't wanna find out," he told them. "We've planted them on every floor of the temple."

The Freemen hesitated. More than one of them took a halting step backward. The whole of the stage curtain was now engulfed and dripping blue fire, so for a moment all was quiet apart from crackling flame.

Fourteen more men were sitting on the prostrate Biggs, pinioning every foot of his arms, legs, and torso. The Freeman with the fire extinguisher approached his head, evidently to crack it with the heavy canister. Erno struggled uselessly against two men. Onstage, Finchbriton spat foam and feeble sparks, and Mick was entirely surrounded.

"Everyone get away from my friends!" shouted Scott. "I don't want to press this, but I'll do it! We all agreed we'd rather die than get taken prisoner! We talked about it in the car."

The man with the fire extinguisher paused. Everyone looked to someone else to make the call.

"It's probably a Nintendo or some nonsense!" shouted an old man from the mezzanine. "He's just a boy! Take him!"

This was all the motivation most of the Freemen needed. They began to advance again, cautiously.

"Scott?" said Emily.

"Yes."

"Is that a flashlight?"

"Yes," he answered, and pointed it at the Freemen like a light saber.

"Is it . . . bright?"

"Not really."

The Freemen grinned easily now; aware that, at best, they were only in danger of being slightly illuminated. Having to squint. Maybe getting their sinuses checked.

"Get ready to run," whispered Scott.

Then the rosette skylight shattered inward, and Scott looked up to see a dark figure sliding down from the rafters on a light and fluidly uncoiling rope, his black mantle unfurling like pure opera, like Batman. It was just the sort of entrance his father would make in a movie, and Scott's heart stirred as Freemen were scattered by fear and falling glass. "Dad?" he said, not too loudly, but breathlessly, as the dark rescuer alighted and turned.

But it wasn't his father.

It was Merle Lynn, C.P.A.

Much to everyone's confusion.

CHAPTER 34

All the Freemen who were not otherwise engaged rounded on Merle, expressions of baffled anger on their faces. This was not how these Initiation pageants went, normally. You could easily miss it, owing to the high ceilings and antique appointments of this theater, but the Freemen Temple was really a treetop clubhouse. It was a fort made of sofa cushions. It was any sort of stronghold dedicated to the promotion of US and the exclusion of THEM. And the 377th level of membership was supposed to guarantee that on a night like this they would mingle only with servants and with Walnut Crescent types who had servants of their own. None of these frustrating in-betweeners. There were not supposed to be children here. There were not supposed to be rabble-rousers. Right now each Freeman should have been holding a glass, maybe his pipe, and speaking with a group of nearly identical men who could really appreciate a funny story about his butler.

Instead they were forced now to subdue a sweatshirt-wearing and possibly crazy old man. And was that a Freeman robe he was wearing? "This," a red-faced Freeman bellyached, "is a *private function!*"

Scott's thoughts were a little more complimentary. He hadn't seen Merle Lynn since their brief meeting three weeks ago, and he realized his memories of the man had not been true: he was not quite the hobo Scott remembered him to be. His square gray beard was tidy. His skullcap was neatly pinned to his thinning hair, which was not anywhere as flyaway as you'd expect, considering he'd just dropped sixty feet through a broken window. He wore the black cloak of a Freeman, which Scott found kind of alarming; but beneath the open robe was only a pair of dark brown corduroy pants and a sweatshirt from Coney Island. He looked to Scott like the sort of well-meaning bachelor uncle who would pull quarters from your ears and forget to close the bathroom door when he peed. But then he pulled a glossy white wand from his sleeve, and in an instant he looked like a wizard.

He lunged with the wand like it was a saber, framed by the raging blue fires and greasy smoke of the proscenium. As a gang of Freemen neared, he flicked his wand and they dropped like marionettes. Two more Freemen rushed him, but with another wave of the wand they

pitched forward and slid headfirst across the floor, eyes shut.

It was getting hazy. The fire spread to the thick columns that flanked either side of the stage. Something on the painted globes was especially flammable, and each Earth blistered and flew apart like a flock of crows.

Merle was moving about the floor now, and even the Freemen who'd been detaining Biggs and Mick and Erno now released their charges and leaped into action, only to fall abruptly asleep the moment they fell within Merle's sphere of influence. But there were too many, and they came too quickly. One Freeman managed to slip up behind Merle and hoist his arms up in a full nelson, and when Merle flicked his wand over his shoulder and put this particular man to sleep, the dead weight dragged both of them down. Merle might have been quickly disarmed had Scott not finally roused himself to action. He dashed between Merle and the final two Freemen, screaming a poorly planned battle cry that was almost "LOOK OUT!" and was almost "NOOOOOO!" but came out something like "Noot." Then, following Emily's advice, he aimed low and tackled one of the Freemen in the groin. The second tripped over the first, and Merle gained enough time to disentangle himself from his narcoleptic wrestling match and put the last of the Freemen to sleep.

Scott could feel all the adrenaline leave him now as if

it were rushing out his ears. He could almost have passed out himself. But Erno and Emily helped him up, and soon Mick and Finchbriton were at his side, too. Biggs snored loudly on the floor.

"Everyone okay?" asked Merle, and then he noticed Biggs. "Must've got him when I doped the guy sitting on his neck. Sorry."

"We better go," said Mick. "More'll be comin' soon."

"More are probably already here," Merle answered. He had no problem seeing and hearing Mick apparently. "Waitaminute," he added, squinting through the haze. "You're that leprechaun who owes me gold."

"No," said Scott. "He's a clurichaun."

"Clurichaun, my eye. This little lepre-conman covered a field with ribbons just so I wouldn't be able to find his stash again. I spent two *days* digging up that field."

Scott turned to Mick, and the elf sighed. "All right, so I'm a bleedin' leprechaun."

"What?" said Scott, a little hurt. "Why did you say—"

"Soon as yeh tell folks you're a leprechaun it becomes all about the gold." Mick sighed. "You might as well tell 'em you're their fairy godfather."

"Not that I'm exactly following this conversation," said Emily, "but shouldn't we . . . ?"

"Right," said Merle. "Archimedes," he added, though this comment seemed to be directed mostly at his wristwatch.

Then there was a sound of flapping wings, and a barn owl descended through the broken skylight, circled the room, and landed on Merle's shoulder.

"That's the coolest thing I've ever seen," said Erno.

"It isn't a real owl." Emily frowned. "Real owls don't make noise when they fly."

"Smart girl. C'mon."

They dragged Biggs to one of the auditorium exits just as a smoking chunk of ceiling crashed down to the stage.

Merle looked up at the blue flames and dark smoke. "Is that dragonfire?" he asked.

"Sort of," said Scott.

"And . . . just 'cause I wanna be sure—we all see the bird covered in frosting, right?"

"It's fire extinguisher foam, and yes."

"Awesome. Okay. Now we just have to find a safe way out. Preferably something near the southeast corner."

"Why the southeast corner?"

"Because that's where I left my car."

"Back to the basement," Emily suggested. "There's a coal chute."

So they dragged Biggs as elegantly as possible down three flights of stairs, and soon they were on level ground again.

"Do yeh think the big guy . . . ," Mick huffed, "would be insulted . . . if I suggested he wear a little sled on his back from now on?"

"How much longer will he be asleep?" asked Emily.

"'Bout another twenty minutes."

At the end of the hall was a door marked BOILER ROOM, and as they pushed through, Finchbriton immediately began ruffling his feathers and chirping in short barks.

"This is where they kept him," said Erno. "In that middle furnace."

Mick ran over and gave it a kick.

"There's the coal chute," said Emily. It was a rusty and curving metal slide from the ceiling to the floor. And this is when she and everyone else suddenly remembered how much Biggs weighed. "I . . . I should have thought of the incline. It'll be tough getting him up the incline." You could see that Emily found her lack of foresight genuinely worrying.

"We'll manage," said Mick. "The bird an' me are stronger'n we look."

"You have a lot on your mind," said Erno to Emily. He grabbed her hand and turned to the others. "Literally. She memorized half a filing cabinet upstairs."

"Doing your *job?*" she whispered to Erno. But she didn't pull her hand away.

They laid Biggs against a pile of coal and tramped up the chute. At the top they huddled together and peeked through the trapdoor to the outside. "Look at all of 'em," Merle breathed. "You see my car?"

Circling the temple was a wide expanse of sidewalk and lampposts. Parked in the midst of all this was a white van surrounded by dozens of policemen in riot gear. Just now the first of three fire engines was pulling up.

"You have a white van," said Scott. Just the sight of one got his heart racing.

"Yeah," said Merle. "It's a good way to blend in. Archimedes, start the car."

The owl on Merle's shoulder swiveled its head all the way around, and, outside, the van's head and taillights winked on. All around, the cops jumped and turned their rifles toward the vehicle.

"Cooool," said Erno.

"That's nothin'. Wait for the good part."

Merle touched his watch; and the van lurched forward, scattered a few police officers, and ran into a lamppost.

"Was that the good part?" asked Emily. "I wouldn't want to miss it."

"Okay, hold on, hold on." Merle poked at his watch some more; and the van backed up abruptly, sent another cadre of policemen flying, and shot forward again and around the temple and out of sight. The cops rushed to their own cars or tore off after the van on foot.

"What now?" said Erno.

"Now I draw the cops away, circle the car around, and pick us up," said Merle, squinting at the little screen on his watch. "Let's get the big guy up the chute; we don't have long."

"How fast is the van traveling?" asked Emily as they skidded back down.

"Forty . . . um . . . forty-three miles per hour, about."

"We have twenty-six seconds."

Merle shot her a look as if he expected that Emily might, at a word, swivel her head all the way around, too. She looked momentarily satisfied with herself again.

Merle guided the van while the kids pushed at Biggs's heels and Mick and Finchbriton pulled him by his lapels. They burst up through the trapdoor to the screeching of tires, and the van ground to a halt right in front of them.

"Quickly! Quickly!" shouted Merle, as if they needed encouragement. They could hear the sirens everywhere. The police were clearly confused and hadn't yet figured out that their quarry had just driven in a big circle. But it wouldn't be long before they worked it out.

After a certain amount of heaving and grunting, Biggs was loaded into the back of the van. Then they turned to close the cargo doors and found two men in black just emerged from the coal chute and aiming guns at their faces.

"DO NOT MOVE!" shouted the more chatty of the two.

"These guys again?" muttered Mick.

"I told you I wasn't good with knots," said Scott.

"SHUT UP! EVERYONE GET IN THAT VAN! NO! EVERYONE GET *OUT* OF THAT VAN! PUT YOUR HANDS IN THE AIR AND KEEP THEM THERE AND PULL THE BIGFOOT BACK OUT OF THAT VAN!"

"With what," snarled Mick. "Our teeth?"

The other soldier turned to his partner. "The elf's right; that was confusing—"

"EVERYONE SHUT UP!" said the other, his body practically humming with rage. "OKAY? AND GET YOUR HANDS WHERE I CAN SEE THEM!"

Merle, wand in hand, raised his arms with the rest of them. But he sort of flicked his wrist in a way that reminded Scott of all those sleeping men inside the temple. The soldiers blinked; the quiet one yawned. But that was all they did. Merle scowled at the wand. "Knew I should have charged it before leaving the house."

"SHUT UP! OR YOU KNOW WHAT'S GOING TO HAPPEN? LET ME TELL YOU WHAT IS GOING TO HAPPEN—"

They never got to hear what he thought was going to happen, though in all likelihood he would have gotten it wrong. "My partner and I are going to be run over by a rabbit driving a Citroën" just isn't the sort of thing that occurs to most people, no matter what kind of life they've led.

CHAPTER 35

"Oh my gosh," Emily murmured through her hands.

"TA-DA!" Harvey postured from the driver's side window. "For my nextht trick—"

Mick interrupted. "Watch me pull a rabbit out o' this car."

"Mick? Whoa—"

Mick flung open the door and dragged Harvey out by the ears.

"*Ow ow ow ow.*"

"Yeh killed these men, Harvey!"

"Bu-but they were gonna kill *you!*" said Harvey as he toddled along on his knees. "They were even gonna kill the children, which I'm largely indifferent about."

"Actually, they're still breathing," said Erno, who was crouching to look under the Citroën.

"You thee?! Didn't kill them. *Maimed* them. I did

the right thing tonight, Mick. Honorable life, that's my motto."

"Yeah, look at you," Scott muttered. "You managed not to *entirely* steal Biggs's car."

"Sun's coming up," Merle pressed. "Police."

Scott wheeled around and addressed the group. "We have to warn my dad."

"Yeah, he was on this list," said Erno.

"I know. And he's supposed to be filming a commercial for Goodco this morning."

"Wait," said Merle. "Who's your dad?"

"Reggie Dwight."

"Reg . . ." Merle coughed. "*Sir* Reginald Dwight? He's in Goodborough? I've been trying to contact him for months!"

"All right," said Mick. "Scott, why don' you and the kids ride with Merlin, here? I'm gonna go with Harvey."

Scott and Erno shared the front bench of the van with Merle and Archimedes. Emily insisted on riding in the back with Biggs, but they could see and hear her through a grated window between the cargo area and the cab.

"Wait. You're not the *real* Merlin," said Erno, who worried suddenly about using *real* and *Merlin* together in a sentence. "You're just some guy. An accountant."

"I am just some guy," said Merle as he peeled away from the Freemen's Temple. "I am also the real Merlin, and I

369

know things. Like that, in the near future, a massive pink dragon is gonna come outta nowhere and start stepping on everything."

"Saxbriton," sighed Scott. "Head west."

"And she's gonna be followed by all the fairies and other magical creatures. And the fairies're gonna command an army of our own children to fight against humanity, and humanity's gonna lose. And the fairies will take over the world."

"How do you know all this?" asked Erno.

"I lived through it. I'm a time traveler."

"That's impossible," said Emily, her face at the window, her little fingers curled around the grate. "Time travel from the future to the past is physically impossible because of—"

"Emily—"

"No, she's right," said Merle. "Time travel from the future to the past is totally impossible. I understand that now."

"But then ... how ..."

"Easy. Have you heard of the Big Crunch?" Merle asked.

Scott thought he had. "That's the one with almonds, right?"

Merle stared. "What? No. The Big Crunch is the end of the universe. The whole shebang collapses into a tiny point. But then the Big Bang happens, and the universe reboots itself. Big Crunch, Big Bang. Big Crunch, Big Bang. Over and over."

Emily shook her head. "I don't believe it. Current cosmological models show that—"

"But wait," said Erno. "Are you saying you're . . ."

"From the last universe. Yeah. The universe reboots itself, and history plays out the same way every time. The pyramids always get built, there's always a Genghis Khan, a French Revolution, the Crusades, Frank Sinatra, the Louisiana Purchase. Not, um . . . necessarily in that order. But every time a me, and every time a you."

"That's ridiculous. Quantum mechanics would make that so unlikely as to be—"

"I couldn't figure out how to time-travel to the past, but I could do it to the future. And eventually I did it so far into the future that I traveled past the end of the universe and popped up in the new one. In Arthurian times."

"And you became Merlin!" Scott said.

"I didn't become Merlin, I *am* Merlin. I'm *always* Merlin. I just didn't know it till I got there. And now I'm here, and trying to figure out how to stop the fairy invasion from happening. It's taken me years to figure out that Goodco had . . . has . . . will have anything to do with it."

"Huh. We know that already," said Erno, "and we've only been at this a couple days."

371

"Good for you. You're very smart."

"Can you teach us to use magic?" Scott practically squealed.

"Nope. Don't know any."

"But—"

"You were right when you said I'm just some guy. Some guy with a few futuristic tricks and an iPhone. Have you ever read the legends of King Arthur? Most of Merlin's 'magic' is just knowing what's gonna happen next. Which I did 'cause I could read ahead."

"But you have a wand . . ."

"I have a Slumbro Mini. It's just a gadget that puts people to sleep. In my time it's what ladies carry in their purses instead of pepper spray. Which reminds me," he said as he fished out the wand and plugged it into the van's cigarette lighter.

"And Archimedes—," Scott began.

The owl turned at the sound of its name.

"Archie's a computer. A kid's toy, really. I souped up the operating system a bit, and he's got a huge historical database; but there's still a lot of stuff I don't know. Goodco was good at keeping secrets. Like what's the deal with their whole two-worlds theory? Why would all the magic be in a separate world? It didn't used to be." Merle craned his neck to look in the back. "Hey, uh . . . kid. Girl."

"Emily."

"Yeah. So . . . did you really memorize a filing cabinet in the temple?"

"From the office of the Grand Ambrosius, yes."

"Seriously?! That's great!"

"I have to write it all down," said Emily. She sounded antsy. "Soon. I'm not taking the Milk-7 anymore. I'm going to forget it."

Merle whistled. "You're one of the Milkbabies. Oh man."

Erno didn't like where this was going. "How did you know to rescue us?" he asked, if only to change the subject.

"I was listening in on the Initiation. I've managed to sneak some hidden microphones around town."

"Turn left here," said Scott.

The van stopped in front of Scott's house; the Citroën stopped adjacent to the van. Scott threw open the van door and ran up his front steps.

After a minute he ran back out, shouted, "They're already gone. Polly too."

The van and the Citroën were taking up the whole street, blocking the flow of traffic. As they sat there, a third car approached slowly and honked to be let through.

Mick exited the Citroën and ran around to meet Scott. "Did your da' say where they were filmin'?"

"I . . . I think he did. Don't you remember? You were there too, under the bed."

"Wasn't really payin' attention, lad, sorry."

The driver of the third car gave his horn another few quick taps.

Scott planted his fists over his eyes, tried to think. Had he mentioned the factory? Or did Scott just think he had because Polly had said something about it on the way home from the airport?

The driver of the third car pressed his hand hard against the horn now and left it there. Scott flew off the handle and ran to the car, grabbed its bumper, intended to lift the whole automobile over his head in frustration. Instead he just sort of rocked it gently. "MY SISTER!" he shouted at the startled driver. Later he'd realize he didn't really explain himself as thoroughly as he thought he did.

"The factory!" he decided finally, turning back to Mick and the rest. He was pretty sure.

"Okay," said Merle. "Let's go then."

Scott crawled back into the van and rode the rest of the way with his whole body closed up like a fist. He thought about Polly. His brain helpfully called up a sort of clip show of every awful thing he'd ever said to her.

"Biggs is awake," said Emily through the little window.

"Awesome," said Merle. "Tell him it was an accident."

"He knows. Merle?"

"Yeah?"

"I think I know why Goodco and the Freemen are getting rid of Knights Bachelor, but it's so ridiculous I don't want to be the first person to say it out loud."

"They're doing it because only a true knight can kill a dragon," said Merle.

"Thank you," said Emily.

"Really?" said Erno. "Only a knight can kill a dragon? What if you just dropped a bomb on one?"

"I don't know. We didn't have bombs in Arthurian times. But back then it was common knowledge that a hundred men could swing at a dragon and only the knight's sword would cut deep. I didn't believe it either until I saw it. And the Knights Bachelor are the only order of knighthood that goes all the way back to Arthur's day, so they're really the only guys who count."

"Even if this wasn't the stupidest thing I'd ever heard, it would still be a lousy plan," said Emily. "The queen can just knight more knights. She could knight all of England if she wanted to."

"She could if the queen was still the queen," Merle answered. "Which I doubt."

"Can everyone maybe stop talking?" Scott breathed. He needed to know if Polly, and to a lesser extent his father, was safe. Or unsafe. It was the waiting he couldn't stand. Then a useful thought managed to emerge through the noise: "Merle, do you have any microphones in the factory?"

"Huh. Yeah, I got one in the foreman's office, overlooking the floor." He reached for what looked like a CB radio kit under the dashboard and turned a knob to channel seven. Then he flipped a switch.

The sounds were faint, but they were the sounds of a struggle. Blunt body blows. Grunts and the clatter of metal instruments. Scott's breathing quickened. He couldn't get enough air. More noises through the radio speaker, and then a scream. A girl's scream.

Scott reached over and turned it off.

REGGIE
Hello! I'm Reggie Dwight, and I'm visiting the good folks at Goodco to see how they make new Peanut Butter Clobbers™!

Ow.

Um, there are peanut buttery bumpers! And melt-in-your-mouth strawberry milk bubbles in every box of Peanut Butter Clobbers™.

REGGIE
OW! Is that going to happen every time I say "Peanut Butter Clobbers™"?

I think that
one was a man.
(cough)
Okay. This . . .
um . . . cereal not
only combines the great
taste of peanut butter
and strawberry milk, but
it's also chock-full of
IntelliJuice™, the magic
juice that makes you
smarter! I wish I'd had
some before agreeing to
do this commercial.

Hey! So, uh . . . try
new Pea . . . try this
cereal here.

And wash it down
with new Strawberry
ThinkDrink™! It's the
punch with punch!

VOICE-OVER ANNOUNCER
Peanut Butter Clobbers—
another good cereal
from the good folks at
Goodco!
There's a Little Bit of
Magic in Every Box!

CHAPTER 36

The van and the Citroën skidded to a stop in the vast but empty Goodco factory parking lot. It was still a holiday weekend, Scott supposed. He realized in a detached and foggy sort of way that he didn't have any idea what day of the week it was. He took off at a run toward the entrance, with its Freemen icons and spiky mascots.

"Wait, what're we doin'?" shouted Mick. "Just blowin' through the front door?"

"There's no time for tricks!" Scott shouted.

"I'll wait in the car," said Harvey.

Mick narrowed his eyes. "Finchbriton, why don't yeh stay an' keep our Harvey company? See that he don't get lost."

Scott paused at the entrance, and he was relieved to see the others fall in behind him. They all crashed through the double doors together and into the lobby, ran past the TV screen and down the hall to the factory floor to find . . . a commercial shoot.

"Hey," said Scott's dad. He wore a pink shirt and white pants and a pleased smile on his handsome face. "You came after all. And you brought . . . friends!"

Assuming that his dad could see Mick, Scott could hardly imagine what he thought of this crowd of gate-crashers. Add a couple of puppets, and they would have looked like a children's television program.

"I'm afraid you're a trifle late, though," his dad added. "We just wrapped. Got it in only three takes!"

"You nailed it, Reggie!" said a seated man in a baseball cap.

"Oh, please. It was good planning. I just read the lines and hit my marks."

There were people all around the huge room, and they all chuckled good-naturedly. Five of them were dressed like the Queen of England. The rest stood beside a big camera on wheels, or next to any number of spotlights on tripods, or by the factory machinery, holding a long pole with a microphone on the end of it.

"Um," mumbled Scott. "Guys, this is my dad, John. Or Reggie. Should they call you Reggie?"

"As long as they don't call me sir," John joked. "Sir is my father's name." More laughter. *Adults laugh a lot,* thought Scott, *even when nothing's funny.*

He drew close to John. "Where's Polly?" he asked.

"Oh, around. She wanted to explore. Do you want to see the commercial?"

John was grinning a lot. Too much? Was he trying to tell them all was not well?

Scott's gang gathered around the camera. Mick whispered, "Maybe I should go find your sis. Get outta here while the gettin's still good."

"Um, I don't know," Scott whispered back. "Let's not all get separated yet." Maybe they were holding Polly captive, he thought. Maybe the crew all had guns and threatened to kill her if John didn't play along.

"This is hilarious," Erno announced as he watched the camera's small display. "The internet's gonna love it."

"There's a lot of punching in it," Emily whispered to Scott. "Might explain the sounds we heard in the van."

Scott, for his part, was barely listening. He wasn't watching the camera screen. He was staring at John Doe, waiting for a sign, some secret message encoded in the dots and dashes of his eyes. But his dad was no longer looking at him. He appeared to be looking everywhere but: at the camera, at Erno and Emily, at Merle, at the commercial crew who no doubt had equipment to put away and lives to get on with but who nonetheless lingered, watching. And then John did something wrong. Afterward Scott couldn't have told you just what that something was: a twitch, a tilt of the head? But while Scott would never have admitted this to Erno or Polly or even to himself, he had made a great study of John Doe. John Doe was his life's work. He'd watched, with fake nonchalance, every movie, every music video, every online interview. From a thousand photographs he knew the cleft in John's chin, the cut of his teeth, the exact former site of the neck mole that John had had removed in the fall of the previous year. He knew the back of his hand like the back of his hand. And this man was not his father.

"THIS MAN," he announced, pointing, "IS NOT MY FATHER!"

Everyone on the factory floor was stunned into silence.

Mick sidled up and asked, "Do yeh mean that in a 'He never remembered my birthday' kind o' way, or—"

"No," said Scott, "I mean he really isn't my father." He glared at the impostor and presented his fists.

"Um," said Erno.

"Kid?" said Merle. "You sure?"

"He's sure," Mick answered. "Let's get 'im."

The thing that looked like John Doe grinned. "The jig is up," it said in a spidery voice, then its skin unzipped at the face and fell to the floor.

CHAPTER 37

The John Doe costume, the perfect suit of clothes and hair and skin, lay in sickening folds on the factory floor. The impostor was revealed to be two short creatures, one perched on the other's shoulders, both still wearing the same terrible smiles.

"Goblins," growled Mick.

They were each perhaps just a half foot taller than Mick, with milky white bodies but startling red faces. Red as if they'd been dipped to their chins in blood and the stuff had dripped some foreign alphabet all over their necks and collars. From top to bottom they had: bald pates, all the worst features of both toad and bat, little gray wool suit jackets with ties, short pants, and chicken feet. The one hopped off the other's shoulders, and they both bowed and said,

"Misters Pigg—"

"—and Poke, atcher service. Specializin' in the 'mpersonation of queens of all stripes."

"And in creatin' diversions, Mister Poke—you know you're quite good at that."

"No better than you, Mister Pigg."

Scott turned when he realized what the goblins were getting at, and saw that the commercial crew had managed to surround them. Even the Queens of England. People came at them from all sides, and Scott felt a poke at his neck. When he turned around he saw the goblins' bodies puff up and scab over like toasted marshmallows. Then the creases smoothed and they were perfect replicas of Scott and Mick, clothes and all. Scott flinched and punched himself in the face. It was a singularly odd thing to have to do.

Behind him Erno and Emily protected each other; Biggs threw crewmen and queens around with gusto, knocking over studio lights and a snack table covered with Danishes. Merle put them to sleep with his Slumbro. One crewman ran to shield the movie camera—he pried it off its stand and ducked beneath the assembly line, then ran off into a darkened wing of the factory.

The goblin-Scott that Scott had punched staggered backward, and Mick head-butted his own doppelgänger in the stomach.

"So what was the plan here, exactly?" sneered Mick. "Didja think I'd get confused an' accidentally hit myself?"

Then a Queen of England got too close to Emily, and she had a fit. Her eyes rolled back, and the lights went out with a crack, and when they came on again there was a donkey wearing a tiara, and Scott couldn't tell which Mick was Mick anymore.

"Emily turned a lady into a donkey," Erno announced.

Emily was shivering on the concrete floor, looking drowsy. Biggs ran to her side. The two or three crewmen and actors who were not already asleep or unconscious ran for an emergency exit.

One Mick pointed directly at the other Mick and sort of vaguely toward both Scotts. "Grab 'em before they get away!" he shouted.

"Why yeh little—" the other Mick grumbled.

The donkey flicked its ears, upsetting its tiara, and wandered over to sniff at a trash bin.

Merle approached. "My Slumbro doesn't work on Fay. I could wave it at all of you, and we'd find out who the real *Scott* is, anyway."

"I don't want to go to sleep," said both Scotts at roughly the same time.

"I think I might have a solution," said a female voice.

Everyone turned. Standing amid the factory lines was a beautiful woman with raven black hair in a smoky night-gown—smoky because it was gray, and smoky because it seemed at once to be both there and not there at all. As if the gown, and the woman who wore it, might only have been a figment of everyone's imagination.

"YOU!" shouted Merle.

"YOU?" said one of the Micks.

"You!" Erno said out of camaraderie, though he wasn't really all that surprised. He knew he'd be seeing his doctor again sooner or later.

She clasped her hands in front of her and said, "Merle Phillip Lynn. Scottish Play Doe. Erno Utz. Emily Utz. Brian Macintyre Biggs. Fergus Ór." A cold flare of light like a slow camera flash tumbled through the room in waves. "There now. I'm afraid you'll find that not one of you can move."

One Mick and one Scott shed their skins and were goblins again. They went to stand at either side of the beautiful woman and held her hands like gentlemen when she ducked under the factory rollers to join Scott and his friends. Closer now, you could see that her beauty was a glamour, and perhaps not as glamorous as it used to be. To Erno and Emily, who had seen her most recently, she looked careworn and tired.

"I cannot believe my good luck," she said. "I'm getting everything I want for Christmas. I'll admit my magic is not what it once was, but I've done some poking around and discovered each of your True Names—does no one learn to keep the old secrets in this world?—and with these I

388

have barely to lift a finger to keep you all in my thrall."

Scott, for his part, was confused. He could move, couldn't he? Sure, he had been frozen with fear there for a second, but the rest of his friends seemed to be genuinely paralyzed. They didn't even blink. Scott twitched a fingertip just to be sure, and he could move just fine. Then he struggled to compose himself as the woman turned to gaze directly at him.

"Forgive my manners, young man. Everyone else here has at least one good name for me, and perhaps a few less savory ones besides. You may know me as Queen Nimue, the Lady of the Lake.

"Merlin," she said, turning to the tense and pink-faced accountant. "Wormed your way out of the earth. The worm that dieth not, it would seem—just how old are you now, wizard? No, don't answer—it was rude of me to ask.

"Fergus—" she said to Mick, and here her face fell, and a little of the glamour came loose, just for a moment. She was an altogether less beautiful but more lovable person in that moment. "I hope by my apples that you'll live to understand what I'm doing here. These are miserable means, but there's an honorable end in sight. Not for me perhaps, but for you, and for all our cousins. You'll see."

She straightened and surveyed the lot of them. "What a class of apt pupils. Let's have a history lesson, shall we?"

"Yes, Miss," said either Pigg or Poke.

"Yes, please," said the other.

"Hm. The Fay were first forced underground by an invading army, you know. Such is the way of things, I think you'll soon find. We were the light of the world, hiding under bushels. Cowering beneath toadstools. We lived for so long in our twilight world that I think even some of our own came to see it as our natural place. Not I. I wanted back some of the world we'd lost. Not so much, really—Ireland could be ours, and Somerset. Maybe Orkney. They were doing practically nothing with Orkney, you know."

"'S a bit unfashionable, Miss."

"Well, you have to have someplace to put the pixies. So I sought to have dealings with a mortal king, King Arthur. I gave him a great sword of enchanted metal: metal that would get into his blood and turn his heart toward our cause. Because here I thought I saw a king to unite all the human world, for good or for ill. But I also hedged my bets, as I think you say. I made sure Arthur begat a son who would be my cat's paw, to replace him if necessary. But then the two killed each other at Camlann. So it wasn't a very good plan, you see."

"Oh, don't say it, Miss," said one of the goblins.

"I will say it. The Fay have always preferred a good story to a well-laid plan. It's a failing of ours. And then came the Marvel—the Gloria. It took me centuries to understand it. The humans, bless them, thought it was just more of their God's punishment on Arthur for consorting with devils and magic. My own people thought it was some black magic conjured forth when father and son murdered each other on the battlefield. I alone knew—it was some trick of yours, wasn't it, Merlin?"

Tears were streaming down Merle's face. But then there were tears streaming down each of the prisoners' faces—they could scarcely blink, could hardly breathe under Nimue's influence. Scott would have to do something, and he flicked his eyes about for an idea.

"We have always been jealous of each other's magics. I never discovered the secret behind your gift of foresight. And you, for your part, made a careful study of any and all things enchanted by the Fay: Arthur's sword, fairy gold—oh yes, I know all about your little experiments on fairy gold. Did you long to be a great alchemist, Merlin? You cared only for the scientific magics with their laws and order, and turned away from sacred chaos and uncertainty. You cast it out of your heart and mind and wished for a world of rules and law, where the human arts were the only arts. You made your wish come *true*, somehow. And you left us to die in a bubble.

"You see, I was haunted by the memory of the Gloria, and the sense I could not shake that the world had been split in two. It was you who put the idea in my head,

Merlin, just before I imprisoned you in that dank cave. You said that Arthur would return, return to a world I couldn't imagine. Where is our dear Arthur, Merlin? Resting up? Do tell him I asked after him."

There were a few things around Scott that could conceivably be used as weapons, and he would have liked very much to get any one of them into his hand without somebody noticing. But one of the goblins (Poke, he thought), would not stop looking at him. Did he know? Did he seriously just wink?

"It took all my skills and half my magics," said Nimue, "but I soon found this new human world through the mists. I was able to part the curtains, just long enough, just wide enough, to make the Crossing. I left a land of feral beauty and wonder and entered New Jersey. It probably goes without saying that I got a bit moody for the next ten or fifteen years.

"But I had a plan. A good one. I would open a door and bring the rest of my people to this world before the bubble burst. I needed power. Influence. I needed more, much more magic than I'd currently had at my disposal if I wanted to open this door. And I knew other Fay had made the Crossing, albeit accidentally, before me. I could . . . I could take their glamour for my own if I had to. Store it away. So I needed an organization that could scour the Earth for magical creatures. If I could not yet have the company of my fellow Fay, then I needed a company of men. I grabbed power the only way a woman in the 1830s could: I married well.

"Zachariah Terribull Goode was not a good man. He was an Old World Puritan, and he did not care for women. In fact he'd made a small fortune inventing ways to shame and torture them: painful headdresses, metal wired to teeth and so forth. . . ."

Here she looked sidelong at Emily.

"But his business was in decline. The punishment of shrews and wantons was falling out of favor. It was I who pointed out that the women he tortured had lovely smiles, when they smiled at all. It was I who saw that the devices were straightening their teeth, I who saw that parents would pay good money to have their children tortured for vanity. New devices had to be tested, and I volunteered to do the testing. I obtained a number of orphans, which was of course much easier to do back then. Not that it's entirely impossible now."

Again she glanced at Emily, with a smile like a knife.

"An honorable life—such is the way of the Seelie Court."

"If y' say so, Miss," said Pigg.

"Have to take your word for it," said Poke, and here he most definitely winked at Scott.

"But stealing children has always been our right,"

Nimue continued. "We take them from their parents, leave behind a changeling. The fairy is raised as a human, and becomes more human. The human is raised as one of the Fay, and becomes more Fay. In the end they're both changelings, in their way.

"I raised my orphans as if they were fairies: I fed them only a bitter stew of flowers and rainwater each morning, taught them about all of the magic creatures, told them that our kind would once again rule the Earth. The symbol of our strength, our great potential, I told them, was the dragon Saxbriton, most powerful of all creatures, whom I had raised myself from an egg. The first of my adopted children. And I filled their mouths with enchanted metal and made little cages for their minds. But in the end too many of them resisted, died, went mad. And I had to admit I had failed, just as I had failed with Arthur. I needed to get my magics *inside* them, to turn them from the inside out.

"I could give Zachariah no heirs, so we adopted my prize pupil, Nathan, as a son. The rest I turned loose on the world. Nathan grew to adulthood, and the memories of his strange childhood faded. But what a proud mother I was when I realized he still had dreams of ruling the Earth. My boy. By chance he was reunited with another of his fellow orphans, Jack Harmliss, who was living a villain's life on the streets of Philadelphia. Twelve years after their orthodontic ordeal I learned I had made some lasting impression on them after all: they both dreamed regularly of the Great Pink Dragon, they both craved dominion over all the peoples of the Earth, and they both had rather strong opinions about breakfast food. It seemed they did not like my flower stew." She sniffed. "Can you imagine?"

"Ungrateful urchins," Pigg sympathized.

"I know."

"And t' think you slaved for so many hours each mornin'," said Poke, "cookin' down the leaves an' stems."

"Exactly," Nimue agreed. "Well, that is, the children cooked their own breakfast, of course. No point slaving when you have perfectly good slaves to do it for you."

"An' what a good mother you were," said Pigg, "teachin' them a trade like that."

"Warms my cockles, it does," said Poke.

"And so my Nathan and this Jack Harmliss had rather an unhealthy obsession with sweet, easy-to-prepare breakfast foods," Nimue continued, pacing among her prisoners.

That's it, Scott thought. *Come a little closer.*

"And they hit upon my best idea for me: a cereal company with a Little Bit of Magic in Every Box. We'd have the humans swallow their poison, and pay for it. They've been doing it for years. But now that we have our Milk-7—"

"IntelliJuice," said Pigg.

"ThinkDrink," added Poke.

"Now that we finally have a concentrated formula that doesn't kill the children or make them grow wings or shrink them or turn them into hairy giants . . . now that we actually have a formula that makes them *smarter?* In a fortnight there will be hundreds of millions of children ready to become my slaves with the snap of my fingers. Child soldiers. Little sugar zombies. Would you like to see what that looks like?"

Nimue stood close to Scott now, but her attention was focused entirely, ruthlessly on Emily. You could see in her face that she was really pushing herself, perhaps to her limit. That whatever she was attempting was going to be dramatic but possibly not entirely practical. Her brow shone with sweat as she raised one delicate hand and Emily snapped up straight like a soldier. The girl's face clouded over; her expression grew vague, as though smudged by Nimue's trembling thumb. Her eyes were pink, entirely pink.

"Who am I, dear?" Nimue asked her.

"My Queen Nimue, Lady of the Lake," said something inside of Emily. Like a ghostly noise from an empty house.

"Oh, that's such a long name," said Nimue. "And so formal. Why don't you call me Mother?"

At this Scott couldn't stand it any longer, and he

grabbed the long pole of the boom microphone that lay next to a sleeping crewman nearby. Nimue flinched, and then Emily did too. The fairy queen turned and backed away from Scott. Scott followed.

"Scottish Play Doe!" Nimue shrieked, and gestured frantically at him. "Scott Doe . . . Scott . . . *what is your name, boy?*"

It wasn't Scottish Play, or even Scott. Not really. His name was Macbeth. His father had given him that name.

"Not supposed to say it out loud," Scott told her. "It's bad luck."

Then he whacked her with the pole.

CHAPTER 38

Nimue stumbled, fell backward, nearly cracked her head against the conveyor belt behind her. Then she scrambled underneath it on her hands and feet.

Scott's friends fell to the floor, too, their bonds cut, and took heaving breaths. Biggs was the first on his feet. Emily looked shaken but mostly normal.

"Pigg!" shouted Nimue. "Poke! Help me!" But the goblins were, suddenly, nowhere to be seen.

"You witch," growled Merle as he got to his feet. He and Biggs and soon everybody closed in on Nimue. She waved both hands in the air as if shooing flies. Then she rose up in the air, her form tumbling like a kaleidoscope, and disappeared.

Merle said a bad word. "I was hoping she wouldn't have enough juice to pull off something like that," he added.

"We still haven't found my sister. Or dad," said Scott.

Then something coughed from the far end of the factory floor where it was dark. Scott and the rest rushed toward the sound, and when their eyes adjusted, they saw Pigg and Poke standing on either side of a utility closet.

"Are you . . . ," said Scott. "Are you on our side?"

"A goblin is his own side, always," said Pigg.

"He's no one's pet," said Poke.

"Now then: one of us always tells the truth," Pigg announced.

"One of us always tells lies," said Poke. "Answer our riddle, and we'll give you back your family."

Scott blinked. "Wh—seriously?"

"Nah," said Pigg. "Just foolin'." He leaped atop the other's shoulders.

"It's been real," said Poke.

"It's been imaginary," added Pigg.

Then they turned into the president of the United States and ran off, whooping and hollering, into the darkness.

Suddenly the door was kicked open from the other side. John Doe was behind it, with Polly just behind him. He had his fists in the air. Then he saw Scott standing there and put them away again. Oh," he faltered. "I thought there would . . . is it over?"

"It's over," said Scott. And because he was feeling especially bold, he added, "You owe me."

John sighed. "I know I do," he said.

CHAPTER 39

They moved as a group and surveyed the factory floor. Biggs carried Emily, Polly clung to John and gaped at everyone else in turn. Everyone, including Mick. *Wait'll she sees Harvey*, thought Scott.

"We should mess this place up," said Erno.

"Quickly," urged Merle. "Nimue will send reinforcements before long."

Merle and the twins knew the factory best, having each taken the tour three or four times. Once again a personal Bigfoot turned out to be a practical thing to have as they directed Biggs to snap conveyors, crush ovens, lift plastic barrels of grain meal over his head, destroy an eyewash station.

"We probably could have left them the eyewash station," said Scott.

"This is mad," said John. "Should you be doing this?

We should call the police—"

Merle frowned at him. "You haven't been reading any of my emails, have you?"

"We should find that Milk-7 business," said Mick. "Flush it down the loo."

"They'll just make more," said Scott. "Won't they?"

"Maybe not," said Erno, and his face was crowded with thoughts. "I'm just remembering something this surgeon said in the temple. That Milk-7 was mostly made from the milk of some animal. Crop-milk, he called it. Do you remember, Emily?"

"I was a little out of it," Emily answered from a dark corner. "Crop-milk is this stuff that just a few kinds of birds produce, to feed their young. Flamingoes and pigeons and doves. They regurgitate it into their babies' mouths," she added with growing distaste.

"The surgeon said it came from *draco* . . ."

"*Draco mythologicus*," Emily remembered, and she made a face. "I'VE BEEN PUTTING DRAGON BARF IN MY *EARS* FOR TEN YEARS?!"

"Here!" called Mick. "Look! The dairy!"

In a far corner of the factory floor they could just make out a large pair of sliding barn doors that were labeled DAIRY. They slid the doors open, and there it was: Milk-7. A great big tank of it. Merle turned a valve, and gallons upon gallons of the pink stuff came down in a torrent and started painting the floor. Scott noticed Emily looking at it with something like longing. *Could anyone ever be willing to be less smart than they already are?* he wondered. *Even if just a little, even if it would make them happier?*

"Wonder how they got it across from the magical world," said Merle.

"Things wouldn't be as hard as livin' creatures," Mick answered. "They could get great batches o' the crop-milk across on November Day an' May Day, I bet. What's with the lad?"

Erno had his hands over his ears and a look of intense concentration on his face, like he was trying to shut them all out to think. "Something that hunter guy said," he told them. "About milking dumb animals. It's reminding me of this clue my foster dad left in his notes."

"You had his *notes?*" said Emily.

"Yeah, but I lost them. Thought it had all been for nothing, but if I could just remember . . .

"'There's a short . . .'"

"No. It was . . .

"'There's a sort of . . . sorting shorthand
both for magic beast and fairy.
All the sly land on the island,
all the dumb land in the'"

"Dairy," Erno finished. "It must be, right?"

403

"It *would* make sense, separatin' them like that," Mick whispered. "Nimue would have no use personally for the magic o' griffins an' dragons. She could only steal fairy magic for herself, so she'd keep folk like me an' Harvey at headquarters on the island. She might keep the animals here, to put their magic in the cereals maybe."

John flicked on the lights, which stuttered to life from caged and naked bulbs in the ceiling. They looked around them. The dairy was a smaller adjoining building with a now-empty tank and a few metal supply cabinets and an old rusty tractor with broken windows and no engine. And a concrete floor covered in four inches of Milk-7, which they were all currently wading in.

"What are we looking for?" asked Polly. "Animals?"

"There are no animals here," said Scott.

"Should go," said Biggs. He scooped up the Utz kids, sending pink goop spattering all over.

"Wait," said Emily. "Does anyone else think that tractor has awfully good tires for something with no engine?"

It was true; the tires looked brand-new. Black, shiny, a little pink goo on the bottoms but otherwise nice. Biggs set the kids down again and pushed the tractor right over, crumpling its cab and breaking what was left of the windshield. Then he started fishing around in the Milk-7 with his hand.

"Kept me in a bunker," he told them. "When I was a boy.

Underground." Suddenly he found what he was looking for and yanked at a metal ring in the floor. A cellar door yawned open, and the Milk started oozing down a set of stairs into a dark space below.

Opening the door triggered the lights, and Biggs led them cautiously down the steps into a wide hall lined on either side by cages.

"They're all empty," said Erno.

"They're not," said Scott.

"Look at them," John whispered. "Amazing."

In the largest cage was a griffin. Its tawny, hungry-looking body ended sharply with a raptor's head and keen eyes that were undimmed by whatever disgraces it had endured here. It stretched back on its leonine haunches and spread its piebald wings and glared.

The griffin shared quarters with a dozen luminous owls and crackling pyrotechnic birds, all of them hemmed in by chicken wire.

In a cage within a cage was the unicat. Beside this an aquarium filled with knotty toads that croaked "OUT OUT OUT OUT" when Biggs grew near.

A third cage held a leopard-bodied creature with a long serpentine neck and head, and slender legs tipped with hooves. It lay on its side, throat fluttering with a hundred distinct voices that whined like a dog pound.

And in a fourth cage . . .

"Is that a unicorn?" Polly whimpered, drawing close to Scott.

The unicorn pawed at the straw and raised its proud head.

"We have to get it out," said John. "I can't stand seeing it like this."

"This machine," muttered Merle. He'd approached a grotesque cube of pipes, compressors, pumps, and wires at the end of the hall.

"They use that to get the magic out," Mick told him. "To store it."

Merle winced at the hoses and arms and tubes of it with a glimmer of recognition in his eyes.

Biggs ripped the door off the griffin's cage, then shielded the twins as it hunched low, uncertain, then scrabbled out into the hall and through the cascading pink goo up the stairs, surrounded by a dazzling flock of birds. Everyone pressed close against the sides of the hall to let them pass. There was a great clatter above, then the crash of what must have been a skylight.

"Mr. Wilson has some explaining to do," Emily said to Erno.

"He's sick," Erno answered. "He needs help."

Next Biggs released the unicat and placed its lean gray body in Scott's arms. It didn't protest.

The toads stumped up the stairs (croaking "LIBERTY

LIBERTY LIBERTY"), and the leopard-thing slunk out behind them.

Finally, the unicorn. It emerged from its cage, minced through the goop, and then took off at a run, its radiant body ascending effortlessly up the stairs and into the factory darkness. Scott caught his breath, and found he was standing next to his father. They shared a glance.

"It's time to go," said Merle. "Seriously."

They sloshed through the Milk (which seemed to be simmering now, almost boiling, though it felt no hotter against their feet) and up the stairs. Then they followed the unicorn's trail out the exit into the parking lot.

"That felt good," shouted Erno. "We've ruined all their plans, right?"

"Don't bet on it," puffed Merle as he ran. "We slowed them down a little, maybe. They still have their factories in California and Europe."

They neared the van and Biggs's car. Harvey and Finchbriton watched them approach. The pooka called, "Did we win?"

Then the factory exploded behind them.

Everyone, even Biggs, was knocked forward. A jagged column of flame and smoke rose from the center of the factory. A rippling flood of hot air blasted through the front doors and started blistering the pink paint right off the dragon over the entrance. Steaming bits of factory and marshmallow shapes rained down everywhere.

"Is everyone all right?" John was shouting. "Is anyone hurt?"

Everyone was fine. They got to their feet and watched the building blaze for a moment, lighting up the sky orange, like a second sun rising in the east.

"Wow," breathed Erno.

"Yeah," said Scott. "Wait. Why did it explode? Was that something we did?"

"Beats me," said Merle.

One of the grain elevators toppled and pretty much smothered the fire.

"Huh."

"Well," Scott added finally. "What should I do with this," he said, meaning the cat.

"Probably just stick it in the bushes somewhere."

Scott went and stuck it in the bushes, but it followed him back.

"Okay, I guess we're taking the cat. Should we go?"

They went.

CHAPTER 40

They ended up at Merle's place. They believed, and for good reason, considering the week they'd had, that if Goodco knew anything about Merlin living as an accountant in West Goodborough before tonight they would have broken his door down already. But they all knew they would have to leave soon. They were going to run, make plans, strike back, foil the invasion. John had actually used the phrase "save the day" more than once and didn't even seem embarrassed about it.

Scott traipsed around the tall house, up and down stairs, just getting the feel of the place. Nearly all of the rooms and hallways were clogged with books, filing cabinets, stacks of papers. Merle's owl-shaped supercomputer could handle a *lot* of people's tax returns, freeing up Merle for world saving and a lot of breaking and entering.

Scott found Polly sitting at the breakfast table, alone.

Usually when he came upon her like this he'd find her whispering to her little prince, but His Tiny Highness wasn't making an appearance today.

"Hey," said Scott.

Polly didn't respond right away, or even seem to recognize that he was there, so deep was she in thought. When she finally turned her head, she looked so serious, adult. It was an unseemly sort of look for a seven-year-old. *I had a few days to get used to all this business,* thought Scott. *She got it all at once, and in the worst way possible.*

"Dad's looking for you," Polly told him.

"I'll find him later. I want to email Mom first. So . . . what happened to you guys in the factory?"

"I don't know. They all jumped on us as soon as we came in. Dad fought a couple of them off," she said, and her voice rose in both pitch and volume with this last bit of news, "but there were so many. Then the pretty woman said our names, and we couldn't move, and these two terrible but kinda polite little monsters came over and touched Dad's face. Then the men tied us up and put us in that closet."

Scott thought. "We didn't untie you. How did you get loose?"

"My little prince cut us loose. With his sharp sword."

Scott smiled, and he went to hug his sister awkwardly, where she sat. "I'm glad you're still weird," he told her.

She pushed him away, but when he stepped back she

was smiling. "It runs in our family I guess," she said. "You smell like corn."

"*You* smell like corn." They *all* smelled like corn. Turns out, if you stand near an exploding cereal factory it just happens. "Where *is* your little prince, anyway?"

"He wanted some time to himself."

"Uh-huh. Is that the door to the basement?"

"Yeah. Emily and Erno and Biggs and the old guy are down there."

Scott went through the door and stepped down the creaky wooden stairs to a vast unfinished basement. The walls were concrete to his chest, brick above that, and then a hanging labyrinth of beams and pipes. Merle was sitting on a plastic milk crate, facing Erno and Emily. Erno sat in a torn and battered chair from an old card table. Emily sat on Biggs, her legs draped over his shoulders, a notepad propped atop his head. It was a nice scene, like one of them had finally gotten the father she deserved.

"I have no idea why the elves are in some separate universe now," Merle was saying. "We all shared the same world back in Arthur's day. I just thought they'd been hiding. Like, underground or whatever. Hey, kid," he said when Scott approached.

"Then why did you tell Nimue all that about Arthur coming back in another world?" asked Erno.

"I just meant the future. 'A world you can't imagine.'

A world with cars and celebrity dance competitions and really small dogs. The future. It's the legend of Arthur, you know, that he's the 'once and future king.' He's supposed to come back when Britain needs him most. So I got the idea of bringing him into the future with me—to slay the dragon, and maybe even lead the world against the Fay. We left Avalon together, but when I reappeared here in New Jersey a few years back, I was all alone."

"I wonder what happened to Arthur," said Emily. As she listened to Merle, she was writing rapid lines across and down the yellow pad of paper. As Scott watched, she filled a page and flipped it over to start on the next. Archimedes was perched on a nearby lamp and appeared to be reading over her shoulder.

"I don't know," sighed Merle, and he looked down at his hands. "I don't know *what* happened to Arthur. If I . . . if I killed him . . . well. He was gonna die anyway without some twenty-first century medical attention. Mordred stabbed him pretty bad."

"But Nimue really trapped you in a cave?" said Erno.

"Yep," said Merle, and he actually brightened at this change of subject. "Of course, I *knew* she was going to, 'cause I'd read the books. With all her powers, I couldn't have stopped her from doing whatever she really set her mind to, but I could make sure she put me in the exact cave where I wanted to be put."

"How could you do that?" asked Scott, but he didn't sit down with the rest. Instead, he circled around them, eyeing the back stairs.

"Nimue wasn't kiddin' when she said the Fay like a good story. They think story's the magic of the universe or some bull. So I checked out a bunch of caves around Avalon on my own and found one that had a good back door. Then when Nimue and me are walking one day, I point out the cave entrance and tell her this tall one about two ancient lovers who got closed up inside. There was no other way out, I tell her, and the cave became their tomb. Then I say—get this—I say, 'What a chilling apparition I see there!' So of course she asks, 'What apparition?' and I say, 'Why, I see my own fetch (that is, a specter of my own death) above the door! But what harm could possibly befall me in Avalon when the Lady of the Lake herself is my consort? Ha ha!' And Nimue laughs, too, but I can see it in her face: she's just found my tomb. There's *no way* she's gonna trap me in any hole but that one, 'cause otherwise it'd ruin the joke. You know?"

Scott excused himself and left them still talking as he ascended the back stairs. He came up through the concrete floor of an enclosed porch that overlooked the scant and weedy backyard. Mick, Harvey, and Finchbriton were sitting on a vinyl sofa in front of an old television set.

"'Lo, lad," said Mick. Finchbriton whistled. Harvey

flicked his ears in Scott's direction but otherwise didn't turn away from the set. "We've been havin' a long talk, the three of us."

Scott had to take Mick's word for it. To the casual observer it looked an awful lot like they were watching cartoons. "Everything okay?" he asked.

Mick shrugged. "It's a lot to take in. An invasion. Saxbriton comin'. One o' the Great Queens o' the Fay, of the *Seelie Court*, doin' the things she's done."

Scott nodded. "So . . . uh. Do you know what you're going to do? Where you might go if you . . . go anywhere?"

"Think we need to stick together on this one," said Mick. "An' I still owe yeh."

Scott shook his head. "You don't owe me anything any—"

"I think we all of us owe one another somethin'. All the time, like. I think that might be the way t' live," Mick said as he turned his attention toward the start of another cartoon. "Honorable. Your da's lookin' for yeh, by the way."

"I know. I'm going to send my mom an email first."

"*Shh*," shushed Harvey. "Thith ith the one where he'th a bullfighter."

Scott left the room and walked back to the staircase in the center of the house. At the top of the stairs he heard a sound like *whoop*. After a pause he heard it again.

Merle had shown Scott a laptop he could use. Email

had to go in and out through Archimedes for security's sake, but at least this computer had a keyboard. Scott did not yet feel comfortable dictating personal letters to a superintelligent owl.

The laptop was in a mostly empty room in the corner of the house. So was John Doe.

"Thought I might run into you if I stayed in one place long enough," said John.

"You have a sword," said Scott just as John brought the blade of it down and around, slicing through the air. *Whoop.*

"Haven't you heard? There's this rumor going around that I might have to slay a dragon."

Scott didn't answer but thought privately that there must be *some* Knight Bachelor left who wasn't an actor or a singer or some pampered billionaire.

"You know they found Sir Gordon Maris this morning, dead of a heart attack?" said John. "He was a jockey, years ago. Seventy-nine years old, no threat to anybody. I just *saw* him. And now he's dead."

Whoop.

"Merlin thinks I might be one of the last men knighted before Goodco replaced Her Majesty with two goblins in a queen suit," John added, and Scott could see his father already starting to buy into the movie make-believe of it all. Already casting himself as the leading man.

Thing is, Scott had believed it, too, for a moment. In the dairy. He tried to remember the way that felt.

"I forgive you," he said quickly. He'd had no idea he was going to say it until he said it.

John started, and lowered the sword to his side. "Oh . . . good. Um. For what exactly?"

"For, you know, running out on us. On me and Mom and Polly." Polly herself appeared in the doorway, and Scott thought, *Good. It's probably better she hear this.*

"Wait," said John. "Run out on you? Scott, I *never* ran out on you. That isn't what your mother told you, is it?"

Of course it was. Wasn't it? It had been so long ago.

"He didn't run out on us," said Polly. Of *course* Polly would know the truth. She and their mother probably talked about it every other day. While eating ice cream and watching movies with lots of kissing. Scott wished he hadn't brought it up, not like this.

"I went off to Toronto for eight days, to film a movie," said John. "*Treacherous Intentions*, did you ever see it? No, of course not; it's rated R. But I came home to find that your mother had moved out and taken you both with her. We'd been having problems. . . ."

"Mom says it was a lot of little things," said Polly. "Do you wanna hear them? Thing Number One: she—"

"Ah, you know something?" John interjected as he watched Scott's face. "We don't need to talk about this now. There's time. I bet Scott only came up here in the first place to use the computer. That's right, isn't it?"

And just like that, John was Reggie Dwight, hero of stage and screen. "Yeah." Scott sighed happily. "I have to email Mom." John smiled at him. He smiled back. And was he actually getting teary now? No, of course not, that would be stupid, Scott thought, blinking his eyes. He coughed and sat down at the computer.

There was still the question of why his dad had never visited. Or why, with all John's money, Scott didn't own at least one speedboat. Nobody was off the hook or anything.

"Okay, remember," said John. "Don't tell your mum anything about all this."

"I know."

"She's still down there working for Goodco; they *need* her, so maybe she'll be safe if they think she doesn't know anything—"

"I *know*. I mean—I know. Thanks."

He had a couple emails from her, one from New Zealand and one from Antarctica. The last read:

Dear Scott,

  Hope I hear from you soon. Are you mad I left? You know I wouldn't ever leave you if I didn't have to. You're probably just very busy. Well, so am I! You would not believe

419

Antarctica. It's like another planet. I've seen lots of seals and skua. Remember we looked up skua? No penguins yet.

There's this phenomenon down here called the Fata Morgana—it's an optical illusion, like a mirage. It makes the horizon look smeared and distorted in a weird way, but otherwise it's nothing special. Except there's this strange spot where the Fata Morgana isn't behaving like it should. That's all I can tell you right now, but it's very exciting. I haven't even begun to understand these readings we've been taking.

Write back soon. Be good to your father. Be even better to your sister—she loves you.

It'll be January before you know it.

Love,

Mom

It made Scott feel sad and good in equal measures. He was pretty sure John had been reading over his shoulder, and trying to seem like he wasn't. Scott turned his head slightly, and John set himself in motion.

Whoop.

They were going to have to flee Goodborough. Go into hiding while they made their plans. There had been some talk about a boat. Never before had Scott had so much to say and so little he could write.

Dear Mom,

I can't wait to see pictures! Why don't you start a blog where you can post a picture every day? Make sure you're in it. Every day. Or else Polly will worry.

Sorry I haven't written before now. You're right, I've been busy. I won't bore you with the details, which are boring. But I made some new friends. And visited a tree house. And saw a play. And learned about history. And about how commercials are made. They do a lot of it with stunt doubles, it turns out.

I'll write more soon. I promise.

Love,

Scott

Whoop.

**A sneak peek at *Unlucky Charms*,
the Cold Cereal Saga Book Two**

CHAPTER 1

Samantha Doe was going to miss her big red coat. It was by far the warmest thing she'd ever worn, and she'd worn it every day for more than three months, and you couldn't help getting attached to something like that. On the inside it was furry, like a pet. It even had the word DOE on the pocket. Samantha loved her big pet coat. But she was going to have to give it back.

She'd been in Antarctica for fifteen weeks—twice as long as she'd been told. She could swear near the end that Goodco was just grasping at excuses to keep her there. And then there was that business with her laptop.

One of the Goodco people, one of the big men who didn't seem to have any scientific credentials at all, had come to her dorm room and asked why she hadn't been sending any personal emails to her children.

Samantha had, in fact. She'd sent Scott and Polly each

an email every day since the Saturday after Thanksgiving. A hundred letters. But she said, "Well . . . since it's *personal* emails I'm not sending, I don't see how it's your—"

The man brushed past her and grabbed her laptop off the bed.

"Hey!" Samantha said. But she stepped back. She was suddenly afraid of this big man. He'd just come in from the cold night, wearing the same sort of coat Samantha wore, that everyone wore. Red on the outside, furry on the inside. On him it looked like an animal he'd turned inside out and was flaunting, like a warning. He scowled at the screen.

"You haven't sent an email to your kids since December first," he said. "And they've never emailed you back?"

Samantha wanted to fold up into herself. Scott and Polly wrote her all the time—what was this guy talking about?

"Here—" the big man, this massive man, told her. "This. Where did you get this software?" He showed her the screen, and a file she'd never seen before. It was called 2003 TAXES, and it was nested inside three folders named for sugar-free candy recipes and a fourth titled PHOTOS OF MY UNATTRACTIVE AUNT. She'd never noticed any of these before, either. Her laptop had a lot of garbage on it.

"Why . . . why does it matter?" Samantha asked the man, who was heaving, who could not possibly be

2

getting larger, could he?

"It matters . . . it *matters* because it's counteracting the spyware *we* put on your computer. How did it get here?"

Samantha didn't know, though her mind turned back to a drawing Polly had sent, months ago, that took a suspiciously long time to download. Anyway, the big man dropped her laptop carelessly on the bed and thundered out before she could answer, or get indignant, or even ask what he'd meant by *spyware*.

She stood awhile, aware of the shallow tide of her own breath. She wasn't so sure about this Goodco anymore. She didn't care how beloved their cereals were.

Afterward she checked, and it was true: all the old emails to and from her kids had vanished off her computer, as if they'd deleted themselves. All of Scott's curious messages, wanting to know every last thing about the strange phenomenon she was studying. Even Polly's drawing of a cat with a unicorn's horn, gone. She sat on her bed and thought for a long time.

The next day she demanded to leave on the next plane out, and over the following weeks Goodco delivered one feeble excuse after another why she needed to stay. But then finally, when they gave their permission, an unscheduled flight made ready to leave right away—a woman at the Kiwi base had slipped in the shower, and Samantha could hitch a ride on her medical transport. She landed in New

Zealand, and gave back her red coat, and caught a plane to Los Angeles, and then another to Philadelphia. Scott and Polly and their father, John, would be meeting her at the airport—or so they said in an email she could no longer find five minutes after she read it.

She deplaned into the terminal, exited the secure area, and almost didn't see the chauffeur holding a sign with her name on it. She wasn't looking for her name, after all; she was looking for her family. But she approached the uniformed man with a little frown on her face.

"I'm Samantha Doe," she told him. "I wasn't expecting a driver."

The chauffeur tucked the sign under his arm and fished something shiny out of his pocket.

"I've been instructed to give you this," he said, and handed her a small gold octagonal hoop.

She turned it in her hand. "What is it? It . . . heh . . . it looks like a miniature particle collider."

"Put it on."

"What?"

"I've been instructed to tell you to put it on."

"Instructed by whom? My ex-husband?" she said as she slipped the thing onto her wrist. Then, wincing, she asked, "Was it always glowing?"

And then she was gone.

● ○ ★

5

Thirty feet away, Scott gasped. He couldn't help it. There was no flash of light, no puff of smoke. His mother was just there, and then she wasn't. She wasn't anywhere. She wasn't anywhere in the whole universe.

"GO GO GO GO!" shouted someone in the crowd, and then ten ordinary-looking men converged on the startled chauffeur and seized his arms—Freemen, laying in wait for Scott and his friends to show themselves. Members of the Good and Harmless Freemen of America, a secret society of creeps who did Goodco's bidding. Scott's heart started pounding against his chest like it wanted out— and why not? The last time he'd seen so many Freemen in one place, they'd tried to dissect his friends.

"What the—" sputtered the chauffeur as the Freemen held him fast. "Lemme go! What happened to that lady?"

The surrounding men, in their plain clothes and scarves, looked to an older Freeman in a black cowboy hat and duster, who stood apart and scanned the faces in the crowd. Then he turned to the driver.

"Who hired you?" Scott heard him growl.

"Some old guy," said the chauffeur in a high voice. "Look, what's this about?"

"It's the wizard's work," the man in black told the others. "Must be. Fan out, he might be close."

The man in black was both right and wrong—the wizard was close, but the wizard wasn't a wizard.

Scott started to move, but Merle laid a hand on his shoulder.

"Stay put," the old man said.

Scott's wig felt itchy. His fake glasses felt fake. In his black wig and big black glasses, he felt like Clark Kent. A kind of bizarro universe Clark Kent who removes his glasses and for some reason his hair to reveal that he is actually a perfectly ordinary blond boy with a mild peanut allergy.

Well, not so ordinary, really. He was part fairy, on his father's side. Plus he had a leprechaun in his backpack.

"Is he really Merlin?" another Freeman asked the man in black. "They say he turns people into animals."

"I *wish*," huffed Mick, the leprechaun. Merle could only do a few cool things, and he was already doing most of them.

"*He's* the reason all the magic left our world," another man told his fellow Freemen, glancing around, his voice the reedy voice of the True Believer. "*Merlin*. He's why it's all trapped in another dimension with the elves and fairies."

"Not true," Merle muttered under his breath.

"And now he's trying to ruin the Fay's Grand Plan to bring the worlds together. Him and his friends. He's *powerful*—"

"He's just a very old man who knows some card tricks,"

insisted the Freeman in charge. "Nothing more. But . . . assume he could be anyone. Check the women for Adam's apples."

The so-called wizard just to Scott's left in the gift shop was not Scott's father. This man in a Mets sweatshirt and an identical pair of thick black glasses was a time-traveling scientist named Merle Lynn, and the glasses had been his idea. Each pair had a tiny light in the bridge that flashed thousands of times per second, too fast to see, and did something weird to the occipital lobe in the brain of any person looking directly at them. Scott didn't understand the details, but the upshot was that anyone staring you in the face would be transfixed by your glasses and not really notice anything else about you. These glasses were your secret identity. So even though there were evil men in the airport looking for Scott and Merle right this second, they paid no attention to the old man and the boy in the wigs and glasses standing stiffly by the Ben Franklin bottle-cap openers.

The Freemen were splitting up, showing people fake badges and asking them questions. Or maybe real badges—the Good and Harmless Freemen of America had a wide reach.

"They're coming," Scott whispered. "Why are we just standing here?"

"If we let 'em come to us, we'll look like a couple a'

8

nobodies with interesting glasses. If we move, we'll be a boy and an old man trying to leave. Your call."

Scott exhaled slowly as a Freeman in khakis and a pink shirt walked right through the gift shop and showed them a very authentic-looking police badge. Scott's wig felt like a pile of hay. He tried to maintain eye contact without looking like he was trying to maintain eye contact, which was quite a trick.

"Sorry to bother you two," said the Freeman. "But we're looking for a person of interest. Elderly Caucasian male? Mind if I ask you why you're here?"

"Waiting for my brother," Merle answered. "His flight's late."

"And which flight would that be?" asked the Freeman as he produced a smartphone from his jacket.

Had he really been paying attention, the Freeman might have noticed Scott and Merle tighten up inside their winter coats. Even the backpack flinched. But the fact that he hadn't yet registered that he was already looking at an elderly Caucasian male meant the glasses were doing what they were supposed to.

"From Dallas," said Merle.

The Freeman frowned at his phone. "You're in the wrong terminal. The only flights from Dallas are arriving into D and F. This is C."

"Son of a gun. Well, thanks for the help."

"Sure," the man told them. "You're free to go."

But they didn't. Outside the gift shop an old woman was shouting, "HOW DARE YOU?" to another Freeman who had apparently just asked her to prove she wasn't secretly a man.

"Whoop. That looks like trouble," the pink-shirted Freeman said. And he turned to leave, but here were these two people with glasses, still staring at him like idiots. He turned back.

"Everything all right?" he added. "You don't want to keep your brother waiting."

"Right," said Merle, and he tried to back away without looking away and accidentally knocked a City of Brotherly Love snow globe off a low table. And still he did not look away.

"Oopsie," Scott said weakly.

"Brilliant plan, this," said Mick, knowing he could only be seen and heard by a very few. "A disguise that requires eye contact. Maybe later I'll tell yeh abou' my idea for a bulletproof necktie."

The Freeman backed up. He squinted. He peered at Scott and Merle as if they were one of those posters that look like noise but that reveal a dolphin jumping over a heart if you cross your eyes just right. Then he took a picture with his phone. A picture of Merle and Scott in which their glasses would not flash but would rather perch awkwardly on their suddenly recognizable faces.

"Um," said the Freeman. Then Merle waved a white wand at him and the man fell, snoring, in a heap.

This wasn't magic, either. It was more like a futuristic Taser, Scott recalled as he and Merle plowed through people and Liberty Bell ashtrays and dashed back toward the parking garage.

"There!" shouted the man in the black hat. "Those two!" Nine men peeled away from whomever they'd been interrogating and sprinted after them.

"YOU ARE NOW ENTERING THE MOVING WALKWAY," said an electronic voice as Scott and Merle scampered shakily onto a low-walled conveyor belt for people who didn't appreciate having to walk a tenth of a mile to get to their cars.

"Your fault," yelled Merle. "Just sayin'. No reason we had to get this close."

"I had to see her," Scott answered, probably too low to hear.

"Archimedes," Merle said into his wristwatch. "Bring the van around."

The narrow moving walkway created some confusion for nine men running abreast, so a number of them ran down the center of the carpeted hall instead and fell behind.

"Any o' them wearin' those pink goggles?" asked Mick.

"I don't think so," Scott answered. He didn't want to look. "I think they're trying to blend in."

"Aces," Mick said, and he zipped his cauliflower face out of the backpack. Then he hopped atop the black rubber handrail and ran back toward the Freemen.

"What's he doing?" shouted Merle.

Scott watched Mick curl into a ball and tumble down into the narrow alley of the walkway.

"I think he's bowling."

Freemen tripped and knocked against one another and bounced off the handrails.

"YOU ARE NOW EXITING THE MOVING WALKWAY."

Scott and Merle vaulted onto the carpet again and through the exit, and then they were standing in an alcove, a recessed bay of doors set into the airport building where it met the edge of the four-floor parking garage. They stepped out among the concrete pillars and ramps of the garage, where they were joined by a barn owl and a white van. The former flew to Merle's shoulder as the latter screeched to a halt in front of them.

They had no intention of getting in the van, though. The parking garage only had one narrow exit, and it was sure to be guarded. Mick caught up, and the three of them ran right around the van and hid themselves behind a huge gray column between two SUVs.

Merle spoke to the mechanical owl, Archimedes, and Freemen began pouring through the doors in time to see the white van peel away again.

"Blockade all C garage exits," one Freeman said into a walkie-talkie as the others moved to pursue the van.

"Wait!" said the man in the black hat. "He's tried this trick before. There's no one in that van."

"Great." Scott sighed. "They're getting smarter."

"Listen," said the black-hatted man, and the others listened. "Silence. He's still on this floor."

The Freemen stepped lightly, spreading out, bending to check under cars. When one drew close, Merle put him to sleep with the Slumbro and Mick helped drag him behind the pillar.

"Can you bring the van by again?" whispered Scott. And with his fist and a pair of running finger legs, he acted out a little scenario.

Merle raised his eyebrows and nodded. He gave the Slumbro to Scott and set about trying to explain the plan to his supercomputing robot owl. Scott flicked the wand when a second Freeman rounded the pillar, and they stacked him on top of the first one.

"Gettin' cozy back here," said Mick.

Scott heard an engine rumbling close, closer, but then it was only some lady in a blue hatchback. He whispered, "How long before the van gets back?"

"Maybe a minute."

A minute felt like a long time just now. The Freemen seemed to be everywhere—had more arrived? Maybe some of them were only passengers. A flight attendant pulling a pair of suitcases passed too close, and Scott put her to sleep before he could stop himself.

"Shoot, sorry," he hissed. "Sorry." Mick put her with the others.

Then Scott felt the van's congested engine draw near. Merle was hesitating.

"Can't do it yet," he groused, and nodded at a clutch of passengers entering through the alcove that separated the terminal from the garage. "Regular people in the way." Then they cleared and he added, "Archie, peel out."

Nearby they heard the fuss of the engine, the shriek of tires, the high whine of a belt that probably needed replacing. The van lurched forward, and so did Scott, Merle, and Mick, four bodies running at once toward the same finish line, and Scott really hoped Archimedes had a firm grasp of the geometry of the situation.

"There they are!" shouted someone, and a dozen undercover Freemen in their polos and chinos began to crab walk back through the sea of cars toward the terminal entrance. The fat white van hurtled around the corner, and Scott, Mick, and Merle crossed directly in front of it at top speed, with Archimedes flapping behind.

The van was braking now, filling the garage with a kind of angry whale song.

They threw themselves back into the bay of doors, pitched through those doors and into the terminal, then turned just in time to see the reeling white van parallel park itself neatly inside the alcove.